JEFF LEAVELL

Accidental Warlocks

Accidental Warlocks
Copyright © 2018 Jeff Leavell. All rights reserved. No
part of this work may be reproduced or utilized in any form or
by any means, electronic or mechanical, including photocopying,
microfilm, and recording, or by any information storage and retrieval
system, without permission in writing from the publisher.

Published in 2018 by Lethe Press, Inc.
6 University Drive, Suite 206 / PMB #223 • Amherst, MA 01002 usa
www.lethepressbooks.com • lethepress@aol.com

ISBN: 978-1-59021-581-4

This novel is a work of fiction. Names, characters, places, and
incidents are either products of the author's imagination or are
used fictitiously. Any resemblance to actual persons, living or
dead, organizations, events, or locales is entirely coincidental.

Set in Janson and Times New Yorker
Designed By: Frankie Dineen

✖

"In the middle of the journey of our life, I came to myself in a dark wood, for the straight way was lost."
Dante's Inferno

"Any two particles that have once been in contact will continue to act as though they are informationally connected regardless of their separation in space and time."
Bell's theorem

"Every man and every woman is a star."
The Book of the Law I:3

✖

For my mother, Beverly Leavell.
You make the world endlessly more beautiful. Full of
Magick. You gave me everything.

For Reiner Beelitz, who came into my life when
I needed him most. I have no idea how I convinced you
to stay on this crazy ride, but I'm glad you have. You
are one of the best things that has ever happened to me.
I am forever grateful and lucky.

For Alex Rondon. My brother and my best friend, you
helped me find my way back to myself. Regardless
of where life takes us, you will always be mine.

For Amy Klein, my writer guru, my soul mate, you
have taught me how to live.

And In memory of Jon Nelson. My love and my best
friend. Without your love and support this book never
would have been written. I only hope I can be as great
as you believed I was. I will miss you every single
day. You are always by my side. Forever. Fly safe, baby.
I will see you soon.

And this is only mostly true.

x

Accidental Warlocks

Bewitched

When I was a child, my mother would take me up to the edge of New York City, Washington Heights, to the Cloisters, a grand, magical castle made up of five disassembled European abbeys which had been sent to America and reassembled on a hilltop overlooking the Hudson. On the subway, she would read T.S. Elliot to me. I remember singing along with her when she reached the lines, "In the room the women come and go talking of Michelangelo."

I became obsessed with *The Hunt of the Unicorn*. My mother would always remind me that the seven tapestries had been stolen from the La Rochefoucauld family during the French Revolution and used to cover potatoes. She would then laugh, without ever knowing how much the idea of something so beautiful, something cherished, could be taken away. The idea that, at any moment, someone might come along and steal my mother, terrified me.

My favorite part of the trip was when she let me sit all alone outside in the cloistered gardens while she wandered the museum. From different vantage points you could see the river, dark clouds moving slowly, the promise of rain. I would lie on the stone floors and close my eyes, imagining I was a prince and that this was my castle. Or I would memorize lines of Elliot to impress her on the train ride home. She had reddish-blond hair and was from LaGrange, Georgia, and she wore jewelry the size of meteors, throwing herself at life with such wild abandonment and hope, her fearlessness could send you swirling for days.

My mother never forced a bedtime upon us when I was little; we would stay up as late as we wanted, sit with adults, listen to my mother and her friends drink and tell stories, watch them spread Tarot cards. My mother threw wild and sprawling dinner parties for intellectuals and artists, musicians, among whom were several gay best friends. Enthralled, my brother and I hid under the table. They would argue politics and religion and books, my mother stealing people into candlelit corners to read their cards and reveal their futures.

During these affairs, kids always got dessert before the first course was served; she would set up a table in the kitchen and place a cake, or a huge bowl of ice cream, or a pie or some other elaborately made treat in the center; we used no forks or spoons, but attacked the treats with our bare hands until we were satiated. I remember stuffing huge pieces of cake into our mouths, throwing it at one another, smearing icing or pudding on foreheads, laughing and running around, tiny, crazed and euphoric on sugar.

Once she found a mattress on the side of the road and made me and a group of neighborhood kids drag it home and onto the porch so we had something to spend our summer days jumping on. It was en vogue to drag dirty mattresses home for children to play on.

And one night my mother took a small group of us to a hilltop graveyard where she told us a spirit possessed her, changing the color of her eyes from blue to green. I watched again at distant river shrouded in fog. Dark clouds obscuring the moon. I listened as my mother laughed and walked among the dead. She told us of mermaids and ghosts and unicorns that could be found not in tapestries but in the wild places. Everything we had ever imagined and more existed if we wanted it. I realize now that was the key. You had to desire something, ache for it. Magic exists but comes with a price.

Among the graves she stopped. Wisps of fog wrapped around her in an eerie, golden light, and she smiled at me as if she had stumbled upon the greatest treasure in the whole world, as if something remarkable had been hidden and now revealed. I felt embarrassed at how she stared at me, and turned away from the intimacy.

X

In my twenties, she would tell me how she often could not sleep at night because of terrible dreams where I would be found dead, the needle still in my arm. She worried I would one day overdose. I told my mother everything; we kept no secrets. She once had a violent premonition of a lover of mine she didn't like standing over me with a bloody knife looking down at my dead body. She knew he was feeding me pills and liquid Oxy.

She would one day meet him: we ate dinner at an Italian restaurant on 6th Avenue and 4th. He was a dark and moody man, punishing and haunted. I had wanted her to love him as much as I did, but she couldn't. When I called her later that night, terrified because he had brought a knife into the room, screaming at me, screaming at the walls, she had told me to run, east, toward the river. "Water will keep you safe. And I will be there as soon as I can."

I stood on the edges of another river, at another time in my life, and my mother pointing out ripples in the water, screaming and laughing because it was a mermaid. She lifted me into the air, soaring, and I swear I saw it too. In that moment, I saw everything she did.

When I was thirteen she handed a copy of Larry Kramer's *Faggots*. "I think this might help you." I would spend hours locked in the bathroom jerking off to sprawling fantasies of orgiastic parties and dreamed of knowing friends, all inspired by that book.

She and I would take long walks, looking into other people's houses, making up fantastic stories about who might live inside. We would sit in her kitchen and talk to spirits, channeling them until I was so frightened I couldn't go pee by myself, making her stand just outside the bathroom door, talking to me the whole time. In those moments, her voice would change, conjuring the entities we were calling on, and her eyes would take on a strange, slightly darker hue, and she would smile. Everything was always going to be all right. That is the lesson the spirits had for us: that life would always, ultimately be okay. That was the great secret. If we were stronger, we might have taken comfort in that.

We would go on endless nighttime drives, tracking down her lover who she swore was cheating on her. Once she even tried to run him over, my brother and I in the back seat, her best friend in the seat next to her. And then we would go eat at late night diners and laugh and talk about anything and everything.

Years later, I made the decision to give up being a lawyer, having security, financial freedom, the course of my future, all while sitting on the Grand Canal in Venice with my mother, drinking dark chocolate in the cold air, talking about the sense of feeling haunted that came over us first in Rome and now along those darkly shadowed canals. She told me that the air felt saturated with previous lives, memories of all the people she had once been flooding her.

Europe was suffocating her. Rome felt almost threatening in its familiarity. Venice was an intoxicating swirl of ghosts and lost memories.

I didn't want to be a lawyer. I was looking for a way to make those around me proud, to prove I had succeeded. I wanted everyone to stop worrying about me, the high school dropout, the junkie now ex-junkie, the liar and the cheat, the under-achiever. I just wanted to find a way to make it possible for everyone to finally look at me and think, *There he is, he made it. Finally, he will be okay. There is nothing to worry about anymore.*

And yet, I didn't want what they wanted for me. I didn't want to be anything but the one thing that was so far out of my reach it seemed impossible. I didn't want to be anything but a writer, a career that would most likely leave me poor, never living up to all the endless expectations of those around me.

Looking out over that ancient city, my mother haunted and trembling next to me, a choking fear swallowed me, gnawing at the edges of my mind.

We would be getting on a train for Paris the following day, leaving Italy and all its haunted distractions behind, but first we would sit, the lingering taste of squid ink pasta and dark chocolate burning in my belly, a world full of uncertainty and fear raging in my head. Blinded.

So much of my adult life was out of focus, dark, and yet I kept looking for that ray of light, that hidden secret, that promised outcome, that moment when suddenly the world would be flooded with meaning and wonder and magic.

I have always been slightly predisposed toward optimism. Even in those darkest moments, when the demons howled the loudest I believed something beautiful was happening. I believed my life had a meaning.

We walked slowly down a maze of ancient streets toward Plaza San Marcos, my mother stopping periodically to run her hands along stone walls or to stare up at a broken angel hanging precariously over a doorway, communicating with the elements, breathing heavily into a fractured moonlight that filled the empty spaces.

"I feel so alone here." An old woman looking down at us from her store-front window filled with white meringue clouds and strange cream filled pastries. "I think I drowned here in a past life, in all this water," My mother whispered, her voice soft, the smell of the canals stagnating, the air drenched in sea water. "I can feel it in my lungs, I can see it when I close my eyes. I am a little girl running barefoot across large empty rooms, throwing herself against darkly painted walls, moonlight bursting through heavy clouds, and I am sinking, falling forever into that deepness."

She told me she had been murdered. The two of us were standing in some small lost plaza with looming windows and arched doorways, splinters of moonlight and fog dancing against strange rhythms. She had been murdered by her father, or maybe a brother, some male relation, and she remembered clearly the sense of betrayal and fear. We were staying at a small hotel just behind Plaza San Marcos, slightly removed from the rest of the tourists, each of our rooms overlooking a winding, lazy canal. I sat alone in my window looking down at the arched bridges, the swaying of the water rocking the boats tied to black posts, dim light fracturing the late-night mist that had settled over the city.

I was lost. At thirty-eight, I had no sense of direction anymore. No sense of who I wanted to be.

The next evening, we boarded the train for Paris. We each had our own first-class compartments with an armchair facing large windows, a bed, and a private bathroom. I sat in my room, reading Henry Miller as we sped north to Paris. Outside the night was frozen and empty, the only sign of humanity the desolate stations we broke through, never stopping, racing through the night. We had rooms in a small but elegant hotel in the Marais. My mother and I sat on her balcony, looking toward the Seine, the spirals of Notre Dame in the distance, the hills of the Left Bank and the Latin Quarter, the air thick with the sounds of the city.

"I feel safe in Paris." She wore a lime green turban-like scarf around her head, her fingers wrapped in jewels that sparkled in the lights of the Marais. A whole world moved on the street below us, chaotic and loud and full of mystery. "There were too many demons in Rome, and Venice was full of death and fear, but Paris… everyone is gay in Paris."

I laughed. "It's just the Marais. Everyone is gay in the Marais."

She grabbed my hand. We didn't touch a lot. Despite my deep love for her, I don't think either of hugged one another more than a few times in my entire life. Her hand felt cold, a dead woman's hand. A drowned woman's hand. "I don't think you should be a lawyer," she said.

Below us two men were kissing, a woman was yelling in Arabic at a cab driver, someone was laughing, kids were riding by on bikes, their shrill bells echoing through the streets.

"Even if it means you fail. I'd rather you fail trying to do what makes you happy than see you succeed at something you don't want."

The following year we met in Amsterdam. We had house boats on the Herengracht Canal. My mother and I sat in the rain. I had stopped trying to be a lawyer and given up eleven years of sobriety, and I was slightly drunk and stoned. She looked at me, her hair wet, the air cold, rain turning to snow. "You have no idea what you are doing, do you?" She reached out, pulling the hood of my jacket up over my head. A boat full of drunk musicians floated past, men singing to each other in Dutch, playing guitars, passing a bottle of amber liquid back and forth.

"I know exactly what the fuck I am doing."

"No, you don't, but you will." She smiled.

I knew I was disappointing her. Even though she would never say that. She was right, of course. We would both come to regret the truth of her prediction.

※

We ended up in Paris again, but I ignored her for the rest of the trip, hiding from her, refusing to go with her to the Picasso National Museum, or walk up the hill to the Sorbonne, or to eat fondue in the small basement restaurant she loved. I was mad at her. I had no idea that was going to be the last time we would spend together in Europe. She would be diagnosed with cancer, and I would find out I was HIV-positive, both events changing the course of our lives forever.

When I found out my mother had cancer, it was breathtaking, so startling in its scope I still can't seem to fathom its meaning. Her lying in the hospital bed, frightened, betrayed, trying to be brave, blue eyes a little stunned, repeating over and over, "This just isn't what I thought would happen."

And I wonder if anything will ever be able to break my heart in just that way again.

Life has a way of moving forward relentlessly, like those various rivers I spent my childhood on. I was always waiting for the right moment. The right time. I was always waiting for the stars to align before I decided what I should be doing. Now I know what my mother was trying to tell me. Nothing matters and everything matters. Both things are equally true. And it is better to fail at something you love than to succeed at something you hate.

Because all these people we love, all these events and all these moments, all the possibilities, all the love and fury and joy and pain will fade. Disappear. Everything and everyone I have ever loved will one day disappear.

We will all die.

※

I once dreamed I had found a way to build a time machine. But every time I went back into my past, I found something different, something I had forgotten. Nothing was as I remembered it. The people I loved were somehow all wrong—the way they spoke, their mannerisms, the lighting, the way shadows were cast. I kept reaching for something familiar, but each time I came up empty.

x

I woke up in my bed in Los Angeles, sleeping next to me were my husband, Alex, and our boyfriend, Jon. I had that sense of drowning, of having swallowed too much too fast. It took a few moments for the world to begin to slide back into focus. I kept repeating, *I am here. I am here.*

I got out of bed and, naked, I went to the backyard, sitting on a stone bench, the air sweet with jasmine. It was still dark out. Somewhere in the distance a helicopter hovered, its light like a beacon in the nuclear sky. I was still intoxicated from my dream of time travel, the past whispering in the shadows, the faces of those I loved like neon messages shining bright before burning away.

We are here, they seemed to be saying to me. *We are all right here.*

Mermaids

Most of what I know about sex I learned cruising parks and public bathrooms. There is a kind of beauty to the anonymity of being inside a stranger or having them inside you, feeling them as they come, their arms tightening around you, the way their breath changes. There is an intimacy even in the most degrading moments, even when kneeling on a dirty bathroom floor, gagging on a stranger's cock shoved all the way down your throat, the feeling as it throbs right before it shoots into your mouth, filling you with that inescapable feeling of having been used and loving it.

I have spent endless hours engaging in the most intimate acts with thousands of men in parks, bathrooms, and sex clubs. I can still taste some of them, the way they smelled, the way they kissed. I can feel the secret rush of energy moving between us, connecting all of us like some grand matrix—pinned to the floor of the bathroom at The New School in the West Village, someone standing guard, as one man pounds his cock into me, holding my head up for another man to shove his cock into my mouth. I am lost. I am nowhere. Three a.m. on Hyperion in Silver Lake, my turn to fuck the young Latin guy who is bent over the car, a line behind me, other men dripping out of him. He is wet and open. He moans as I fuck him. I pull him back, licking the back of his neck, salty and masculine. We are reckless and dangerous. We are without morals. Beautiful and brutal. I feel myself empty inside him, connecting me to all the other men who have been here.

There is a history to this. A culture. There is an art to it.

There is a magic to this.

And there is a kind of love to be found.

Something about the way the jasmine smelled, sweet and innocent, mixed with the summer car exhaust, the choking, breathless L.A. smog, something in the way the darkness felt against my bare-naked skin, the way my heart ached reminded me of the way Raphael kissed me.

As a teenager, I would spend weekends at my best friend's place on Central Park West. We would spend Saturday mornings watching the Robyn Bird show. I would suck him off before going out to cruise the Rambles at Central park. I can still see his dick, the shape of it, short but thick, stubby, the smell of sweat, the smell of him. I can still remember the way it slid perfectly down my throat. I remember teasing him, the way he would moan, telling me to go slow. *Not too fast Jeff, not yet, I don't want to cum yet.*

The Rambles might be better referred to as an Island of Misfit Boys, a place where the straight jocks from my high school, the mean kids, my father and step mother, my brother and step sisters, none of them existed anymore. This place was just for me. A place where I could be whoever I wanted, feral and desperate, starving. A place where I could find relief, where I no longer had to pretend to be something I wasn't. Even in the strange little lies I told about my age, my name, where I was from, who I was—even then I was more honest in that place than in most places I have ever been.

Once I followed a well-dressed white guy wearing a dark suit, and a black guy in jeans and a leather jacket across the bridge down a path and into the bushes. I stood, transfixed, as I watched the man in the suit drop to his knees before the black guy, the black guy unzipping and taking out his cock. Just as the black guy was letting out a loud gasp, I heard someone whistle from above me and say,

"Hey, blondie, whatcha doin'?"

I looked up, and a dark-skinned Dominican kid with black, curly hair was sitting precariously on a tree branch, smiling at me. He dropped down next to me with a thud so loud it startled the two guys. They ran off.

"What the hell you doin' out here watchin' the faggots suck dick? You miss the bus back to New Jersey or somethin'?"

I was momentarily offended that he had just assumed I was from New Jersey, and I said, "What are *you* doing out here?"

He grinned—he had a sexy grin, big and wondrous—and he held up a pack of Marlboros. "Smokin' cigarettes, man, and watchin' the faggots suck each other off." He held out a cigarette for me. "Want one?"

I took it. His name was Rafael, and his mom cleaned houses for people who lived in the mansion apartments of Central Park West.

"I'm pretty sure I'm a faggot too, you know? So, this seems like a good place to come and learn shit. See what the faggot life is all about." He was skinny and wore a used army jacket a few sizes too big for him. "You cold?" he asked, taking the jacket off. "You cold, you can wear it."

"I'm not cold."

It began to rain and Rafael jumped up, tossing the jacket over both our heads for protection. "Que quete conjo! Yo, you smoke weed? Wanta smoke a joint with me?" His hands moved fast, full of a lightening nervous energy, his feet always tapping, dancing back and forth, always moving. He laughed easily and smiled at everything I said, even when what I said didn't warrant a smile. "What's your name?" he asked, passing me the joint.

"Jeff."

He laughed; I wasn't sure what was funny. "That's a good name. 'Jeff.' A strong name." He tapped his fingers on my chest. "I really like that name. Really, I do."

"So, you learn any tricks out here?" I asked, stoned and full of courage.

"Yeah, man, of course I do. But not like I needed to. I already knew tricks." He smiled, his arm reaching around the back of my neck and pulling me into him. "You know what I mean?"

I was laughing almost uncontrollably now. "Naw, I got no idea what you mean."

He pushed me away and stood tall. "Look, it's serious business you gonna do some shit like this. You don't just fuck a dude or some shit. You gotta treat him nice. That's what matters, you know? The quality of the experience." He winked. "You gotta tickle it a little before you go stickin' it in."

I wanted to turn away, to hide the pink blush flooding my face, but I knew it was too late by Rafael's laughter.

"Pendejo!" He slapped me upside the head. "Look at you blushing and shit." He leaned in and kissed me quick on the lips, his tongue brushing against the edges, gentle and yet forceful. "You are too cute." He didn't pull away, just stayed there, his forehead propped against mine, his lips brushing against mine, his fingers intertwining with mine. I can still remember how he smelled. Musky but not rank, like a guy who had been out all day and was now caught in the rain. Sexy. His breath was spicy, and he pulled me into him, kissing me again, deeper this time. "Goddamn," he whispered into me, his breath making my mouth hot. "You gonna be comin' back around here tomorrow?"

"Yeah, I can be here again tomorrow," I said without thinking about how complicated that might actually be.

"Meet me here. At the rock. 3:30." Then he looked at me, serious. "And don't think I'm letting you stay here after I leave. We are gonna walk outta this park together, you get me, man?"

I smiled. Yeah. I got him.

He held my hand all the way out of the park, insisting I wear his jacket. Just before walking north up Central Park West, he kissed me on the cheek and said, "Okay, baby? Ima see you tomorrow, right?"

"At the rock. 3:30."

His smile grew, his eyes blazing. He leaned in quick and kissed my lips, looking around after, making sure we hadn't been seen. He punched me in the chest and was gone, running across the street, weaving around cars.

The next day I arrived at the rock a few minutes late. Rafael was already there waiting with a red rose, the kind you bought at corner bodegas for fifty cents, in his hand. He was wearing khaki pants and a blue, button-down oxford and scuffed black work boots. He smiled when he saw me, pushing black curls out of his eyes, and he handed me the rose.

"You got me a rose?" I asked, embarrassed.

"Fuck ya." He kissed me quick, his lips so warm. "I wanted you to know you were special to me." He looked around for a moment, men leaning against trees in predatory stances, watching us. "I was thinking maybe we could go downtown, you know? Check out a movie or get some ice cream or some shit. What you think?"

The sky was a dark grey, summer transitioning to autumn, a light rain beginning to fall. He took my hand in his. His skin was so hot, it almost burned.

"We can walk. Or take the train. Whatever you want, baby."

I had never really been on a date with a guy before. No one had ever given me flowers. Or held my hand for as long as Raphael did, all the way from 72nd Street and Central Park West to Washington Square Park. He pointed out places his mom had worked, telling me about the lives he had seen when she would take him with her.

"You got no idea, baby, how crazy some people are. They do crazy shit, and they think they're normal. This one woman won't ever leave her house. I mean ever. I'm serious. She has people bring her food and groceries, and if she needs to see a doctor, they come to her. She's afraid of everything. She's afraid of dying so bad that she don't know she's already basically dead living like that. It's fuckin' insane. Think about that. All her windows are blacked out. She don't even know there's a world out there no more. Lives right there on 5th Avenue. Richest place in the world, and it don't do her no good at all. I'm not shitting you. Crazy fuckin' people out there." He squeezed my hand. "They don't know about life." He leaned in, smelling me, his lips brushing up against my neck. "They don't know about this." He pulled me close and for the first time he really kissed me, deep, his mouth locked to mine, tongues searching and exploring. He smiled and pressed against me, and I could feel him grow hard. He reached around and grabbed my ass.

And then we were moving again, and he was talking on and on about things, anything, whatever happened to pop into his head at the moment, as if he were afraid that if he didn't get it all out, he might not get another chance.

We ate falafel at a place on MacDougal and got ice cream from a vendor in Washington Square Park, sitting on stone benches and telling each other stories. I tried to tell him something important, talking about my life with my father and step-mother, about school and how I felt alone most of the time, with no one to talk to.

"I think that's part of bein' a faggot," he said, grabbing on to my hand. "I think it ain't easy, you know? These people, they don't know us. Not like we know each other. The whole world is built for them. They don't even know we are the way we are, you know? If they did…" His eyes became distant, losing focus. "My dad caught me once. With this kid I go to school with. It was nothin', man. We were just jerkin' off and shit. Harmless. Nothin' like what I've done in that fuckin' park. That son of a bitch beat the shit outta me. Seriously. I had to go to the hospital and get stitches. Whole time my older brother telling me that I'm breakin' my father's heart. Ruining the family. Get my shit together. Me sittin' there bleedin' with a broken arm, and it's *their* hearts that are broken."

I kissed him. The buildings around us lit bright in the fog that had settled over the city. I wrapped my arms around him, holding him as tight as I could, and I wished I could have kept us there frozen in time like that, in a world that never changed. Rafael laughed, biting my ear, kissing the lids of my closed eyes, nipping at my nose. We made out for what seemed like an eternity, except it wasn't enough.

"I gotta go," I said, hating myself the minute I spoke. "I gotta go home."

"Where you live?" He had yet to let me go; his arms claimed me.

"Jersey."

And then he pushed me away. "I fuckin' knew it!" He laughed.

"Shut up." I tackled him. We didn't care who was watching, or that the pavement was still wet from the rain, or that we had no place to go, no place to be together. No real place to fuck.

He walked me to the PATH train at Christopher Street and asked me when he could see me again.

"Whenever," I said. "It's no big deal getting here."

"What about school?"

"Fuck school." I smiled.

We spent a few more minutes making out and then made plans to meet again at our rock the following weekend.

I took the train back to Madison and walked up the hill to where my family lived in our large house like some isolated castle cut off from my world, the only world where I belonged, and locked myself in my bedroom, and cried.

x

Those years in Madison were lonely. I felt like I didn't belong anywhere. I had no idea how to speak to anyone, like a foreigner who had accidentally walked into a distant land where the language and the customs were all different. People looked at me like I was a stranger. There were times when all I could do was scream, standing in the middle of the kitchen and yelling, trying to communicate something that was impossible to get across.

I remember terrible fights with my father where I just howled, wanting to rip at myself, pull myself apart, until nothing was left. I had dreams of setting the house on fire and disappearing, dreams where I found guns hidden under my pillow, and late at night I slipped into the rooms of my brother and stepsisters, into my parents' room, killing them all, shooting them point blank in the face. Horrible dreams where I was taken into custody and locked into asylums for the criminally insane, forced to live with the guilt of who I was. A monster. A killer. I would wake screaming, alone in the basement bedroom on Woodland Road and think about killing myself, as if that was the only option left to me. I would lie awake at night, afraid that if I fell asleep I would kill them all with a knife from the kitchen and then wake from what I had done covered in blood, everyone dead.

Once, sitting on the edge of the pier off of Christopher Street, I told these things to Rafael, afraid he would think I was evil, monstrous, terrible. After I was done, he looked at me and I saw he was crying.

"What's wrong?" I asked, wanting to run away.

"You are so beautiful." He ran his fingers over my lips. "And you aren't no fuckin' killer. Fuck your family. Fuck everyone. Fuck this whole fuckin' world."

Raphael told me how his father had found some porn under his bed, how he had thrown his mattress across the room, ripped his posters from the walls, and shredded the journals where he wrote poetry

"He came at me, you know? The guy came at me like he was gonna beat the shit outta me, but fuck that, you know? Seriously, fuck all of that. I ain't no little kid no more. So I beat the shit outta him."

I looked at him, stunned.

"My mom, she told me I couldn't stay there, you know? That I couldn't be their son. So I been movin' around."

Everything inside me hurt. I wanted to reach out, to hold him, to save him. I wanted to change the world. "Moving around? What does that mean?"

In a few days, it would be Halloween. The River was a dark and furious thing. Men were cruising the piers. Teenagers were smoking joints. A man in leather chaps, ass exposed, was making out with a skinny guy with bright pink fingernails. The West Side Highway roared behind us.

"My older brother, Carlos, he used to tell me there were mermaids in the water, you know? In the River."

I looked at him. He was so beautiful in that moment. Golden. His eyes seemed to capture the light of the city, all the beauty and all the pain of the world reflected back at me.

"Mermaids?"

"Yeah, you now, chicks who are half-fish?"

I laughed. "I know what mermaids are."

He smiled at me. "Yeah, well, you know, for most of my life I believed him. I thought, fuckin' New York City, man, of course there were mermaids livin' in the River." He lit a cigarette, the burning red lighting up his face. "But now I know it was all bullshit, you know? Ain't no ~~god~~damned mermaids in the River. Not one magical fuckin' thing in this ~~god~~damned city."

We curled up together and fell asleep, holding each other tight against the cold and the wind. In the morning, we ate eggs and bacon at a diner on 7th Avenue and then he stood with me while I waited for my PATH train.

"Where you gonna go?" I asked.

"Around. You know. I'll be good."

"When can I see you again?"

He looked older, his eyes darker, his smile more restrained, less full of wonder. "Come up next Sunday. 2:30."

"At the rock?"

"Yeah. At the rock."

My train was pulling in. He kissed me, holding on to me for a moment. And then he let me go. "I miss you," he said, as the doors closed.

"I miss you too," I said, the train pulling away so he couldn't see the words as they left my mouth.

I knew that he wouldn't be there, but I went anyway.

I spent three hours on that rock before I gave up.

Storm Breaks

I'd like to tell you that when Rafael didn't show up I searched the oceans for him—perhaps he had been stolen by an envious mermaid. But I didn't. My heart was broken. Devastated. I hurt in ways I didn't know was possible. So, I did the only thing I knew how to do. I wandered the trails of that park, sucking off any guy who let me, fucking as many guys as I could, looking for an escape from the pain.

I sometimes wonder if Rafael might be lurking in the bushes, watching me. I think at one point I caught a glimpse of him in the trees. I don't think he would have been mad. I think if anything he would have understood. *This is who we are*, he once said to me as we watched two guys suck each other off. It was getting dark out, no need to hide in the bushes any more. I dropped to my knees before him, taking his cock out. He had a beautiful dick. Long and thick. It was always so hard. Always so ready for me. I blew him as he watched those guys fuck. We would do that. Spend hours in the park, me blowing him or him fucking me. Watching other guys fuck. *And I love who we are*, he would say.

x

I had a friend, Laurent, who called that moment where you meet someone in the most random of places, out of nowhere, and, in that moment, you see them for who they are, he thought of that moment as accidental love.

My husband, Alex, was never meant to be someone I loved. He was just some trick I was going to fuck. Another big dicked Dominican I met on Scruff. The first time he showed up at my house in the hills of Silver Lake, a rambling mansion falling apart around me. I was newly sober, broke and dependent once again on my father. Alex looked so beautiful, so strong. Those first few seconds as he stood there in my doorway, I knew I was going to love him.

I knew that night when he fucked me, relentless and dirty, beautiful in a way that was animal, pulling out of my ass and cumming into my mouth, holding my head down, forcing me to lick him clean. The way he made me take him to dinner first, not allowing me to be just a fuck. The way he smiled. He was so young, neither of us really knew how to talk to each other yet so I did what I always do. I didn't shut up. I just kept speaking, hoping that he would see what I was trying to say somewhere in all those words. The way after he fucked me, he put on some 80's horror movie, and then fell asleep next to me. The sound of his breathing, the wind blowing through the door that led to the balcony that led to the night, to those hills lit up so bright they seemed to burn endlessly.

I remember climbing out of bed and standing naked on my balcony, looking out over the night. Hollywood was to the west, downtown just barely visible to the south-east, Sunset Boulevard like a river of neon reds and oranges, the glow of cars, the never-ending parade of life.

x

New York, another city drowning in the stunning beauty of light, to nights blanketed in snow, to accidental loves and to Elly and Daniel and Wonder Bar, a neighborhood bar where you could go fuck your neighbors and still share a drink. Now it's called Eastern Bloc. A different kind of place, but for me Wonder Bar was paradise. At least for a few nights. When it snowed.

Wonder Bar was located on 6th Street between Avenues A and B. It had a back room, a small dark room next to the bathroom where you could get your dick sucked or fuck or do any of the other lascivious and sexy things gay men used to do in gay bars. Wonder Bar's back room had a kind of neighborly innocence to it. You might get a kiss or a polite pat on the head after giving someone a blowjob. They might even say hi to you and buy you a drink in the front bar.

The last time I was there was back in the early 90's during a blizzard that had settled over the city in a surreal and blanketing quiet. Like a silent black and white movie, the world felt transformed. I was there with my friend Elly. We lived together in Brooklyn and had known each other from boarding school. She drove a Mercedes station wagon her father had bought her and had cold, startlingly blue eyes. We had tried dating in high school, fucking once in the attic bedroom of a friend's farmhouse on Nantucket, but it hadn't worked out.

I was much more interested in fucking her friend, Charles, whose family owned the large Nantucket beach estate, and she had a special place in her bulimic heart for donuts that eclipsed all else. She was blonde and beautiful and full of dark lonely desires, just like me. We both came from a similar casually rich background, and were lost, set loose in the world with no real responsibilities. When confronted with a blizzard and an unlimited supply of cash, it made perfect sense to drive her forest green station wagon across the Brooklyn Bridge to Wonder Bar in the East Village.

Elly had spent much of her life in a self-controlled bubble built carefully over the years to protect her from the chaos and pain of the outside world, but she let go at times, screamed uncontrollably at the night and shook her fists madly at the stars and danced and got fucked up in a royal way. On those nights, Elly was the most fun person in the world.

There were other kinds of nights. Dark nights. Elly's moods were dramatic and dangerous things. You never knew where any one thought, any one action might lead you. I have seen Elly standing naked before the bathroom mirror with scissors in her hand, threatening to cut away pieces of herself, "All this fat!" Her eyes looked dark and burned with fury. "All this ugliness." She spat at her refection. "I hate you!" Her fists struck her own face, her lip splitting, blood thickening. "*I hate you!*"

I'd had to tackle her, grabbing the scissors and throwing them into the other room.

She fought me. She was strong, fists swinging, legs kicking. "I'm going to kill you for this!"

Later that night, over a bottle of whiskey and a pack of Marlboros, she said, "I could kill you in your sleep, you know? Then you wouldn't be able to stop me. Then there would be nothing you could do."

I knew she loved me. I knew that most likely she would never hurt me. And yet I locked the door when I went to sleep.

x

The city was ready for an apocalypse, a blizzard to end all blizzards. The night was clarifyingly cold, street lamp's golden halos obscured by blinding white. We drove along abandoned avenues. New York was like a lost kingdom, empty and pristine, the sky filled with the promise of flying horses and magical gnomes and wish-granting wizards. We parked, and I told Elly I would meet her in the bar in a few minutes.

She gave me that look, and then she shook her head. "I'm having fun, tonight, Jeff, no matter what."

"Me too," I said. "I'm just picking up a few bags. To cut the edge."

"The edge of what?"

I laughed. "Everything."

"Whatever. Just make it quick."

I ran to 7th and Avenue B, walking the long, lonely stretch to the stoop where the dope dealers hung out. I always prayed during that walk. To God, to the spirits, to whoever would listen. I had been having a running dialogue with the elements for my entire life. Begging them to help me. To save me. Making endless promises that tonight, God, would be the last night I would do this. I just need it tonight. To get through. To get around. Just tonight. To survive. Over and over, I repeated my mantra until I was standing, veiled in a swirling white, before the dope man. There was a line, even in the middle of a blizzard, and the guards were walking up and down. "Cash out, assholes, have your money ready." One of them, probably fifteen, stopped and looked me up and down. I knew he was thinking I didn't fit in. Too well-fed, too rich-looking, too something. I knew he was considering kicking me out of line until one of them recognized me and nodded his head, a silent act of approval.

I had been going to that spot for over a year now. They better fucking recognize me.

I bought a bindle of heroin for a hundred bucks, stuffed the ten bags into my pocket, and ran back to Wonder Bar and Elly and our lost night.

Elly had already made friends with a few older queens, true New Yorkers who had said fuck you to the storm, refusing to compromise their lives for anything, and a beautiful Saudi Arabian boy named Shahid. Shahid had curly black hair, darkly golden eyes, and tan skin. He was model gorgeous—almost too gorgeous—tall and muscled, thick eyebrows, strong jaw. He smiled at me, trying to tell me something in a strangely lyrical accent. His eyes were so golden, they seemed to emit a light like some radiant pirate's treasure waiting to be found. He told me a glittering jeweled tale of Saudi Arabian wealth and royalty. Of not knowing what it meant to be gay, of what he was feeling, of these strange, monstrous desires he had.

"I fell in love with a man who worked for my father. He was a father himself with a wife, very devout. He believed in Islam and Allah, and he was honorable and loyal to my father. And yet I knew, when he would look at me, this thing that passed between his eyes, I knew that he wanted me. How do I know this at sixteen years old? How do I know what this thing was when I didn't even have a name for it? I will never know the answer to this. I just knew it. I felt it. Like a pain in my chest, a gnawing at my stomach, self-loathing and a hunger that pulled me in the direction of those eyes. I wanted him to look at me, to see me. I wanted to feel his words and the sound of his voice. One day I was alone studying. My father and brothers were in meetings. Something important. They were always involved in things of great import. Things that did not involve me. I was to be the smart son—not a warrior or a womanizer, but a lawyer or an accountant. A philosopher maybe. This was good for me. It meant they left me alone. And alone is what I wanted. Alone meant time to pursue my thoughts and my fantasies in my strange and dark little world."

The music vibrated around us. The door had swung open, a blast of cold followed by white flurries of snow like tiny fairies bursting into the void. The bar had gotten busier. Men danced and kissed, the light a warm amber broken only by the glittering sounds of the men as they talked and loved and laughed. Elly was making out with a tall Italian man who insisted he was bisexual and loved women. I could hear her laughing somewhere in the corners of the room. I knew her so well that I could understand the variations in her tone, what each gasp and giggle meant. Were we light or dark? Happy or sad? Was there to be joy or fury? Elly was a constant puzzle always reshaping herself, never allowing herself to be complete, never slowing down, a chaotic whirlwind endlessly moving until the time when it all ended and she would lock herself in her room, in darkness, sobbing, talking of suicide and quoting Sylvia Plath.

I hated Sylvia Plath and everything she represented. Sad girls and dark rooms filled with torn letters and shredded memories.

"I was in the downstairs library," Shahid continued, oblivious to the world around us. "We had a very large house, a palace with many rooms and levels. I sometimes wondered if I would ever be able to explore and discover all the possibilities in that house. I think the moment I found the library, I just stopped. Everything I had ever wanted was in that room. Books banned in my country, forbidden ideas, long novels, collections of letters, books of philosophy and law and art, literature from all over the world. I could spend my life in that room, locked with those books, fed by my family's servants, and I would never be freer anywhere in the world." He smiled. It was strangely sad. "I think I might have been right. But you cannot spend your entire life in a room with books, can you?"

I smiled and reached out, the tips of my fingers touching the tips of his, a moment of electricity and knowing. "I'd like to think that's where I'll end up one day."

He leaned in and kissed me, his eyes open and full of a kind of wonder that can only fade with time. His lips were soft, his breath wet with whiskey and cigarettes and pizza. He grabbed my hand and leaned down, his head against my forehead, our lips touching gently, and he began whispering. I couldn't hear what he was saying, but I could tell by the vibrations it mattered.

"What are you saying?"

"It is a poem. In Arabic. A love story. But one always dies. I am always saying it, hoping it might change by the end."

I liked that idea. That somehow, maybe, he could change the ending of something that already existed, something that was solid, but might become malleable, changeable in time.

"I felt safe in that library, and when the man who worked for my father came in, looking at me with his eyes full of intent, I felt like I could expand into anything I wanted to be. Like maybe I could be free. He was so handsome, like a movie star, or the captain of some great adventure. I don't know what words he said to me that first day. He just came into the room and closed the door behind him, locking it. Our house was filled with guards. My father was very paranoid. Nowhere was exactly safe or private. Nowhere but that library with its books and its paintings."

His breathing had changed, his eyes focusing momentarily on the past.

"He was rough, but I liked it, do you know?"

"Yeah. I know exactly what you mean."

"At first it hurt, but then I wanted it to hurt, needed the hurt. He thrust into me, his breath hot against my neck, his body smelling like a man, sweaty. His cock wasn't long, but it was fat, and for a moment I felt like I was losing myself, pinned underneath him, there for his pleasure only."

He smiled and lit a cigarette. "We are so stupid and romantic when we are young."

I wanted to tell him we were still young, but maybe I didn't even know it at the time. Maybe it is just forty-eight-year-old me now in Los Angeles, who wishes I had said it. *You are still so young. You both are. Life hasn't even begun to destroy you.*

"I believed he would leave his wife and family to be with me. Oh, he left them to sneak away, to bend me over couches or chairs, to throw me onto the floor and use me. And I enjoyed it. I believe there is an honor in being used like that, by a man, to give him pleasure. I received pleasure every time I felt him come inside me. But when it was over, he would leave me like that. Alone. To do what I wanted with myself." He shut his eyes for a moment. Then he looked at me, smiling. He was too handsome to have that look of vulnerability: he should be ruling worlds, starring in TV shows, on billboards in Times Square. Not here in a blizzard at Wonder Bar, propped up against me, telling stories of his past.

I leaned in and kissed him. He opened his eyes, and then he pulled me to him, his breath mixing with mine, and we held each other, kissing.

"I told my family I wanted to study in New York. Not London. Not Paris. New York City. I believed everyone in New York would be sophisticated. Metropolitan, intense, and beautiful. I believed the city would be full of intellectuals and artists. There are more bankers and lawyers than I was expecting." He smiled. He kissed me again.

I remember my dick getting so hard it hurt. I looked to the back room for a moment, wondering how to lead us there. To relief.

"My father was furious. He hated America. It was the West in ways that Europe was not. It was fascist in its commercialism. It was Christian and Jewish and everything ugly. My father wanted nothing to do with the U.S. But he knew something was wrong with me. Something that would embarrass him. So instead of fighting me, he said maybe the U.S. with its Jews and its naked women was the best place for a boy like me. In a way I think sending me to this place that he hated, to the Unclean Land, the Godless People was an act of kindness. He was setting me free. If I had stayed, I would have been devoured by his world. If I had allowed myself to be who I am, I would have been eaten alive. NYU and New York and the Unclean World became my salvation. And here I am, living my life as a beautiful gay man in New York City."

I looked to the center of the room where Elly had taken her top off and was dancing braless, in a circle of cheering gay men.

"We are nothing but animals," he whispered into me. "Brutes. I would like to fuck you the way he fucked me, brutal, relentless, filling you with my cum. Here, in the dark, in the back room. And then I am going to leave you. Would you do that?"

"Yes," I said, knowing what it would be like. Used and left, an object to be enjoyed, the knowing made my dick hurt even more.

When he fucked me, I could feel his loneliness. It was violent and cold, detached, and I wondered what it would mean for him to make peace with who he was, if that were even possible. I wanted to tell him we were more than animals. We were more than anything I could ever explain or say. That we were lost, sailing alone in the dark, castaways. Instead, I let him fuck himself into me, pounding at me relentlessly until he was gasping and holding me tight, filling me with everything he had.

After, he didn't leave me there like he had promised. We returned to the main room, Elly now in her underpants, her bi Italian in a white jock strap, her grabbing onto his hairy ass, and Shahid and I dancing, holding each other close. He whispered into my ear, and I smiled, kissing the side of his neck, smelling him. Sex and cum and ass. Boy.

It felt good to be held. The music was perfect. Everyone was happy. I walked Shahid out when he left, making out with him in the snow, both of us too drunk to notice how cold and desolate the night was. We exchanged numbers and made plans to have dinner.

Half an hour after Shahid left, an older couple—in their forties, younger than I am now—hairy and well built, came into the bar. One was in leather chaps, his ass large and on display. When he bent over, the cheeks opened, inviting, and I knew I had to have that hole. We cruised each other for a few minutes before I followed them into the back room. They had the kind of asses you couldn't say no to. I fucked them both the way Shahid had promised to fuck me, and then, trying to make sure they both got a little bit of my load, I left them waiting for more.

Nights like that are rare. Glimpses at inherent possibilities. Drunk and stupid, Elly and I drove back across the Brooklyn Bridge through that spiraling blizzard, laughing and smoking cigarettes, talking the whole way. I have no idea which one of us drove or how we made it home alive, but I clearly remember blasting the B-52s and bouncing around the car, her eyes so bright in that darkness, radiating out toward me. That really was an awesome night.

I called Shahid once. He called me a few weeks later. We made awkward chatter, promising to hang out. But we never met again.

x

During another snowstorm, I took Elly's station wagon. Once again, the city felt like it was in some kind of preparation, locked down for disaster. The sky was a heavy, brightly lit silver, the air frozen and still. A hush had spread over Manhattan, turning it into a fairytale kingdom of dark shadows and sparkling lit paths, ominous leafless trees like strange looming giants storming the gates. A flurry of snow had begun to fall, painting the world in white and gray.

I was driving to Chelsea to fuck a guy I had met on a phone sex chat room.

He was deep in the West Side. Not yet glamorous, the meatpacking district still seedy, no High Line to walk, no fancy piers. Decay and threat and cruising. The West Side of the Village and Chelsea was filled with male prostitutes, leather daddies, sex clubs and porn shops. Cars lined the streets, driven by married guys from Jersey and Long Island looking for dick.

It was sexy and dirty and full of promise.

As I drove down the street, heading west, a strange apparition appeared on the road ahead, shrouded in fractured street lamps. He was tall, his shoulders held back, his hair stringy and brown. He was naked, his hands and feet burnt and swollen red. I slowed down. He turned to me, and I felt like screaming and laughing, both afraid and safe at the same time, as if I had stumbled into some alternative universe of angels and elves and goblins.

He was in his early twenties, grotesque and battered, his forehead too big for his face. His nose sat wide and crooked, his hands large to the point of being out of proportion to the rest of his body. His eyes, though, were determined and sure of themselves. This was a man on a mission.

I rolled my window down, pulling up beside him. "Are you okay?" I should have just kept driving. This was not my business. He was clearly insane.

He looked at me, stopping for a moment. His skin was raw from the cold. He looked martyred. Tortured. Displayed suddenly in the world. A reminder of something important we had forgotten.

"Are you okay?" he mimicked back at me.

"You should go inside. Go somewhere."

"I am inside. I am everywhere." A shudder went through me as I realized no steam rose from his mouth when he spoke.

I am not an uncommonly generous man. I am not necessarily kind. When I said, "Do you want my jacket? It's fucking cold out there," I surprised myself.

"Do you know what is ahead?" He pointed uptown, toward Chelsea and Hell's Kitchen and the Upper West Side. Toward the future. "Darkness. And it will prevail. It will swallow us whole. And we will be afraid. But we will also be complete. Because we are darkness. We are shadows. We are discarded pieces."

Parked in the stillness of the falling snow, I sat there and watching as he walked away from me, down the street, further west toward the water. For a moment I thought of oblivion and of death, and knew I needed the brief and furtive connection that a hook-up promised a gay man.

I drove into Chelsea and parked the station wagon on a side street just east of 10th Avenue and stepped into the snow. The buildings of the city glimmered distantly in a swallowing fog, devouring concrete and steel. I was outside, and it was wet and cold. I was on my way to fuck some guy I had never met.

Across the street from me, casting a lurid and ominous glow over the glaringly muted white of the snow, I saw a red-light bulb blinking above a small door. Below the red neon open sign was a small wooden plaque that read, *Store of the Occult. Darkness and Light. Books and Artifacts.* The wood was worn, and the words were written in a dark, mangled green. There was no window and no way to confirm that it was, in fact, open, but I trusted the sign. Drawn inexplicably by the strangeness of the red light, I turned the knob and opened the door.

I stepped into a dimly lit room filled with shelves of books, oversized arm chairs, Persian rugs, and grinning skulls. Candlelight flickered in dancing shadows along the walls; a black cat lay atop a stack of books, its two front paws draped over a copy of Israel Regardie's *My Rosicrucian Adventure*. Hector Berlioz's "Symphonie Fantastique" played quietly in the background, and a tall man with black hair and pale eyes sat at a desk. He read a leather-bound book with no words on the cover, just symbols carved as if into flesh. His hands were long and thin. He was a little older than me, but he looked alien to me, foreign and ancient.

His smile had the effect of making me feel comfortable and uncomfortable at the same time.

"Anything I can help you with?"

"Just looking." I said and wondered how many other people had told him that, and how many ever bought anything from the store.

"I considered closing up, but then I thought, you never know who's out there on a night like this."

Something about the way he said it didn't put me at ease. But it didn't send me running either.

He had an eclectic collection of books: Keats and Burroughs and occultists Regardie and Crowley, Jack Parsons and Dion Fortune, strange bound books with archaic symbols on them lay next to Dostoyevsky and Henry Miller; tortured looking artifacts and monstrous drawings, a wide collection of poetry alongside books on spells and histories of magic and the occult. I looked at two stunning charcoal drawings flat on the desk, each making my heart hurt. They weren't of anything special: one of a woman with long hair and sad eyes and the other of a naked man lying on his side, reaching his hand out, his face full of expectation and loss.

"I'm Daniel." When he stood up I saw he was impossibly tall, rail thin. He wore dark slacks, a black Dali's Car t-shirt and wing-tipped shoes he had probably bought on St. Marks.

"I'm Jeff." I smiled. I have a nice smile. People like it. "I hadn't meant to come in here. I was meeting a friend. But you were open."

"And you just thought you'd check it out?"

He stepped from behind the desk. I noticed Aleister Crowley's Thoth Tarot deck spread out on the desk. Alongside the cards was a copy of *Dante's Inferno* in a beautifully bound hard copy edition. I wanted to pick it up and hold it in my hands. Books had that effect on me. They impacted me in ways that nothing else ever has.

He pulled a bottle of Jameson out from under the desk and looked around for two shot glasses.

"Wanta have a drink?" His voice was deep, the kind of voice you felt as you heard it.

"My friend. He's probably waiting."

He poured himself a shot and raised it to me. I smiled again. "I'll probably be open for a while. If you want to stop back in."

x

The guy I was meeting lived in a run-down apartment building just a few blocks up the street from Daniel's bookstore. I buzzed his apartment and was let up. His place was hazy with incense. Over the speakers, monks chanted and played almost silent bells. The room was lit by one dim light covered with a red handkerchief. He was thick with a black beard and salt and pepper hair. He wore a black leather vest and worn-out blue jeans with the ass cut out. A porn VHS played silently on TV, two muscle men in a field, lifting bags, slow motion turns, the camera catching glimpses of their bodies. Cut to a barn. One of them had his suspenders pulled down, bent over a tractor, holding his butt cheeks open for the other man, a large cock sticking out of blue jeans, slowly, slowly it enters the ass, they begin to fuck. It is a strange scene against the backdrop of the monks chanting.

Outside his living room windows, snow fell silently, blanketing the streets in stillness.

"I have to wake up early," he said to me, pulling his pants down and turning around, revealing a plump white ass. He bent over the coffee table, spitting, and rubbing his fingers over his hole. "Fuck and then go home. If that's cool?"

On the TV, the dick had been replaced by fingers then by a fist then by the blunt wooden end of a shovel. The bottom's face was hidden, the top was furious and full of anger and desire.

I dropped to my knees and licked his butt, tasting the sweat and funk of him. It tasted good. He moaned. He had a pink hole and white cheeks, and when I slipped inside him, I felt my whole world fade away, everything centered in my cock. The air was heavy with incense and smoke and silently chanting monks. My dick was buried deep inside him. He pushed against me, begging me to go harder, to really fuck him hard, which I did. I fucked him as hard and as fast as I could. I liked seeing him bent over like that, his hands balled into fists, thick grunting noises. When I came, I made sure to push in deep, holding my dick inside him, until I knew it was done, there was no more.

He dropped to his knees, and took my dick in his mouth, cleaning it off.

I'm not sure why I went back to Daniel's bookstore after. Maybe because I felt a little sad as I walked down the stairs from the nameless man's apartment and onto the street. Or maybe because his shop had been warm, the candlelight romantic.

Something about being around all those books would also help with the impending anxiety of having just fucked a guy without a condom. AIDS still felt far off and impossible, something barely mentioned outside of the gay and lesbian center, but I knew what I had done was risky. I was beginning to make bargains I'd never keep with the Universe, and the idea of whiskey and books and Tarot seemed like a pleasant distraction.

When I walked, in he had a shot of whiskey waiting. I sat on the couch against the wall and across from the desk and did two shots in a row.

Daniel smoked Dunhills, and he offered me one.

"I had a feeling you'd be back."

"Like a psychic feeling?" I was being a smart-ass. It's something I do when I'm feeling suddenly insecure.

He laughed. "I figured you were gonna meet a trick."

"A trick? What made you think that?"

"I don't know. Just something about the way you stood. The time of night. Who goes out in the middle of the night in a blizzard except a guy looking for dick?"

"I could have been homeless or crazy." I thought back to the odd man I'd seen earlier that night.

"You still could be. All I know is that you got laid and then came back here. The rest…well, you're still a mystery."

I didn't feel very mysterious, and the fact that he knew I had gone out on a night like this looking to get laid made me feel embarrassed and stupid. No way I was going to tell him I had driven an hour through this weather from Brooklyn.

I asked him for a reading, offering to pay.

"I never let anyone pay me for reading the Tarot, but I should warn you, I don't play nice. I will tell you what I see, even if what I see is dark."

"I think I can handle it."

"My ex broke up with me because all I saw was failure. Ruin. Stagnation. Self-induced banality. He wanted success. Passion. Love. Adventure. Every card I got predicted the opposite. He said I was cruel, that I should have lied. I'm not going to lie. To him or to you. If you can accept that, fine. I'll give you a reading."

Dali's Car was playing on the stereo. *The Waking World.* The room smelled of tobacco and something else, something deeper, muskier, familiar. Peter Murphy's voice reminded me of high school and friends who had disappeared. It reminded me of Sarah Lawrence and the first time I did heroin, falling in love with Ashton, lying next to him and listening to his breathing, slow, in and out, the sounds of the rain as it fell against our dorm windows. Music can carry me backward until I get lost in the present moment, forgetting who I am.

x

The last time I had seen Ashton was in Chicago. We had gone home with a Puerto Rican bartender named Juan. The next morning, high on coke and coffee, eating pop tarts, Ashton told me he had fallen in love with Juan.

"That doesn't make any sense," I said, my nose hurting, a slight swelling in the lymph nodes, something that happens to me when I snort too much coke, my head pounding, my ass sore from endless hours of fucking with no release. "We just met him. He's some one-night thing…. He's some bartender."

Juan stood at the counter pouring Lucky Charms into a yellow bowl. Outside another snow storm raged. I tried to remember why we had come to Chicago. What day it was. I tried to remember exactly who I was.

It all made sense to me, suddenly, what had happened:

It was winter. February. New York was cold and bleak and felt dead. Ashton and I were doing three to five bags of dope a day, sometimes more like six to ten. We weren't going to class anymore. We would sit in our apartment on 13th and 1st Avenue and pretend to be together, pretend to be in love, pretend to care, when we were dying, lying around waiting for the checks from our parents to arrive so we could go out to eat and do laundry.

We decided to drive to Chicago. We bought twenty bags of China White each, a few bags of coke, a carton of cigarettes and got into Ashton's BMW and drove west. It had made sense. In a way. South might have made more sense. In Miami, he wouldn't have broken up with me for a Puerto Rican Goth bartender. In Miami, we would have stayed in till sunset then gone to the clubs and laughed at all the fags.

But I had said I had never been to Chicago.

So, there we were. I'd called my dad. He bought me a plane ticket home. I left Ashton with Juan. When I got back to our apartment, the snow had melted and there was the hint of sunlight. New York suddenly seemed bearable, and I didn't miss Ashton as much and I had thought I would.

X

The day I got back, I packed a bag of dirty laundry and got on the train at Penn Station and went to see my mom. She was living in a beautiful little row house just blocks from the Delaware River in Lambertville, New Jersey. She didn't have cancer yet, and I wasn't HIV positive, and life had a kind of hopeful glow to it.

"You look like shit," she said.

"I feel like shit."

We drank black coffee and ate a ham quiche she had made, and she read my Tarot.

"The Guys are pissed," she said to me, holding a card so I couldn't see it. The Guys is the name she'd given to the guardians who watched over us and guided us. "You are stuck."

"I want to be sober," I said, knowing what she was referring to. "I keep meaning to be sober."

"Meaning to do something doesn't mean anything does it?"

Outside icicles caught the sunlight and turned it into sparkling jewels that played along the stones of the small back patio. My head hurt.

"Are they mad at me?"

"They aren't mad. They are concerned. They are worried"

"Will I get sober?"

"Only you can answer that."

"Then what the fuck is the point of having Guys or reading the Tarot?"

My mother didn't like it when I cussed. Even though she swore all the time.

She pulled three cards. The Tower. Death. The Magician. She sighed and shook her head. While it wasn't exactly fatalistic, it existed within the same genre.

"It's up to you what's going to happen. There are two roads. You keep coming to a fork. Eventually the fork will be gone, and the road you choose will be the life you live."

I spent a week at my mother's house watching bad TV and eating quiche and a hunter stew my mother served with a thick toasted bread with melted brie. I went for cold walks along the canal by myself, praying to God and the Guys. Asking for help. I spent hours in cramped book stores and slept twelve hours a day, and was able to not get high for six whole days.

When I got back to the apartment, Ashton was there. He had a black eye and a split lip. The same Dali's car album was playing, the record scratched and worn, skipping slightly.

"Juan's a dick," he said. "Where have you been?"

"My mom's."

"I thought you had left."

"All my stuff is still here."

"Like that means anything."

I remember we fucked, but neither of us could stay hard so we walked east and copped bags of dope and sat at Sin-e on St. Marks getting high and drinking lattes in tall glasses.

A few weeks later, Ashton would move back to his parent's house, a large, modern glass structure on a cliff in Malibu, where he would eventually hang himself off the balcony, his feet dangling forever above those rocky beaches.

x

"What do you think?" Daniel asked me, breaking through the memories. "Do you still think you can handle it?"

"I can still handle it," I said, suddenly feeling very hot and unsure of myself. What if Daniel stumbled upon the darkness? What if he told me my future was finally foretold? That my mother had been right, and I'd run out of forks. Destiny had been called into existence.

What if I had made all the wrong choices?

x

Being in Daniel's shop was like being inside a different world. You had no way of knowing what was happening outside. No other world existed anymore, just this one. It was beautiful, elegant in its disrepair: an old steam heater rattling and clanking like angry ghosts; scratched and gouged hardwood floors; books piled everywhere without regard to author or subject; and pieces of art hung along the walls.

I sat down in a straight-backed wooden chair across from Daniel's desk and tried to ignore the itching in my dick and balls. I imagined millions of tiny crab-like insects hatching eggs and climbing over my skin, an assortment of crawling, slithering terrors unleashed by nameless's pink hole.

What if Daniel told me I was going to die? Or that I had gotten AIDS or cancer or some other horrible illness? Or what if my mother was going to die? Or my brother? Or a friend?

Or what if I, like the ex, was destined to fail? Never really achieving anything? What if I ended up spending my whole life working in some endless job with no meaning in some ugly, poorly lit office? What if I was never going to be anything special? What if I would never amount to anything? Just some guy. Like all the other guys out there in the world. Nothing more.

I made a promise to myself that if he told me I was going to end up as just some guy, just some normal man with a normal lover in some small, crowded apartment with a job I hated, bored, I would kill myself. Before it ever happened. I decided I would rather die then and there than end up living some banal existence.

x

Daniel pulled the cards into one deck and held them, closing his eyes. His bohemian chic was handsome and tragic. The radiator clanked and howled, spitting off great gasps of hissing steam and heat.

In those moments, back in those days, you had to love New York. It was beautiful and decadent and flawed and full of possibility. Full of stories. Anything could happen to you back then.

"Now you," he said, handing me the deck. "Hold them and really focus. Focus on what you want. Who you want to be. Focus on your life."

Terrified at the thought, I considered throwing the cards at Daniel and running out of the book store back to Elly's station wagon and driving home, fast and reckless.

I held the cards in my hand, and I tried to focus on anything but the fear, yet all I *had* was the fear. I was nothing but terror. I tried to imagine my life as I wanted it to be. But I had no idea what that even meant. I suddenly had no idea who I was or where I was going or what I wanted.

I put the cards down, my hands shaking.

Daniel watched me. "You're right to be cautious."

Daniel had pale gray eyes like a wolf. His lips were thin and red and wet with whiskey. He pulled the cards toward him and shuffled them, and then without warning, he pulled two cards: The Hanged Man, followed by The Tower.

He told me my future. Some of it was beautiful, some of it was terrifying, and most of it turned out to be true. Daniel had a way with magic. A way with breaking the veil. That's what he used to call it. Breaking the veil of this reality for the larger one beyond. Daniel liked to believe that magic mattered. That it was important. He used to tell me it provided a doorway to bring some action into the world, to affect our lives, to change the course of our destinies.

Sometimes I thought he was full of shit. Sometimes he proved me wrong. I did see magic during those days with Daniel. That is the truth. I saw strange things occur, things that should never have happened, happened. I'm just not sure how seeing any of it has actually changed my life. I'm not sure that knowing magic exists, that it is real, actually matters.

He put the cards away, poured two more shots. We shared the cigarette, the burn and warmth of the whiskey settling in like fire. We talked about Keats and Dante. I tried to convince him Hart Crane was the greatest American poet, but he refused to hear me. He insisted it was Walt Whitman.

"Without Whitman there would be no American poets. No fucking Hart Crane. Whitman was a man. Crane was too sensitive. Too frightened. No one would have beat Whitman without ending up with a few bruises."

"That's not fair. Whitman lived in the woods. Crane, what happened to him…he didn't have a chance."

"He just jumps off the side of a boat and dies because a bunch of sailors wouldn't let him suck their dicks?"

"That's bullshit, and you know it. You're just being an asshole. Anyone who has ever suffered for being gay should look at Crane as a fucking hero."

Daniel read to me what has now become one of my favorite poems, *When I Heard at The Close of the Day:*

> *When I heard at the close of the day how I had*
> *been praised in the Capitol, still it was not*
> *a happy night for me that followed,*
> *And else when I caroused—nor when my favorite plans were*
> *accomplished—was I really happy,*
> *But the day when I arose at dawn from the perfect*
> *health, electric, inhaling sweet breath*
> *When I saw the full moon in the west grow pale and*
> *disappear in the morning light,*
> *When I wandered alone over the beach, and undressing, bathed,*
> *laughing with the waters, and saw the sun rise,*
> *And when I thought how my friend, my lover, was on*
> *his way coming, then O I was happy,*
> *Each breath tasted sweeter—and all that day my food*
> *nourished me more—and the beautiful day passed well,*
> *And the next came with equal joy—and with the next,*
> *at evening, came my friend,*
> *And that night while all was still I heard the waters roll*
> *slowly continually up the shores,*
> *I heard the hissing rustle of the liquid and sands, as directed*
> *to me, whispering to congratulate me,*
> *For the friend I love lay sleeping by my side,*
> *In the stillness his face was inclined toward me, while the*
> *moon's clear beams shone*
> *And his arm lay lightly over my breast—and that night I was happy.*

After reading the poem, he opened a door in the back of the shop. Daniel had a small one-bedroom apartment filled with antique kerosene lamps and a fireplace, a dark oriental rug over wood floors, and windows that looked out onto an alley in one direction and the corner of the street below, where a red neon "XXX and Video Booth" sign flashed on and off, sending obscure messages across the floors and walls from other universes trying to reach out to us, to connect to us.

The room was overrun with books and pieces of art, old wine bottles used to hold candles, antiques in various stages of disrepair and repair, large comfortable chairs found on the street and re-upholstered in a mix-matched fashion, and a tooled tin ceiling with a beautiful wrought iron candelabra chandelier that hung in the center of the living room, its eight lit candles throwing shadows across the room. Hand-drawn archaic-looking sigils littered the walls, hidden in corners, barely visible behind pieces of furniture. The letters were a secret code, reminders of a path chosen, but not always followed.

Daniel didn't turn the lights on. "Candlelight is a way into the soul, a pathway to another world," he said. "If you just sit and watch it, if you let it seep into you, it can guide you down new and strange roads. There are other universes out there, other worlds. The past and the present and the future lie over each other in textured patterns. There are times, sitting and staring into candle flame, I can almost feel them, all the me's from the past and the future, all the me's in different universes, all the endless possibilities. I can sense them and hear them, and I know they are just as aware of me as I am of them."

The slow and steady way he said those words, I almost believed him. He made a pot of his homemade opium tea, mixing spices to cut the flavor and the strength, and served it in small golden white chinoiserie tea cups. The effects were slightly hallucinatory and calming. The room felt warmer. I felt connected to Daniel through some hazy substance in the air.

The room and the tea heightened my sense of time travel, of having moved through universes, having entered new worlds. Daniel reminded me of a dream I have had off and on ever sense I was a teenager.

X

I am riding my Big Wheel down a long, narrow road between two vast fields. The sky is lit by stars, like jewels thrown across a sprawling darkness. There is a farmhouse and a lake behind the farmhouse. Beyond the lake, the forest is dense with dark, sentient trees. They shimmer supernaturally in the moonlight and breeze, lush and full and aware. It is warm out. I am sixteen, I am always sixteen in the dream. My mother is somewhere down the road in her car, calling my name. I am riding away from her, and she is looking for me.

The moon is full and bright and golden, reflected in the waters of the lake. The night is quiet. Peaceful.

I hear whispering, and a giant finned tail splashes in the water followed by the crescent leap of a merman—diamond-shaped moonlight glistening on his body like Christmas lights, the night suddenly full of magic and potentiality. I am not afraid, I am not lost, I am aware of myself as I have never been before. I feel connected to something larger than anything I have ever experienced before. My life, for that one mythopoeic moment, has meaning. It has redemption and salvation. I am no longer just Jeff, but I am a part of all the vastness, the infiniteness, the endless story.

I leave my Big Wheel on the road and I walk toward the farmhouse. I know this place. It feels safe. Something important waits for me. Inside, the cycle will be complete. I know this because I have been here before. I have made this exact journey a hundred times over the course of a hundred different nights and I still find myself mesmerized. Like Shahid's love poem, I am looking for an alternative ending, a change in the inevitable. I am looking for a change in events that have already happened and will happen again, in exactly the same way.

A side door opens onto a stairway, always that exact side door opening onto that exact room. I can hear my mother calling my name in the distance, but it fades as the door shuts behind me.

But these stairs are circular. This is a slight difference. The stairs are the only thing that ever changes. Sometimes they are grand antebellum staircases, sometimes they are dirty New York tenement staircases filled with homeless and drug addicts, sometimes they are narrow, broken, and scary. This time it is a metal winding staircase leading up. They always lead up.

At the top of the stairs, a large loft-like room opens out onto the lake. It has three walls, the fourth nonexistent. The moon glows bright in the dark waters. I can hear the murmuring of the merman as if he were singing to us, whispering to us. I always wonder what he is saying. Is it kind or is it a warning? A blessing? The shadows of the trees are reflected green in the moonlit waters, as if they were in sunlight and not hidden by darkness.

There is a boy. He is also sixteen. He is so beautiful that every time I see him, I have the sudden terrifying sensation of falling. The world explodes around me, everything going quiet and still. He is the most beautiful boy I have ever seen. It breaks my heart to look at him. He uses a paintbrush to write words in red: *He Falls Gently Through the Trees*. He is naked. I want to wrap my arms around him and hold him and keep him safe. I want to keep us both safe, to freeze this moment forever, to find a way into this dream and never return, because it is a puzzle. I know that. I knew it the first time I had it. This dream is a puzzle trying to tell me something of great importance, something huge and vast and endless and yet I can never quite figure it out. It always eludes me.

And I know I can't keep him safe. What is coming is coming. That is just the way of things.

He turns to me. His smile shatters my existence. I feel everything I have ever known, everything I have ever been, all my memories destroyed by that smile.

"I love you," he says, and then he steps over the ledge and through the missing wall and out into the night, walking slowly on the night air, on beams of moonlight, walking away from me.

And then he is gone.

Every time I have that dream, I wake up crying and alone.

x

Something about Daniel reminded me of the boy in the dream.

The sky was a shimmering silver outside the window, the endless lights of the city refusing to let complete darkness settle, windows rattled in the wind, swirls of snow occluded the presence of reality.

It is strange to think of time travel in this context. To be here, in Los Angeles, remembering me then and recreating the world as I think it was, as I hope it was, as I want it to be. The truth merging with fiction re-emerging as the truth. I create new memories and new realities, new existences that replace the old ones, layers upon layers until one past or one present or one future is no longer possible. All things have become possible, all things are recreated, each one just as real, just as true, just as valid as the other. Each one has occurred, calling into question reality and truth and fiction as well as identity and self-awareness and history. It calls into question the assignment of meaning and the creation of reality.

It calls into question my sense of self.

Daniel told me a story about a man he had met in India. This man claimed he had never been born and never lived and never died.

"He kept telling us what lived inside the flesh was not human, even if the flesh itself was. This little old man, with his wrinkled skin and his tiny, round dark eyes, smiled and said over and over, that we are aliens. Aliens inhabiting flesh. Spirit trapped inside a body. This guy, he fucked my head for months. I couldn't stay in India. It was too crowded and dirty and hungry. Every time you ran into an American or a European or an Australian, they'd tell you how beautiful the beaches are or the ashrams or the gurus, but of course, that isn't the real India. That is just the white man's India. The real India is chaotic and in turmoil and is constantly becoming. It has nothing to do with beaches or gurus."

"We are endless," Daniel said, his voice lost inside an encroaching darkness. "We are bound only by the thoughts we think. And we choose those. That is what I think that old man was saying. I mean, it probably isn't. He created a charity, a board of trustees, a corporation. He created entities that fed into his bank account. But I still think maybe some of what he said was magical, you know? I think even greedy men have great magic. He spoke of really big thoughts, big ideas, he taught me how to see these ideas, these thoughts, as actual kingdoms, universes, places that existed not just inside me but outside of me, all around me. Every thought I have evolves into creation." He moved next to me, his body touching mine. "I know it sounds stupid. Ridiculous. Like New Age crystal bullshit, but I think it's more than that. I think it is magic. I think thoughts are like making curses, casting spells. I believe we are magicians, sorcerers. Accidental warlocks."

The tea made me feel distant yet connected. It made me feel less and more real at the same time. Daniel was stroking my head, our legs touching. Naked, he was so skinny I could see his ribs, and he was hairy up and down his stomach, all over his chest and shoulders and back. He was nothing I would normally find sexy, yet I found myself lost in him. I wondered if my dick would taste like the last guy's ass. When he got on his knees, I hesitated and he looked up, eyes playful and decadent. "I don't care. It's hot that you have another man on you."

I let him fuck me. For a tall man, his dick was short but thick, the kind of stubby, fat cock I have a fetish for. He started out gentle until I convinced him he didn't have to be. I liked it hard. If I'm the bottom, I want to be taken, owned. I want to get him off.

He fucked me for what felt like hours, moving in and out of dreams, wrapping ourselves in stories, his cock moving through me, growing larger inside me, rooting me to a place and a time, creating a space for me to exist. He fucked me into reality, he drove himself into me, and when he came, holding me down, pinning me there, to that spot, to that place, he called my name, his body jerking over me, and I felt it, all of it, unload inside me.

Afterward, his cum dripping out of me, we lay on wood floors sipping opium tea and smoking cigarettes, watching the smoke play in candlelight, the windows open, snow dancing and fading in the air around us.

"I always wanted to be a magician," he said. "Like Crowley or Parsons, like John Dee talking to the angels, Solomon building cages for the demons, but I was never able to find the magic. It always felt so far away. Drifting just out of reach. I could see it. I knew it existed. But I could never catch it."

X

After India, he moved to Thailand and then China, then Egypt. He spent a few months in Turkey before moving to Paris. I told him that Paris was one of my favorite cities. Saying it made me feel embarrassed, uninteresting. Of course, I loved Paris. It was Paris. It was obvious.

"I met a guy in Paris," he said, almost as if he hadn't heard me, his hands tracing lines in my face, following strange pathways, writing new stories. "He was a Satanist." Daniel laughed. "Which is an even bigger crock of shit than the worst kind of Christianity. It's just Christianity in reverse which makes it gross, uninspired, and yet all these stupid Satanists think they are being punk rock, you know? Living on the edge. They are on the edge of nothing. They are right in the fucking middle. Satanism is just another stupid middle-class, bored white person's dilemma. But at the time, I didn't know that. I was chasing the magic, hunting Hermes."

Outside the windows, daylight was forming itself into bursts of light. Daniel rolled two joints, dipping them each into a dark, oily substance and setting them to dry. My eyes followed trails of light, strands of color that bounced off the walls, forming roadways through the smoky room.

"His name was Lucas. He was tall and gorgeous, black hair shot with gray-blue eyes. He was older than me, forty-nine, rich and handsome and stunning. He told me things that sounded like secrets, like he was revealing a great mystery to me. He told me he would show me the way. Help me to open my heart. That is what he said to me. That my heart was closed, forced into seclusion by society and Christianity. Lucifer would open it for me, show me the real world. He took me to a gathering in Madrid."

I remember being a kid and spending summers in Georgia with my grandmother, Sadie. We would stay up late into the night, casting spells and talking to spirits with the Ouija. Sadie told me that magic was anything I wanted it to be. That the world was steeped in mystery and wonder. Sadie was tall with long red hair and drank Jim Beam and smoked Salems and when she was mad her anger turned into a destroying force that was unstoppable. One summer night, Sadie held my hand and we closed our eyes and she made me repeat a strange series of words strung together not for meaning, but for structure. She was building a doorway with sound, unlocking a portal, calling something forward. When it was over, both of us breathless and stunned, I asked her if it had worked.

She said: "We won't know. Not for a long time. But one day you will wake up in the dark, and you will feel him and then you will know."

"We stayed in an old castle outside of Madrid. There was a lake in the back and a forest and a room Lucas called the dungeon filled with slings and giant dildos and all kinds of bizarre sex toys. During the nights, groups of rich men and women would gather in robes out back, chanting and praying, and then they would line up and walk slowly to an old stone house in the trees where they would drain the blood of a goat and paint upside down crosses on each other's foreheads, weeping and laughing. Some nights they would all fuck. It disgusted me. This one old woman tried to get me to stick my dick in her ass. I almost puked. I love girls but not pussy. I'm just not one of those gays.

"One afternoon I took my book and went into the dungeon and read, trying to piece together the meaning of each of the objects but the harder I tried, the more abstract they became. There was nothing of pleasure, nothing of pain, just some lost banality. The whole thing was beginning to feel desperate, but I couldn't see it yet. Not exactly. It was just this feeling, a malaise that had settled over me. He let me borrow his car, an Aston Martin. One of the most beautiful cars I've ever driven. I drove it into the Chueca, the gay part of Madrid and found a bathhouse a friend had told me about. I was tired of spells and magic and deciphering Crowley. I wanted real release. I wanted real magic. I spent five hours in that dark little hole of a place, my eyes closed, bent over, letting anyone fuck me who wanted to. I took so many dicks that day. I lost myself in it."

He stood up and pulled black curtains down over the brightening dawn. His body looked emaciated and breathtaking, wrapped in the shadows of the room. He took a joint and lit it, inhaling deeply.

"Be careful," he said as he handed it to me. "That oil is a strange mix of things I don't understand. It's made for me by a shaman in Arizona. I've met some really weird beings smoking that shit."

Here is something important to know about me: I didn't even hesitate. I didn't even wonder what strange things went into that black oil made by esoteric priests out in the desert. I just took the joint and smoked it and let the drug wash over me, whatever it was.

"I sometimes think sex, pure and violent and forceful, is the best magic out there, because it grounds you. It places you in your flesh. Sometimes I think that is the important thing. We aren't spirits, we are mammals. We aren't boundless, we are bound. Caged. Trapped. The only way to any real freedom is to remember that." Daniel said, lying down next to me, spouting a new philosophy, contradicting everything he had said to me earlier.

x

Daniel's body was warm. I felt the drug dark and lazily crawling over my skin, moving around inside me, possessing me. "I'd like you to sleep with me," he said. "For a while."

I didn't know what to say. I was never a fan of the sleepover. And yet, something about Daniel made me want to say yes. He was the kind of guy I was never attracted to, but all I wanted was to get him back inside me. He was the kind of guy who made me want to have a sleepover even though I hated sleeping over. He was the kind of guy who reminded me of a boy in a dream that had walked on air, disappearing into the night.

We smoked the rest of the joint. The drug lead me down dark passages and hidden corridors in my mind. I felt myself in those neural pathways, the fingers moving through the back of my head, down my spine, exploring different points of entry, bursting centers of light and energy.

I fell into a dream, in and out of semiotic story lines filled with subtext, a dark and romantic music playing softly throughout the room, Daniel's breathing heavy and raspy and gorgeous.

In one dream I walk through a dark forest following a glowing white horse in the distance. I saw its wings, its horn. It knew me. I had to touch it, to talk to it. I wanted to say something important, but everything felt meaningless. The forest ended at a steep cliff. I stood looking out into night and empty air. The world dropped off, but the pegasus hovered just over the chasm, wings beating against the night, eyes piercing and gray.

"Life is full of torments," it said to me, his voice deep and lyrical.

A tiny man in a black suit sat on a rock. He had a flute in his hand. Little balls of light hovered around him. Daniel sat high above me on the branch of a tree. The tiny man began to play the flute, the balls of light faerie's dancing in the darkness, illuminating us.

"Life is full of torments," the pegasus said. "We are born to suffer."

I was trying to find my way out of a burning building. All around me people are screaming. Smoke fills the air, scorched with the scent of burning flesh and despair. I hear someone calling my name in the distance. The voice is familiar. It rises above the screams. The walls and floors are melting into flames. The world is disappearing.

I sometimes wonder if that voice is Alex's, calling my name from the future, trying to get my attention, to pull me toward him, warning me. The familiarity of the voice in my head is his. I am sure of it now. I am sure that in that moment in Daniel's dark apartment, high and twisting in time, Alex reached out to me, pinned me. Made me his.

And then I am alone, standing under a twisted, iridescent shimmering tree. The night is aglow in its halo. The tiny man in a black suit is still sitting on a rock, playing a violin instead of the flute. At his feet is a long, mean-looking snake. The man's music is sorrowful, full of pain. The snake hisses, slithering around his feet. Behind them are the giant ruins of a house. Three children hang from the rafters, their bodies twisting in the night air. Above them, a shadowed man hovers in the clouds, his face hidden in darkness. I know he is watching me. He has been looking for me all along.

I know he is coming for me.

X

When I woke, the bed next to me was empty. I found Daniel in the kitchen. He made me pumpkin pancakes for breakfast with chocolate chips and fried bananas and sugar on top. The sky was a slate gray, the snow heavy and thick, endless. NY1 was predicting more snow today than the day before.

I called Elly. She wouldn't need her car for a few days. She was snowed-in in Greenwich with the married doctor she was seeing while his wife was in Barbados.

I helped Daniel open the shop. I found a collection of Paul Bowles stories and sat down on his large couch and read, a cup of coffee next to me while a few customers brought the cold and snow into our little sanctuary.

Sometime in the afternoon, Daniel rolled a cigarette with Kief and hash and we got stoned and listened to The Velvet Underground and watched the snow fall. At times, I thought it would never end. Maybe this was the apocalypse everyone had been promising. The final days of life as we knew it.

We made a cabbage and kielbasa soup and watched old Charlie Chan movies. A young couple came into the store. The woman was looking for crystals. Daniel told her he didn't sell any, and she became angry, calling him a fake and a fraud. She stormed out. A gay black couple came in, each of them dressed in tuxedos, asking if they could use the phone. Their car was snowed in, and they were supposed to be meeting one of their sisters in mid-town for her engagement party. We offered them soup and whiskey, and they stayed a while. We talked about music and theater. One of them was a writer and had a play opening at a small theatre down the street. When they left, I told Daniel I kept thinking we were going to all end up fucking.

"Why would you think that?" he asked, non-accusing, just curious.

"I don't know. It's just the way I think."

"Do you fuck every guy you meet?"

I paused, then laughed. "I fucked you."

"You're right. After you fucked your trick."

"God, I'm a whore."

He kissed me. His mouth tasted sweet and sour at the same time. "You're my whore."

I wanted him in me so bad at that moment I didn't think I could stand it. I made him fuck me bent over his desk, his cock jerking inside me as he came.

Later that night, we braved the storm and walked over to the Ninth Circle Steak House. It was no longer a steakhouse, but I had heard in the 60's it was the place to get the best steaks in New York City. In the 70's, 80's, and early 90's, it was the best gay bar in New York, because it was exactly that: a bar. It had a juke box, a downstairs with a pool table, and a tiny outdoor cement garden where you could smoke and buy any drug you wanted. It was a neighborhood spot frequented by closeted celebrities. You could hear Donna Summer followed by Sonic Youth followed by Iggy Pop followed by Rick James on that juke box. Guys danced and did poppers and fucked and laughed and came back and did it all over again.

X

One wild night I got fucked up and fucked all night long with a boy named Orlando from Bennington College. Years later, I would find out he died of an AIDS-related illness that his rich diplomat father covered up.

The thing I remember most clearly about that night with Orlando from Bennington was the way he lined up the candles in his apartment, telling me the meaning behind each one, blessing the light and the smoke, blessing us. He had a shelf of books dedicated to serial killers, and another to magic, and another to porn and sexy literature. I woke up to find him standing over me, his eyes painted in dark circles, his lips a lipstick red, black sheer panties and high heels. I fucked him bent over the couch, his high heels still on, a hole ripped in the sheer black panties, as he begged me not to forget him.

"Please," he whimpered, "remember me. Always remember me."

I rarely thought of Orlando.

x

Daniel and I ordered drinks at the downstairs bar and watched as the boys filed in, shaking off the cold and the snow, and lined up to cruise, gossip, buy drinks, and play pool. We made out with this tall Columbian guy with a dark beard. We kept saying how he looked like this poet, and when he would ask us which poet, we would both break out laughing because it was just this poet, just any poet. That guy really looked like some fucking poet. We gave him a blow job in a dark corner by the pool table, each of us taking turns with his dick until he came in my mouth, and I kissed it back to Daniel.

We walked a circuitous path home through the snow, stopping to stare up at the Jefferson Market Library on Greenwich and 6th. I used to always pretend it was a castle, or a house, and that I was a prince, or just some really rich guy who lived there. I would keep it empty except for really big chairs and books and lots of candles and heaters, and friends would come and spend decades there, cooking dinner and drinking wine and reading. No one would ever die or get sober or leave because we were happy and life was perfect.

I told Daniel this, and he smiled.

"We weren't meant to be happy," he said, his eyes sad, his smile full of some unexplained meaning. "We were meant for something else."

And I told him how crazy that was because that was exactly what the pegasus told me in my dream, and we laughed and held hands and walked west, toward the water, toward the end of the world as we knew it, and climbed into his bed and fell asleep and woke the next morning to a break in the storm, a blue sky, and melting snow.

x

Daniel took me to dinner for my birthday on a warm night in May. Spring had arrived, the air filled with the perfumed hints of flowers and car exhaust and piss. We sat at a table outside of a French restaurant on Perry Street, and Daniel told me the world was changing.

"I keep having these dreams, and in them the world is changing." He kept scratching, so I knew he was high. I ordered a carafe of red wine and picked up the books he had bought me: a history of the Tarot, and a hard-bound collection of poems by Hart Crane, a galley edition that had never gone to press. I reached out, the tips of my fingers touching his. He felt cold. Distant. "I think a darkness is spreading. An infection eating at the world."

He had been speaking this way a lot lately. Talking of darkness and demons and mind control. Everything he was reading centered around conspiracies and elite cabals bent on world domination.

He was getting thinner. He told me he wasn't eating. Food was toxic. The world was toxic.

Sometimes after these talks, after too much time spent with Daniel, I began to believe him. I began to believe I was toxic. Daniel had that effect on me. I wanted him to be okay. I wanted him to be happy.

I wanted us to be okay.

"The world is a spinning abyss," he was saying. "A sphere of chaos."

The waitress was displaying a beautiful plate of profiteroles and Tarte Tatin and mini-opera cakes and crème brulees. The air was warm. You could smell the river on the breeze. Lavender colored flowers were sprinkled in between the desserts. The Maître d' was speaking to a handsome young couple in French. People walked past us, laughing, talking, on their way, moving. The city was alive, breathing, its heart beating. Daniel was no longer talking, he was ranting and gesticulating wildly. In the middle of it all, I stood up and walked away.

I cried for a few minutes, ducking into a doorway on 7th Avenue, just before the entrance to the 2 Train. And then I stopped crying.

Elly made us cucumber and cream cheese sandwiches, and we sat on our roof top on Court Street in Brooklyn Heights and watched the lights play in the sky. We each snorted a bag of China White and let the world melt away. Later we went for a walk down Montague Street toward the promenade. Manhattan rose before us like some mythological city of kings. A land of gods and monsters, of warlocks, a land where battles were fought and lost for the souls of mankind. Daniel was alone in that vast oasis, raving and ranting, screaming, howling, falling.

Elly held my hand, and it began to rain. A warm spring rain. Winter and the snow were gone. We closed our eyes, and I felt myself contained by that inner darkness, and I heard Elly singing. She would do that sometimes. Sing to me.

I was never more aware of how far-reaching that darkness inside me went than I was in those moments when I was high, with Elly singing and the rain falling, a city of kings burning bright before us. It seemed to reach out and expand into the forever, into the infinite, pulling at me and taking me with it. I could disappear into that darkness, just like Daniel had done, fade away until nothing was left but the insanity, the raging voices, the screams.

x

"Magick is real," Daniel said to me that night of the first blizzard. "It moves inside us, around us, it affects us and we affect it. Whether we believe in it or not. Magick is real. And vampires are real, and there are monsters and angels and great cities in the sky where many gods live. What you really want is all real."

Candlelight flickered in darkening shadows along the walls, a ballet of false images. He held me. His arms felt strong, and I wanted to believe everything he told me was true.

It was the sort of moment people refer to as magical.

But it was doomed to end.

Possession

I often wonder about the demon Sadie called forth that night long ago in Georgia. About the entities my mother talks to. I wonder about synchronicity and about magic. About destiny.

I grew up in the time of gay cancer and AIDS and HIV. I was never careful. I was always foolish. My dick has taken control on almost every single occasion. Those times when one of us decided to wear a condom, we usually gave up. Sex is about feeling, and it feels better bareback. I don't even like porn that has condoms in it. It is no surprise at all that I am HIV positive. The surprise is that it didn't happen sooner than forty-four. But I wonder what would have happened if I had found out I was positive when I was nineteen, or twenty-five, or thirty-seven. I might not have survived it. The timing of my sero-conversion is so specific, so perfectly planned, it is hard not to imagine that what my mother has always told me is true. We are pawns, characters in a bigger story told by the gods.

My mother and I like to create myths out of our lives. We like to assign vast meaning to otherwise normal life occurrences. When she found out she had stage IV cancer and they told us she only had weeks to live, she gave away all her jewelry. Seven years later, she admits that was a mistake. She believes she has been kept alive by a lady who comes to her at night, hovering over her bed, healing her. This lady does not talk to my mother. She has no interest in being my mother's friend or confidant. Her only purpose is to manage my mother's disease.

We like to joke that we are probably insane, except for the fact that we are both alive. Being alive the only proof we have that maybe we aren't insane.

I have made a whole philosophy of life around dick and ass. Around cruising. Around sex. HIV was just the natural outcome of my choices.

And I think back to that voice I heard in Daniel's apartment, to Alex calling me in 1991, reaching out to me from 2012, calling me forward to this moment.

That moment when my whole life changed.

December 24th, 2012, I was at Alex's mother's house in Huntington Beach. We had rented a house in Idyllwild for Christmas. I wanted to be in the snow. I was tired of the sun. I was tired of LA. I wanted to be somewhere quiet, in the trees, a place blanketed. The plan was we would wake up Christmas morning and me, Alex, and his mother would drive out of L.A. and up the mountain into the snow for a few days of movies and reading.

But on that night, December 24th, I had the strangest dream.

I dreamt Alex and I were in a house somewhere in a forest. I could hear the wind outside, the breath of the trees. I was alone in the living room. Two candles burned, one red, one black. An elaborately designed golden bowl sat on a mosaic table, and inside the bowl was a solid gold ball. I heard Alex whispering in another room. I knew, in the way that you know things in dreams, that he was playing pool with a stranger. I could see them. Alex was beautiful and bright, but he was frightened, his eyes filled with a strange panic, and the stranger was nothing more than a shadow, a shimmering darkness on the edge of vision.

This stranger reminded me of something important at the fringe of my memories, from another dream a long time ago, someone who had visited me once late at night when I was a child.

A woman sat in the chair across from me. She had long, curly black hair shot through with grey and wild fiery eyes. Her lips were a violent red, her fingernails long and claw-like, digging into her legs. She was whimpering and chanting, staring at me as if trying to convey something of great importance to me. She kept looking at the bowl.

Desperate. I knew she was communicating to me in a silent language from some far-off land, from another dimension. She was there to help me. To help us. I picked up the bowl. It was cold. The ball inside shimmered in a golden sunlight. I heard Alex calling my name, telling me to hurry because it was trying to get in. That soon it would be inside, and it would be too late.

Everything was filled with an urgency I didn't understand. The ball began to spin, around the upper edges of the bowl, and I had to keep it going. If the ball stopped spinning, whatever monstrous entity was fighting to get inside me, would win. The moment the ball stopped, hovering suddenly just above the frozen golden bowl, it robbed me of all feeling. I felt it descending. I could smell the stench of what was coming. The witch woman stood, her body shaking, her eyes full of blood red tears, her clawed hands tearing away at her flesh, devouring herself until she was nothing. I sat there, the sound of Alex sobbing from the other room, knowing I had failed.

He had reached all the way into the past to warn me, and still I failed.

I woke up. I didn't fall back asleep. I had the terrifying sense of a strange and dark entity hovering in the shadows of the room. The next morning Alex told me of a dream he had about a monster trying to possess me. He had spent much of the night watching the door, terrified something was trying to get in.

We had both spent the night awake and terrified, guarding against evil forces, trying to take care of each other.

I wouldn't find out I was HIV Positive until the following October but I knew the exact moment it had happened. October 2012. Just a few months before the dream of the demon entering my body, before the night I became possessed.

People will tell me I am wrong, HIV is not a demon, it is not a monster. Like my mother's cancer, it is a disease. It is science. Like everything else in the world, it is rational and understandable and not a part of the world of fairies and unicorns and mermaids. They would say to me I am lucky. I contracted the virus now, at a time when science and medicine prevail. I am healthy, I am undetectable, I am just like normal.

Just like normal but not.

The HIV virus doesn't actually leave me. It hides in my belly or in my brain, waiting for its moment to get in. Waiting for me to let the ball stop. Waiting for the witch woman's chants to falter, for Alex to lose the game of pool with the Stranger.

They are all right, of course. I am lucky. I have always been lucky. I was born under a lucky moon. The stars aligned to bless me. Angels sang songs for me on the day I was born.

HIV is not a demon. It is not a monster. I am not possessed. I know that. But it does separate me. I remember jokes made, or ugly comments about people we all knew with HIV, when people didn't know my status. I remember people writing terrible things on bathroom walls about coworkers who were positive. I remember being rejected by guys on PrEP because they only fucked negatives. I remember a boss of mine saying, "These fucking people with AIDS can't even get out of their deathbeds to come to a benefit in their honor." I remember all the casual cruelties, like being in a room of white people making racist jokes because they feel safe—we are all the same here, right?

But we aren't all the same.

We aren't all just like you.

What most people don't get is the momentous power of the fact that I know a monster is buried inside my belly or my brain. A destruction. A death. And nothing anybody says will change that fact. This demon isn't just HIV; it is the alcoholism, the heroin, the thoughts that are constantly destroying the world, shattering myself, tearing apart every aspect of my existence. Some days, it seems that buried deep inside my heart at the core of my soul, I am possessed by monstrous entities bent on my destruction.

And then, I will look up from my dark constructs, my castles built on bloody moors, my wildly howling harpies, and I will see my husband, Alex, laying on the couch reading, our dog Paco at his feet, sunlight sprawling lazily along the blond wood floors. Our boyfriend Jon will send us a text that he is eating ice cream and French fries for lunch, and that he loves us. He loves me, they both love me; I was born under a lucky sign; the stars all aligned for me, and they still do. I will eat the five slices of bacon Alex made for me, and I will stand guard against the thoughts, against the monsters that live in my head, and for a moment I will see the world as bright and good and full of promise. And for a moment, darkness will not prevail.

We Are All Beautiful

In the early 90's, Wednesday nights ruled NYC with Disco 2000 at Limelight. I was at Sarah Lawrence the first time I ever went. Micah, who later OD'd on heroin and had a strange and unsettling write-up in *Seventeen Magazine* after he died, would drive us in his 1960 Alfa Romeo roadster, top down, racing from Bronxville into Manhattan. Elegance and glamour went hand in hand back then. We wore dark suits and make up. We never had to wait in line. We never had to pay. Somehow, we always ended up on the guest list. I always felt scared and out of place, like I wasn't pretty or interesting enough. It always came down to not being enough. Micah once took my hand and told me I was beautiful. He smiled. "We all are. We are all beautiful."

I used to walk around the catwalk on the balcony above the main dance floor, high out of my mind, looking down at all those dancing people and all the lights, and I fell madly in love with New York City. The world seemed to shine and swirl in its beauty. People didn't just dance, they lost themselves down there like angels trying to forget the truth, that life wouldn't be waiting for them, that it just kept moving on.

Afterward, we would take a taxi down to Save the Robots on Avenue B where I would sneak out to buy heroin from the guys who manned the line in front of a stoop on 7th Street between B & C. After Save the Robots, we went to dinner at Florent in the meat packing district, where I always ended up eating escargot and French Fries, a magic hangover combo.

I still find it hard to fathom that they turned Limelight into a mall. Sometimes I miss Micah. I'm sorry most of you never got to meet him. He was incredible and weird and absolutely gorgeous. And he had this way of making you feel like you were more than enough. Like you were the most beautiful person in the whole world. I'm also sorry most of you will never get to have the escargot and French Fries at Florent. That was a New York nightlife institution.

We lived in a swirl of lights and a fog of magic and glamour. We danced on cracked streets and flung ourselves about in tiny railroad apartments. We fell in love and fucked and got high and we danced, the music an endless and bright beacon calling us away from our personal squalor and into its layered, ecstatic depths.

A few years before Save the Robots closed, I met this super tall German boy with red hair at Limelight. I took him to Robots. He wanted to eat breakfast on the Brooklyn Bridge after. We bought egg, cheese, and ham on Kaiser rolls and sat on the Brooklyn Bridge, watching the people as they walked to work. He told me America was wild and beautiful. He was so tall, his hands long and thick. His eyes were a stunning, almost too-blue blue.

"This country is wild!" he screamed, standing up, startling a mother and her children walking past us. "This country is wild and endless and beautiful!" He fell down next to me. "I fucking love America!"

On my roof in Brooklyn, Manhattan blazing on the horizon, I fucked a man I cannot remember much except his cum tasted sweet, and he laughed as he shot into my mouth. He moved in with me for the last two weeks of his stay. Everything made him happy.

"I am sad for one thing," he said to me the night before he flew home. We were sitting on the fire escape outside my bedroom window on Sackett Street in Carrol Gardens.

"What is that one thing?"

"When I return, New York will no longer be like this." He smiled at me. "You can feel it in the air. Everything is about to change."

Micah had shoulder-length dark hair and was beautiful. He had pale skin and golden eyes and was a boy in that puppy-dog kind of way. Always bounding over to you, running at you, jumping on you, and hugging you. Always in love. Always wanting your approval.

x

We spent a weekend together during a school break. He came to my father's house in Madison, New Jersey. My dad wasn't there. We took acid, and he got in the bathtub and told me he was dying. I sat holding his hand and falling in love with him, wishing I could save him. The lights were too bright, the tile too white, and we lit candles and drew a bath more cold than hot, and he lay there convalescing, talking to me in whispers. At one point, I left him to go outside. It was spring, a chill in the air, and the trees were beginning to show their green.
 The night felt like it was whispering to me, trying to reveal its secrets.
 I felt like I was connected to the wind.
 Micah was so fragile in that tub, it made me feel large and clumsy. He was like a finite poem, and I like a screaming novel with no end.
 Micah had a thick cock. It wasn't long, but it was super thick, too big to wrap my hand around. He had the kind of dick I loved to worship. Medium length and beer can thick.
 I once felt guilty after he died, because I jerked off thinking about him and his huge dick. It was a fantasy about Micah and Eric, this big black guy I had met in the East Village. They fucked the hell out of me. They fucked me into the ground. That kind of fucking that changes you. It was strange fantasizing about someone who was dead and someone I was sort of dating. After I came, I had the sudden terrible realization that this could never happen. Ever.

x

I met Eric one night, walking endlessly around Tompkins Square Park waiting for the dope spot to open up. I was horny but didn't want to go into Crowbar by myself. Eric was tall and muscular and dark, and he smiled at me and made me feel safe. I followed him back to his apartment on 11th Street where he fucked me in the stairway that led to the roof because his mother was visiting from Barbados. Eric had a huge cock. It took me a while to get used to it, but he was gentle and after he came, he sat on my dick and slowly milked my cock, kissing me the whole time. He made me feel special. Like I mattered.

We fucked off and on for a few years, until one day, broke and dope sick, I stole his wallet while he was in the shower.

Sometimes I still jerk off thinking about Eric.

x

Micah and I spent the rest of our vacation in New Hope, Pennsylvania, near where my mother was living at the time, driving around at night along those dark river roads drinking whiskey and trying to find songs to listen to on the radio. Micah cried sitting at the edge of the Delaware River, watching the water rush by us, and I hated him which was tied to loving him. Everything felt so dark out there, so muted compared to New York City. The stars felt farther away, colder, less obtainable. We wandered into local gay bars full of middle aged men with bellies and skinny younger guys, shiny drinks in their hands, disco balls and colored lights.

"These people," Micah said to me, whispering against the pounding music. "Who are these people?"

"They're just people," I said. "Just everybody people."

Micah looked so sad. "We could be so much more. They could be so much more."

"Not everybody wants to be more."

"Then what's the fucking point? Watch TV, jerk off, and die? What's the fucking point if this is your whole life?"

I've spent a lot of my life not liking myself. Finding fault with everything I did, the way I spoke and moved, how fat I was or how skinny, how smart or dumb. I let other people define me. I defined myself by who they were, how they behaved, by what they had. I have felt so alone most of my life. Disconnected. Lost. I didn't just not know who I was, I didn't seem to have the framework to go about finding out.

"Remember that night we thought I was dying?" Micah said to me, the tears streaming down his face. We were in a small park off Main Street, the dark river rushing by, the stars malignant and cold, a wind whispering through newly formed leaves.

"I never thought you were dying," I said.

Micah took my hand in his. It was so warm, so intense, so alive. It made me want to run, to hide. It made me want to hit him.

"I will one day," he said, that heat and intensity finding its way into his voice. "Die one day. I will die one day."

Everyone thinks they are going to die young. We have romantic notions about our deaths, not realizing that most of us will die old and alone, bodies riddled with cancer, aching and pointless, but for Micah it was true. He would die young and tragic, of a heroin over dose, falling into mythic proportions almost by accident.

"And then who will you be? I'm so high right now, and you—you are so gorgeous, so handsome. You should be something. When I die, don't be like those people. Promise me that." He brought my hand to his lips. He was so beautiful, it was hard to look at him. Like maybe if you looked too closely, he would burst into flames right there in front of you. He was that kind of beauty. Shocking. Not meant for this world.

"It's terrible," he said. "When you think about it. It's really fucking terrible." And he was sobbing. His whole body was shaking.

And I did not take him in my arms. I did not hold him. I did not comfort him. Instead I just sat there, my own arms wrapped tightly around my chest. The world felt too big that night. Too unsure.

We couldn't take care of the other in that moment. We didn't know what was coming.

Death Musings

When I was a teenager, my best friend, Ashley, and I would take long dark drives through the vast estates of the town we lived in. We would blast The Modern Lovers or the Cure or The Psychedelic Furs, and bounce around the car, the windows down, smoking endless cigarettes. Some nights we would break into a local country club and go skinny dipping in the midnight waters of the lake, the lights of castles sparkling all around us, our destination a large dock in the middle. We would skinny-dip, terrified of the twisted cold-hearted creatures that lived in the depths, until we were safe on that rocking wooden plank.

The world was magical and endless. Night times were vast. Some nights we would smoke joints or eat bags of mushrooms, drinking bottles of whiskey, and some nights we were sober, talking about AA and the Twelve Steps, while still trying our best to be fifteen or sixteen or seventeen. We would talk endlessly. I moved in a pack of girls, all beautiful, all slightly crazy. We were wild back then, unafraid, or maybe too afraid. I'm not always sure of the difference. We believed everything was possible.

We were not cynical. We were not angry. We were full of hope. We cast spells against our enemies and made love potions and stayed up all night doing the Tarot and talking about magic. We believed in every possibility. We drew sigils and sang songs and worshipped strange and magnificent gods. When things went wrong in the world, it was directly related to demonic possession, and when things went right it was equally related to some form of magic. We spoke to monsters and met in crumbling graveyards at midnight and tried to talk to the dead.

Here are the things we never discussed: the time our friend's father raped her, or the time I OD'd, or the fact that his dad beat him so bad he couldn't stand, or how sometimes the only way they ever let you know they loved you was all the money. They threw it at us, forgetting that we were their children, the way they disappeared for months at a time leaving us with strangers who turned into lovers, the way her mother cleaned for hours, scrubbing till her fingers bled, all the nannies and cleaning ladies and bored fucked out of our mind family trips. All the drugs.

We lived in castles. We ran wild. We did what we wanted. We drove drunk through the suburbs with the lights off, looking for flying saucers in the night sky. We drove madly through the city looking for heroin and devils and guys to fuck.

Those were dark, magical, beautiful, terrifying days. We lost a lot of people along the way. I always think of Avishai, dying while everyone stood around watching, no one really knowing he was dying, or of Micah, trying to prove a point and getting so high on dope he fell away forever, all those people dying right before our eyes.

Lately I've been thinking about my death. That sudden moment, right before I fade away, when I am still aware, when I still exist and know what is happening. That moment as you are dying when you think, *I am dying*. Sometimes I picture myself in bed with Jon and Alex. They are asleep. They have no idea what is happening to me, and as I disappear I think, *There is still so much I wanted to say to them*. This vision is heartbreaking, but it is also comforting knowing I had been loved so much and I got to love as much as I did.

Sometimes I see it as an accident, in a car or falling out a window or through some giant hole in the middle of the street. Sometimes I wonder about opportunistic diseases, cancer, or what would happen if suddenly my meds stopped working. All the illnesses that might tear away at me, slowly, torturing me.

Slow painful deaths trapped alone inside my head.

Because it is inescapable. We will all die. I am powerless over that. I hope that in those final moments, I will remember how lucky I was. How incredibly beautiful my life has been. I have lived the life of a prince in a fairy tale. I have been spoiled in many countless ways. Even in all the pain, even with all the loss and sadness, I hope I recall all the love.

It is stunning to know that in the end there will be only me. That I will face that moment all alone.

Or maybe they will all be there with me. All the dead. All the demons and angels and monsters, all those gorgeous flying beings. Maybe they will hold me safe in arms that feel like Alex's, holding me in place, making me feel like the most special man in the world. In kisses that feel like Jon's, opening secret places in my mind, kisses that remind me that I am loved, kisses that are like spells always coming at the exact moment I need them most. They are my home.

Or in Avishai's laugh and Micah's stunning eyes. In Max's stories as we walked through Tompkins Square Park to buy drugs from 7th Street stoop dealers. In a sandbox on Nantucket where you first told me you loved me.

These people, they are all my home.

I hope this is what happens.

Even if it is just chemicals, just a comforting figment.

Near This Wild Heaven

We are here...we are all right here....

When I was a senior at Sarah Lawrence College, I stole my father's car and drove to New Orleans with Chrystal and Amber. We drove through the Holland Tunnel, music blasting, singing, feeling suddenly free and without any worries. I had my dad's credit card and money in my pocket.

We stopped in a small town in Virginia and ate fried chicken in a large yellow Victorian house turned into a bed and breakfast. The sense of haunting was so strong in that place, you could feel it crawling up and down your skin. Chrystal and I sat on the large porch next to an old black man in a rocking chair who was eating fried pork skins and drinking a Coca Cola out of the bottle.

Chrystal was on financial aid and didn't have access to the kind of money Amber and I had. Amber was tall and blond, pretty like a strange, Nordic-bird. Chrystal was shorter and darker, sexy in a restless, reckless way.

People in that town knew we were from somewhere urban. Or so we thought. We were sure the whole world was watching us. The truth is, no one probably cared. We were just three more assholes stopping along the way from somewhere, heading somewhere else. But in our heads, we were larger than life. We were punk rock.

We slept at Chrystal's mother's house. Chrystal had grown up in ashrams with her mother, living amongst various cults and yoga colonies, traveling the country. Life and age having caught up to Chrystal's mom, they were living in a small town in a small country house. We sat in the kitchen drinking red wine cold from the refrigerator.

"Like they do in Rome," Cindy, Chrystal's mom, says, her voice high and manic; the warm Southern night buzzing with the endless sound of cicadas. All the rooms were painted in what was supposed to be happy and soothing colors but were, in actuality, overly bright oranges and reds and yellows. Tapestries hung from doorways, along with glittering reflective cloths and strange instruments, incense and Buddhas, and a tortured looking Ganesh. It was a hippy Disney land tableau created by a child on some wild acid trip.

We ate vegan frozen pizzas and carrots and home-made hummus tangy with lemon juice and listened to strange chanting music and talked about astrology and destiny and the possibility of fate. Cindy told stories about the spiritual center she was a part of.

"Dean is so powerful. You feel it the minute he enters a room. He channels a community of multi-dimensional beings who live in the light, a world made up of light, beyond our understanding of physics. But it isn't supernatural in the sense of magic, just in the sense that it is beyond our understanding of what is natural. Dean says the supernatural is just a natural occurrence our science hasn't caught up to yet. This community, The Consortium, they guide us and they help us. They teach us through Dean. They show us a world beyond the illusion of this material existence."

I could tell Chrystal was getting impatient with her mother. She had moved from cold red wine to warm whiskey. Amber was fascinated, encouraging and smiling.

Chrystal was going to be famous. An actress. She was determined to be rich: it was a mission that caused her to chew nervously at her nails and to chain smoke when she drank. She was driven, for her fame and wealth were the only escape. Anything less would mean failure. She had set her life into two distinct destinies. One was built around the myth of her success, glamour and fame and money. In this destiny she was happy and, secure. She had finally made it; she was not her mother.

In the other destiny, she had failed. She was poor, she was alone, she was desperately searching, always playing the lottery or gambling, falling in love with the wrong man, working minimum wage jobs with no chance at ever catching up, ever taking a breath. Chrystal was trapped in a hyper-stasis between these two futures with no room for anything else.

I understood her. I understood that idea of all or nothing. Failure or success. The refusal to live a normal life. But then we were still young, we didn't know anything. Life hadn't had a chance to break us yet.

Amber and I sat outside while Cindy read Chrystal's Tarot. We smoked cigarettes and drank from another bottle of chilled red wine and ate Cheetos. I wondered what would happen if we just kept driving after New Orleans, instead of returning to school. What would happen to us if we just kept going? Stolen cars and credit cards, access to wealthy parents' money. Who would stop us? I always wanted to be moving, never still. I always wanted to be going somewhere. Else. It didn't matter where Else was. Somewhere Else was an idea I was chasing.

Amber was stable and calm, blond hair and blue eyes, like the girl best friend in every movie or TV show you've ever seen: a little too tall and too awkward, but the kind of pale long legs straight guys loved. She was the kind of girl who would stay up all night with you drinking cold red wine and eating Cheetos, pretending that maybe you really would go on some outrageous adventure.

She was the kind of girl who would pretend to run away, but, really, a girl like that had nothing to run away from.

Chrystal and I were more alike. We weren't pretending. We were both running. In any direction we could.

Amber went to sleep. Chrystal and Cindy went into the back yard to meditate with the trees and the stars. I had my copy of *Meditations in an Emergency*. I sat alone on the porch, reading O'Hara, refusing to sleep, afraid I might miss something magical, something beautiful.

That mythopoetic moment when the world suddenly shifts and life becomes what I always knew it was meant to be and what it could never actually be. Perfect. The world would suddenly show itself to me in golden, bejeweled moonlight and rays of shimmering darkness, like a moment in a poem or in a piece of music or in a kiss, when everything is captured and revealed perfectly, and that feeling would extend into forever.

The hint of a Southern night in the air reminded me of my grandmother, Sadie, and of Georgia. Of driving in her Lincoln with James, her best friend, next to her, dressed in some outrageous drag-outfit. He'd be wearing Sadie's jewelry, and a wig matching the long red of Sadie's hair, looking for aliens and ghosts, looking for strangers on the side of the road who spoke in prophecies and held the answers to all the secrets that were hidden from us.

The next morning, we woke and drove as fast as we could, stopping in Memphis for mimosas and bacon, watching all the college kids who were so different from our Sarah Lawrence brethren. They were living a different life, a different experience than we were. We felt urban, smarter, darker. They prayed before they ate, which we thought was hysterical. Slightly drunk and exhausted, Chrystal and I chanted made up prayers to Satan. Amber got embarrassed and went to the bathroom: but when she returned she had written 666 in small black letters on her forehead which really cracked Chrystal and me up.

Sometimes that bitch really could be outrageous.

Three blonde girls with tanned shoulders and big tits held hands with three large blond boys and prayed to Jesus. Chrystal, Amber and I held hands and prayed to Ganesh, and to Cthulhu, and to the Angels of Hell and to various porn stars and anyone else we could think of. We felt punk rock. We felt special. We weren't the MTV generation. We were better than that. Better than everyone. Or at least that's how we felt. We probably just looked like a bunch of assholes, but we wouldn't have cared. We were having fun. We were feeling free.

In Mississippi, we stopped for Cokes and candy bars from a vending machine. We were so close we could feel it. The air had changed. It was warm and wet, the sun bright like liquid gold. People moved slow in the heat, as if through an unseen but felt substance.

Amber went to use the pay phone to call her parents in Vancouver. Chrystal sat on the hood of my father's car and painted her nails a rusty red.

"My mother is so fucking crazy," she said, not looking up from her nails, a Marlboro dangling from her lips. "I'm afraid that I'm going to end up like her."

"You won't." I watched as an old man limped out of the gas station convenience store. He was carrying a six pack of beer in each hand, a carton of cigarettes held tight under his arm. He coughed loudly and spit a greenish black fluid from his mouth.

"I wonder, though. What if she isn't that crazy, you know? What if maybe she's right?"

"Right how?" For a moment, the old man looked like he might fall over. His eyes rolled back into his head and his mouth opened in a slightly horrified ecstasy. I wondered if he was dying, but instead he hobbled away, limping down the road, no sign of a place to be walking to. As if his whole existence was limping endlessly into nothingness.

"Maybe she's right that there is something out there, a meaning and a purpose to life that is bigger than all this." She looked up. In that moment she was breathtakingly beautiful, efficient and divine in the way she painted her nails, smoked her cigarette, and watched me all at the same time. "I want to believe her. Every single fucking time. I want to believe that this time she's found it. That the Ashram and the guru and the cards and the angels and this new dude, Dean and his Consortium, I want to believe that this time is the real time. And maybe it is. It's possible, right? There were times when I almost thought, *Goddamn, this fucker is the real fucking deal.*"

She waved her hands in the air, willing the polish to dry in the humidity, and then she captured her cigarette between two fingers, removed it from her mouth, and hopped off the hood of the car. "Wouldn't that be amazing? Like suddenly the world really was a fairy tale all along. And life was better than the best Disney movie."

Amber was walking back toward us like some ice-blonde Amazonian goddess, hips swaying widely, tears in her blue eyes. Chrystal handed me her cigarette and rolled her eyes at me.

"Why are you crying?" she asked Amber.

"It's stupid."

"So? Stupid is the new cool. Tell me."

"My parents…they're just so fucking nice. I told them what we were doing, and instead of getting mad at me, they told me they were going to put some extra cash into my bank account and to take us all out to a nice dinner on their card and not to worry about the money. Have fun." Amber wiped the tears from her eyes. "I just feel really lucky."

x

A few weeks before going to New Orleans, I had started working with an escort agency called Boys of Summer. I had answered an ad in a gay magazine and ended up meeting the owner, a small, skinny nervous man in his late thirties, at a diner next to the basketball courts on West 3rd and 6th Avenue. I was living with Elly on Court Street in Brooklyn Heights and had taken the F Train from Bergen to West 4th. His name was Vincent, and he was short and hairy with thick glasses and strange rheumy eyes. He was reading a beat-up copy of Anton Robert Wilson's *Cosmic Trigger* when I arrived. I still find myself wondering how he had come across that particular book. Wilson was a mystic, a philosopher, a magician. Vincent was a pimp, but maybe he, like everyone else, was broader than I knew, less one-dimensional. The world rarely seems to fit into my perception of it. I catch glimpses of the truth about people and about reality, but they are fleeting and obscured by my own needs.

And really, who was I, the whore interviewing with the pimp, to judge the books a man reads?

Vincent was worried I was too short and too stocky, not tall and lean.

"You're built like a dwarfish thug." He smiled at the waitress, a blue-haired Polish woman in her sixties with an impossibly thick accent. "I mean that in a good way," he said after we ordered hamburgers and fries. "There's a market for guys like you. I'm just used to the Chelsea boys. Party boys who are too high to get hard." He smiled at me. "I bet you have no problem getting a hard on."

He asked me how big I was and told me we'd have to go back to his apartment where I would have to get hard and let him measure it. Size was an issue in his business.

"Unless you want to bottom. Then it doesn't matter. No one cares if a bottom even has a cock. Unless they have a huge dick, then it's a whole new category. Big dicked bottoms sell well. But you don't have the feel of a bottom. You feel like a top. So, let's hope your dick is top worthy."

The whole idea of going back to his place made me nervous. The weekend before I had gone on another interview with two guys in SOHO who were starting a new agency. One was Italian and the other was black, and they told me they had some other guy on his way over and that the interview would entail him and the other guy fucking us, so they could see how good we were. I was still naïve at the time and I thought that maybe they were telling me the truth.

"Don't worry, though," Vincent was saying, clutching Anton to his chest like the Philosopher's Stone itself. "You aren't my type. I only like trannies. With big dicks." He laughed and lit a cigarette. I'm pretty sure he didn't eat any of his burger.

He lived in a large one bedroom on Cornelia Street he said he had inherited when his grandmother had died. A few other guys, all young, sexy, and well built, were lying around the living room watching porn on the TV.

He introduced me to them and then sent me into his bedroom to get hard.

"Just call me when you're ready."

His bedroom looked out onto a dark, musty airshaft. The bed had a black comforter with bright gold trim and reflective golden hearts. The closet doors were mirrored, reflecting the room back to me in multi-layered harshness. The wood floor was covered in a shaggy white carpet. The ashtrays and mirrors had razors on them, with remnants of a smudged white substance.

I sat on the bed and started jerking off, trying to get hard, but I was nervous. Vincent was right. I wasn't like the well-built, sculpted Adonises in the living room. They were stereotypes of an ideal while I was less than perfect, less idealized. Maybe I had made a mistake. Maybe I wasn't cut out to be a Boy of Summer.

But my dad had told me I needed to get a job, and I was determined. I am a hundred percent sure working as an escort for the Boys of Summer was not the kind of job he was referring to, but it made perfect sense to me. It had the hours I wanted, the pay I wanted, and it seemed like it might be sexy and fun. I closed my eyes and ran through various fantasies. After a moment, there was a knock at the door. In walked Carlos, one of the boys I had met in the living room. He was tall and broad, with curly black hair and tan skin. He smiled and took his shirt off to reveal a tattoo of the Virgin Mary over his heart, the reds of her gown, the weeping face.

"Vincent thought you might need some help."

He sucked my dick and right before I came he called Vincent in, appearing magically with ruler in hand to measure me. Afterward, they both left so I could finish off.

I had passed the size test. I was officially a Boy of Summer.

x

My first date was on Cranberry Street within walking distance of my apartment in Brooklyn Heights. Elly made me give her the address. She even offered to wait for me at the bakery down the street.

"Just in case he turns out to me some kind of serial killer."

"What are you going to do if he is? Beat him with cannolis?"

He lived on the third floor of a walk up and reminded me a little of Lurch from the *Addams Family*, but older and less sexy. He wore a dark suit with a white shirt and wing-tipped dress shoes, and he wanted me to get naked and lie very still on his bed while he tickled me. The point was for me to try to stay as still and quiet as possible while being tickled, fighting the hysterics until I couldn't do it anymore and gave in to a fit of laughter.

The room smelled slightly of sour milk, and long strands of hair stuck out of his nose and his ears. He had a strange yellow tinge to his eyes and when he got excited, he made little choking sounds, as if he were swallowing too much saliva.

It was all faked. I am not ticklish, and as he ran his hands under my arms and up the sides of my chest, I heard movement in the closet and saw the vague shadow of a person watching.

I tried to ignore the heavy breathing from the closet, trying to focus on my performance instead of whoever was watching us. I had a headache, and we were only half an hour into the sixty-minute session Lurch had paid for. It was hard to concentrate on anything else but the throbbing pain and the inane tickling and having to pretend to be squirming and laughing and sort of enjoying myself but not enjoying myself too much.

After fifty minutes Lurch got on his knees and asked me to stand over him and jerk off on his face. I wondered if Carlos would show up to help me out this time, and I realized, that this is what a whore is paid for. Getting hard in situations like this.

I never saw who was in the closet. I just heard their strange whimpering gasps as I came on Lurch's face. I gathered my money and ran out of there as fast as I could.

I walked back home down Henry Street, scratches from Lurch's frantic ticking running red up and down my body, I looked at all the elegant brownstones, catching glimpses of baby grand pianos and shelves of books through windows, and I wondered if it was possible that I might be able to live in one of those places one day, like some young king.

x

My second date was a strange queen who lived on 17th and 8th Avenue. He asked me to pick him up a muffin from Big Cup before coming up to his apartment. He lived on the top three floors of a beautiful brownstone that looked out onto a quiet, tree-lined 17th Street. The bottom floor was a small antique shop that saw customers by appointment only. Boys walked hand in hand in Chelsea, adult book stores were next to bistros and cafes, the sun was bright, and the trees were flowering. Manhattan felt luscious and decadent.

His name was Laurent. He looked like an aging Botticelli cherub, round face, curly blond hair, faded, milky blue eyes. He offered me a cup of rose tea and split his blueberry muffin with me. He wore white satin pants, a pink blouse, and an eggshell blue jacket, like some strange perverted pastel version of a Nagel print.

"I have the cancer," he said, even though by then we all knew it wasn't a cancer. His voice was whispery, as if it were being transmitted over a vast and frozen lake. "So, we cannot touch. But I would appreciate if you got naked and read to me."

I sat nude on the couch, drinking tea and reading Gertrude Stein to him. After an hour, he clapped his hands like some twisted, gorgeous child, and told me I was marvelous. He never asked me to come. He just paid me my money, with a generous sixty-dollar tip.

"Not to be told to Vincent, that greedy little mafiosa!"

And he sent me on my way.

I liked Laurent and saw him at least twice a week for the next few months. One time I noticed a strange purplish irritation on the side of his face that he kept fingering, picking at it till it bled.

"I'm dying, of course." he said, when he saw me looking. He stood up, frail and unsure, and looked about the room. He had Kandinskys and Herrings, photographs of him standing between Warhol and Joe Dallesandro, a bursting vaginal O'Keefe flower. All originals. All worth fortunes. "We are so lucky here, aren't we? Living here, in this wild heaven, with so much possibility. Let the Christians and the straights have their boring suburbs and their endless arguments about right and wrong. Morality is so irrelevant when confronted with the truth of life and beauty. I love being in this decaying paradise." He lit a cigarette, smoke furling around him like a shawl around a black and white film star. "I'm going to miss it all so much."

We listened to Leonard Cohen records, and he asked if I would mind if he got naked too.

"Of course not," I said. I had begun to think of Laurent as a friend.

His body was covered in the strange, purple lesions. Ribs were revealed through his pink-pale skin. His penis was small and shriveled, his balls like tiny marbles.

He rolled joints for us, the tips dipped in some strange clear liquid. He told me he would pay extra if I would do cartwheels across his living room. I was high and told him he didn't need to pay me extra, I'd do the cartwheels for free.

We laughed and read out loud from Lorca's *Poet In New York* collection. He danced around the room naked and sang made up operas in strange, fantasy languages, giggling and falling onto the couch, exhausted. After endless hours of this, I knew Vincent would be mad. Laurent gave me a five-hundred-dollar tip.

He blew kisses at me when I tried to say it was too much.

"Never tell a gentleman who is trying to give you gifts no. It is rude and tacky. Ugly. And you, my dear boy, are anything but tacky." He smiled, slightly sad, nostalgic. "I will miss you," he said, falling back onto the couch and lighting a cigarette.

x

I only met one really sexy guy while working with Vincent. He was a married dad visiting from Oklahoma. I met him in his room at the Marriot in Times Square. It was after midnight. I knocked on the door. A man in his thirties answered, handsome, a strong square jaw covered in a dark beard, a large thick nose, and stubby, thick fingers. He was Italian and said he was from Detroit, not Oklahoma. *Fucking Vincent*, I remember thinking, because he swore he screened the guys before sending us out.

He wore blue boxers and a white T-shirt that didn't hide the thick black chest hair. On the bed was an opened copy of *The Bonfire of The Vanities*, a dark suit thrown across the desk, rumpled pants and argyle socks on the floor. The TV was on mute, a flickering *Soap* re-run.

He told me his name was Andy. He was the only guy I actually ever thought, *Wow, I'd do him for free*. He showed me pictures of his wife and two boys, twins around eight or nine, and we lay on the queen-sized bed and made out. He tasted of whiskey and breath mints. He was nervous, not sure where to put his hands. After a few minutes he said he wanted to brush his teeth. He disappeared into the bathroom. I lay in that room, the hush of the air-conditioning, the distant honking of taxis, the far away removed lighting of the flickering TV. A painting of a little girl with a yellow bonnet walking down a path through a green field hung on the wall above the bed. A white dog was at her feet. She carried a basket of very red and purple berries. It was ugly and somehow frightening to me. I closed my eyes and thought about other things, trying to keep my hard-on.

Andy got back in bed.

"You're really thick for such a little guy," he said. He was taller than me, but felt smaller. "I don't do this a lot. My wife…we just had our third kid. A little girl."

I wondered if this was all that it was going to be. Him holding me and telling me about his family. I thought of the girl framed forever on that path, holding her basket of over-bright lewd berries. She made me feel sad.

It took me a few minutes to realize that the shaking bed was caused by his sobbing. My back was wet with tears. Suddenly he was pushing me down, his hard dick poking through the slit in his boxers. I gave him a blow job while he cried. He came quick. It tasted sour. It turned me on that he came in my mouth.

"Do you have to go, or can you lie with me for a few more minutes?"

I told him I could stay for a while. He fell asleep in my arms, his breathing turning into deep snores. His wallet was on the bedside table. I opened it to a picture of him and his wife holding their newborn baby. They looked happy. It made me think about how little any of us ever really know about each other.

I put the picture of his wife with the newborn in my pocket and left.

I took the 1 train down to Christopher Street and walked over to Vincent's place. The night was alive and full of people. Pizza parlors and falafel stands, bars. The city felt like a breathing entity, a being that moved around us, filling us and devouring us.

Everything around me was in motion.

It suddenly occurred to me that I was stuck. I was the only thing not moving forward. I had somehow fallen, and even though I thought I had made radical decisions like prostitution and heroin, forsaking the "normal" world, it was the normal people who seemed to be living life, while I was just wandering lost on the fringes.

At Vincent's, a group of guys were sitting around jerking off, most of them only semi-hard. Candles were lit. Vincent had drawn a symbol between his eyes and was sitting in the corner of the room, facing a blank wall.

"It's the third eye," he said, reaching up, massaging the strange triangle shape. "I'm learning to see the world outside of my perception." He smiled, the dark of his eyes widening, his pupils huge. He reached out, grabbing my wrist. "Stay," he said, his voice strangely soft and child-like. "We are playing a game."

He turned back to the room of masturbating whores.

"He's fucked up," one of the guys said, his limp dick in his hand. "He bought peyote off some Columbian dude and now he thinks he sees the light."

"There is no light," Vincent said. "Just darkness." He giggled. "That's the game. How to move about inside all this darkness. How not to drown in all this…" He became suddenly silent, his mouth widening, as if he were about to scream, and then he turned away and faced the wall.

I left Vincent's forty percent on the table and took the 2 train back to Brooklyn. It started to rain as I walked down Court Street. I felt the rain moving through the air, like some eclipse, like some vast and overreaching conspiracy, the change in the weather, the change inside me, the sudden moment I realized things were not going as I had planned.

I had ducked into an all-night diner and snorted one of the three bags of dope I had stopped to pick up on the way home. Just as the first winds began to blow, I had to stop and puke. It was late, the street empty. As I stood back up, I saw ahead of me a strange and glowing formation hovering in the empty shadows of the street. A fallen angel trying to regain its balance. It hesitated at the exact moment I noticed it noticing me. Our eyes locked and I knew with a startling certainty that ahead of me was darkness, and that I could not escape it. None of us could. Vincent was right, darkness is the way of things.

I felt like turning and running. I had nowhere to run to. No one to run to. I was suddenly alone.

When I looked again, the angel was gone. Just some trick of the drugs and the lights and my fucked-up mind. And I was alone on the street. And then it began to rain. As the rain fell, for a moment I could see the reflection of the world around me captured in those rain drops like tiny silver holographic balls, glimpses into remote possibilities, endless dimensions.

Again, the world seemed frozen, a tableau of itself, a painting only partially finished, and yet fully revealed and realized in the mind of the artist. The world became so quiet and so still, the rain suspended in a perpetual falling motion, never actually reaching its destination, when suddenly cars honked, sirens screeched, and the world became shattering and wet. I was left reeling in the sudden revelations of nothingness and chaos.

Court Street suddenly came alive all around me, full of taxis speeding in one direction, the sirens howling a few blocks away on Smith, the rain heavy. I ducked into a bodega and bought a bagel, a forty, a blunt, and an egg roll and ran the few blocks home. I locked myself in my room and snorted the remaining two bags of heroin, added weed to the blunt, and lay in my bed watching *The Golden Girls*, drinking my forty, smoking my blunt, sad, missing someone, only I didn't know exactly who.

We drove the 10 into New Orleans. Amber was reading a book on Voodoo history and rites, Chrystal sat in the back smoking cigarettes and drinking Diet Cokes. The air was hot and muggy, smelling of car exhaust, decay, and perfumed flowers. I had gotten us a room at a guest house on Ursulines and Rampart, just outside the Quarter.

Our room was dark and magical, with purple curtains, a large king-sized sleigh bed, hardwood floors, strange paintings of the Virgin Mary and dancing skeletons, candles with black Jesus and writhing snakes. Out back, the courtyard was draped with tropical flowers. Red and mustard colored bougainvillea hung in curtains, falling among angel statues and fountains, wrought iron benches and tables for reading and two black cats that wandered in the dark shrubs.

"This place is amazing!" Chrystal said, lying on her back on the large bed.

Amber took out a joint and lit it. I went into the bathroom and counted ten bags of heroin. I snorted one and went back out. Amber was lying next to Chrystal. They were passing the joint back and forth. I lay on the bed next to them, feeling their warmth, closing my eyes and watching as strange muted colors danced in the darkness of my mind. I felt them and I could hear them. I felt removed and yet intimately close to them at the same time.

"I think this place is haunted," Amber said. I knew she was stoned by the husky tone of her voice.

"I know!" Chrystal jumped up, her leg lying across mine. "I felt it the minute we got here."

I tried to see if I could feel it too. The ghosts. The haunting. I listened to the silence of the spaces around us. The music of birds outside in the court yard. The sound of the fountains and the footsteps along the stoned patios. I felt the darkness inside me grow, and, in that moment, I felt the thing that has lived inside me, buried so deep inside my consciousness that I almost forget he lives with me. Malignant, like a cancer waiting to consume me.

X

I have often tried to pinpoint the exact moment of my possession, the exact moment the demon got in. I often wonder if it had happened when I was a child, whispering to the things that lived in the darkness, dancing with the shadows inside my room, calling forth strange entities without knowing what it was I was doing. Maybe it was something genetic, a family trait passed on from one generation to the next like a giant network of evil that infected us at birth. When I was young, my grandmother, Sadie, gave me a clown penny bank—a metal contraption made up of a leering clown face and a hand. You put the penny or the quarter in the hand and pushed a lever on the back of the clown's head and the arm reaches up to an opening mouth, the coin disappearing inside.

I used to speak to the clown, call it strange names I've now forgotten, talking to it, singing to it, conjuring things inside it.

I was an angry child. Hurt. I was searching for places to hide that hurt. Places to stash away that anger.

Lying on that bed in New Orleans, suddenly aware of my dark traveler, I wondered for a moment if maybe back then, as a child, if one of the beings I called into existence inside that metal clown's head hadn't gotten out and into me.

It didn't matter, of course, where it came from or even whether it was a literal or figurative possession. What lived inside me was darkness and evil and hungry and, for a moment, I touched upon it. I felt it, and it felt me.

"I just hope they aren't the mean kind of ghosts," Amber said, getting up and walking slowly to the bathroom, her long legs strange and disarming. "Like poltergeists or *The Exorcist* or something like that."

"*The Exorcist* wasn't a ghost," Chrystal said. "It was demonic possession."

Amber locked the door behind her. Chrystal looked at me, her eyes raised. First the sink was turned on. Then the toilet flushed. And then the shower. Amber was bulimic. Something we all knew but didn't discuss.

Chrystal lit a cigarette and then handed it to me. She lit another one for herself.

"I hope she's hungry when she gets out of there. I'm starving." She took a book out of her bag. "My mom was teaching me how to draw sigils last night and infuse them with intention. Like I intend to make fifty thousand dollars in the next six months. Or I intend to get an agent or get the part I auditioned for or, fuck me, get an audition at all. She said if I was smart I would draw one for a rich husband. Can you believe that? My hippy mom telling me to use magic to get me a rich husband."

I was sitting up. I smelled incense coming through the window.

"I guess it's better than when she believed everything was part of some giant global conspiracy. Presidents and world governments and aliens and DNA tampering through vaccines. She was fucking paranoid about everything. Now she's worried about getting old and being poor." She inhaled deeply on her cigarette. We heard Amber moving about in the bathroom. "She's whoring me out for her retirement. It's better than thinking the CIA is always watching."

"I'm fucking starving!" Amber said, marching out of the bathroom and sitting on the edge of the bed. "Is anybody else starving?"

Amber had read about a place called The Praline Connection on Frenchman Street on the other side of Esplanade. We took our time walking through the Quarter, wandering through used book stores where I bought a copy of the first volume of Anais Nin's diary, and Chrystal struggled over buying a strange little book by Austin Osman Spare that talked about sigils and magic and philosophy or a strange little book about the Mopses, a German cult that grimaced a lot and worshipped a dog.

We passed art galleries and record stores and stopped for coffee with chicory at Kaldi's Coffee House and listened to some punk band play at a bar on Decatur. At the Praline Connection, I ate fried chicken, mac and cheese, collard greens and sweet tea. We had pralines and banana pudding for dessert. Outside, we lit cigarettes. The sun had set, and there was a light rain. It was less hot, almost beautiful. Street lamps threw a literary light over a city built for stories. Buildings were low and battered, streets were uneven and filled with potholes, people laughed and walked down the middle of roads, ignoring the cars, slightly drunk on food and alcohol, slightly high on the perfumed air.

We got drinks at a small outside bar and carried them down Bourbon Street, avoiding the crowds as best we could. I was drunk and a little high and trying to explain to Chrystal and Amber about the demon who lived inside me.

"I can feel him sometimes, you know? Moving around in there, *thinking*. I can feel him feel me. Every neurosis, every bad thought, every fear and self-destructive impulse comes from him. One day I'm going to find someone to exorcize him. To send him back to fucking hell or whatever other dimension he came from."

"You could draw a sigil. Trap him in it and then set it on fire," Chrystal said.

"Really? Would that work?"

"I don't know, but we could try. I think it's worth a try."

"I read something once about Solomon trapping demons and using them for knowledge. He learned magic and spells that way."

Chrystal and I both looked at Amber. "Where the fuck did you read that?" Chrystal asked.

"In a class on religion. I was doing research. He trapped angels and demons and was able to control them. Or something."

"It's called goetia, the invocation of goetic demons." Chrystal said. "From the *Lesser Key of Solomon*. I had to learn all about it when my mother was involved with the Pagan Coven."

"Jesus," Amber said. "Your fucking mom."

"Whatever. Because of her, we might get rid of Jeff's demon. And I might get a rich husband."

"Maybe you can help me find a way to eat all I want and not get fat."

Chrystal and I shared a look. Maybe I wasn't the only one possessed of strange demons.

X

Laurent had ordered one of those kiddy pools from a hardware store down the street, and we used large pots to carry water from the kitchen sink into the living room, where the pool was set up, to fill it. We sat in the pool and read books and smoked hash cigarettes and talked. It was my job to add hot water when the pool cooled off.

Laurent sat, his legs spread out before him in the water, his head resting on the rim of the pool, his eyes closed, a strange smile on his face.

"Some days I feel so happy," he said, the room saturated with hash smoke, thick and dark. There was a new purple orchid in a large glass vase on the piano. I submerged myself under water, my eyes open, looking at a strange, blossoming bruise on the side of Laurent's leg. "Our bodies are fictions," Laurent was saying as I re-submerged. "They are lies."

I moved next to him, the outlines of our bodies touching, leg to leg, arm to arm, and I rested my head on his shoulder. He felt so cold, so small.

"I am not this thing. This is not the end of what or who I am." He stood, water splashing around me, and held his arms open. "I have half a mind to make you cut me open." He was looking down at me, a strange glow to his eyes. "Make you go digging around inside me until you find it. *Me*. Not this." He waved his skinny arms around the room, down at his body, running a hand through his hair. "It's all such a vulgar fucking lie." He sat back down. "You won't find it, either. No matter how deep you cut, no matter what perverse parts of me you search, you won't find who I am in here. Because it doesn't exist. Not in this body. Not in this room. Not anywhere we can see." He turned to me, grabbing my hand, his eyes now feverish and startled. "You know that, right? Who I am, who you are, it lives somewhere else. We are just bad replicas. Pieces cut from infinity. We are representations of the thing, but not the thing. I, you, we are all so much bigger than these suits of meat."

We ordered caviar and steaks, asparagus and champagne, cheeses and tiny pastries from a French restaurant on 8th Avenue. We ate surrounded by candlelight, wearing satin robes and pink plastic Duane Reade flip-flops.

"I have a girlfriend, Claire, who comes once a week to do my finances. She pays my bills and makes sure my money is all being handled correctly." He spread a thin layer of black caviar over a square cracker and nibbled at it. "It is the price of wealth. All these people protecting you from each other. Someone is always trying to do you damage. But I don't even care, did you know that? I have so much, why not let someone steal a little? I always tell her this. Mr. Webster is taking a little off the top of my investments? Am I broke? Am I starving? Am I unable to pay my bills? These are not losses, but gifts. That is what I tell her. Of course, people steal. And they lie. We all do. But Claire, she gets so indignant. So outraged. But that isn't what I want to tell you about her. The strange thing about Claire is that she is an abductee. Do you know what abductees are?"

"I know what the word means."

"Yes, of course you do, but that doesn't really answer the question, does it? Meanings are so wildly varied. Context is everything." He stood up, the satin robe hanging off him too loosely, as if he were disappearing inside all that elegant fabric. He moved slowly, carefully, about the room, reaching out for a lamp or a table or, a chair as if to locate himself. "We are discussing aliens here. Poor Claire is an alien abductee."

He put on a Brian Eno record, the strange music floating in the spaces between us like the thick smoke from the candles and hash cigarettes.

"They come to her monthly when she sleeps. Through the walls, materializing from empty spaces, appearing as if they had always been there, just veiled, which of course, might be the truth. Claire and I disagree on the substance of these beings, on who they are and where they are from. She believes they have come to earth from some far-off planet, riding for eons in a space ship, to do studies on us. She does not believe they are evil. She does not believe that they intend to hurt us. They are just studying us.

"Which, I, of course, believe is naïve. You do not travel eons to a foreign world to just benignly study. Why bother? Who really fucking cares? We are barely interesting to each other. What would make us so interesting to some advanced, alien culture? But again, that is irrelevant, because I do not even believe they are alien in that way. I do not believe they come from some distant star on space ships, to earth."

He sat down slowly, folding his legs underneath him.

He had such beautiful hands. Pale and long. I always imagined Laurent sitting in front of a canvas or playing his piano, those elegant fingers creating magic and beauty. Magicians hands. Creating fire in the world. Making poetry.

"They are inter-dimensional. Which is why they appear out of nothingness. They are walking through doorways in space, in time, from their dimension into ours."

He suggested we go out and buy fish for the swimming pool. "Great, colorful, violent fish."

When I told him it was after midnight and nothing would be open, he just smiled and closed his eyes.

"Then I shall pretend we have fish. And that they are all around us. Swimming past us right now as we talk, leaving shining trails of reds and oranges and blues. Gorgeous jewels swimming in the spaces between us."

He lit a joint and held it out for me. "The thing about these inter-dimensional beings who come and visit Claire, I'm not even sure she is right about what it is they are doing. I do not think they are running tests. I think they are trying to get her to wake up. To see the world as it really is. To actually be alive. But instead she just lays there, terrified, paralyzed, as they prod her and poke her." He began jabbing at me, giggling, screaming, "Wake up! Wake up!"

I fell away, laughing. "Hey! That tickles."

"And then she just falls back asleep. Can you imagine? She just returns to her bed and falls back asleep and wakes up the next day and goes about her life as if nothing magical, nothing amazing ever happened. We all live our lives like that, as if nothing incredible, nothing amazing is happening. Just a bunch of nihilistic assholes running around jerking off and shitting and acting like everything is pointless. Cynicism is the greatest poison ever invented, next to psychology, of course. Because everything matters. Everything is important. We are swimming in an ocean of jewels, and all we see is a fucking shit swamp."

X

I can't remember exactly where we met Ian and Lucifer, but I know it was on the first night in New Orleans, and it changed the course of everything. Lucifer was intensely handsome, the kind of handsome that left you slightly dizzy and breathless. He had clear blue eyes, long lashes, and a blond Mohawk. He was short, with muscles that came from rough work and a rougher life. Muscles that felt real and earned, not manufactured in a gym in Chelsea. His body was covered in the kind of tattoos you get in your living-room or in someone's kitchen, not done in anything even remotely called a parlor. He was eighteen and had dirt under his fingernails. He wore a black Bauhaus T-shirt and ripped, stained jeans, and red high tops that were falling apart.

Ian was more refined, taller, slimmer, black hair with the green eyes of an acolyte. He was handsome in a classical sense, like a statue or a lost Carravagio painting. He had on black eye liner and dark mascara, smudges of grey on his cheek. He wore similar jeans, green high tops, and a black Circle Jerks T-shirt torn at the belly revealing pale white skin covered in dark hair. The two of them should have been actors or models, not street kids in New Orleans begging for change outside a Circle K Market.

But they weren't actors or models. They were homeless kids.

Chrystal sat down next to them and took Lucifer's hand, turning it palm up. She was going to tell him his future. Amber and I went into to the Circle K and bought cigarettes, two six packs, and a bottle of whiskey. When we came back outside, Chrystal was making out with Lucifer, sitting on his lap and giggling. Ian, strange and awkward, sat next to them, his eyes closed, his lips moving slightly in some secret rhythm, as if memorizing codes or lines of music.

I sat down next to Ian and offered him a cigarette. Amber used the pay phone next to the market entrance to call her parents. Ian took the cigarette and looked at me. Those eyes were like some strange and lost artifact found buried deep in a backwater swamp, pirate's treasure or some stolen alien technology.

"I was trying to meditate," he said.

"Really? In the Circle K Parking Lot?"

"All this fucking neon, man. I thought maybe I could suck up some of that energy, drink in some of that light, you know? Use it to get inside, deep, meditate on the dweller."

He was looking at me intently, waiting, as if expecting me to say something. But I was suddenly speechless, lost in synchronicity, lost in some pattern that had arisen in my life and seemed to entangle me in its web.

Ian stood up and did a strange little dance, and then he was laughing. Lucifer lifted Chrystal out of his lap and joined his friend, the two of them looking like insane leprechauns, dancing suddenly in the manufactured streetlight, the magical red neon glow of the Circle K Market like a monument of despair haloing around them. Lucifer took Ian's hands in his and they began to dance in a circle, singing a wordless song, just sounds, humming and barking, giggling and howling.

Chrystal looked at me, smiling, and I knew she was falling in love. Amber walked over to us, her face a mask of disapproval and sudden adulthood.

"Seriously? Satan and his retarded puppy?"

Chrystal gave her the finger, smiling sweetly. "I think they are adorable."

"Hey, you guys are fucking cool!" Lucifer said, letting go of Ian and turning his blue eyes on us. "We were gonna go get fucked up by the river, wanta come?" He was looking at Chrystal intently, smiling, but I couldn't help but notice a moment where he turned to me and winked, as if sharing some bond between us I wasn't aware of yet.

"You ever hear of the Weimer Republic?" Ian said, moving next to me, his fingers almost touching the tips of mine.

"What?" I asked.

"The Weimer Republic. German. Right after World War One. It was this fucking amazing time in Berlin. All these artists and shit. You know, *Cabaret*. The Mopses Revolution. All that. There were lesbians and fucking gay guys and drag shows and the world seemed really amazing. All these writers and shit moved to Berlin. It was a big deal."

People have a way of surprising you. You think because they are one thing, that everything about them must fit inside this tiny box of an idea, but they aren't one thing. None of us are. We are varied and vast. We contain angles and curves and sharp corners, strange and winding peninsulas, aspects of selves that reveal hidden universes and depths.

"Yeah. What about it?" I had taken a class on German Expressionism and Silent Film my freshman year and did a paper on the November

Group and Dada in Berlin in the 1920's, so I knew a little, but I wasn't sure exactly what this kid was trying to say to me.

"Nothing. Just a thing, right? Something to think about. That fuckin' country is torn apart after World War One, Hitler is on the horizon with his death camps and holocausts, right in between two periods of pain and destruction and here comes this amazing period of art and philosophy. Fucking Einstein and Brecht and Huxley and Isherwood. It all exists in those years. Possibility. Intention. Magic and art and beauty. Then comes Hitler with his dark furies and his violence and experiments creating monsters and black magic, his alien technology and his destruction of a people. He fucking kills it. All of it. All the fucking Jews run to New York or they get put in camps. But those years in between man, they changed the world. Think if Hitler hadn't come along. Maybe we would all be living in some Utopic world, you know? Maybe those demons he was so intent on conjuring wouldn't have been so well fed on pain and blood and maybe the world would be something different."

I looked at this kid, his Southern accent verging on redneck, his post-goth-street urchin-punk rock-look, and I wondered how the fuck he knew about any of this.

"My buddy, he told me that Crowley was there too. Practicing his sex magic and doin' art and just bein' all Aleister Crowley and shit. Can you fucking imagine? Man, I would kill to be there, Berlin, 1922, get the fuck out in '32, you know? But for those ten years, it must have seemed like the world was endless. Dogs, they worshipped fucking dogs. The skies must have rippled and torn apart with the magic going down." He laughed. "You got any smokes?"

I lit a cigarette and handed it to him. "I didn't know about Crowley," I said.

He took the cigarette. "Hitler came along and fucked all that shit up. But why did any of it even happen? What kind of crazy alternative magic brought about that one moment, that time of pure enlightenment between hells? You ever wonder?" He turned to his friend and smiled. "Lucifer knows all about magic. He's all into sex magic, aren't you, man?"

Lucifer was busy making out with Chrystal, rubbing his hand over her crotch, Chrystal's eyes closed. Amber was standing to the side, smoking, drinking from one of the cans of beer we had bought.

"Fuck ya, I am. There's this dude, man, in the Garden District, my buddy went to him. He does this insane shit, man. Like you just gotta give yourself over to him. Dudes go in there, and they don't come out the same."

"What does that even mean?" Amber asked.

"He rapes the fuck outta you," Lucifer said, smiling broad, his eyes sparkling blue in the neon light. "It's how he starts. He takes a guy, ties him up, and forces him to take his dick, you know? Straight up anal rape." Lucifer laughed, deep and rough. "But then, man, he uses that experience to get inside your head. That's when the real raping starts."

"And that's magic?" Amber dripped cynicism. It was hard not to blame her. "Getting ass-raped?"

"It's more than that. He gets inside you, cures you of all the life shit, sets you free. We are all so fucking trapped inside these rules of society, rules of religion: prisons we've built—this guy, he just walks in and breaks it all apart. He fucking tortures you, beats you till you can't walk, then rapes your ass again, fucking with you, bringing you to the brink and then setting you free. It changes you. Gives you a chance to be the man you were meant to be."

"We're going to perform an exorcism on Jeff," Chrystal said, reaching for one of the bottles of whiskey.

"No fucking way," Ian said. "No fucking way. You gotta let me be there. I know all about exorcisms."

We made our way to the river, winding slowly through haunted narrow streets, past bustling bars and strange shops promising futures told and curses delivered, late night restaurants and crowds of drunken tourists, until we found ourselves standing on the dark banks of the Mississippi, the skyline of downtown to our right, the Quarter behind us.

The world sparkled. The lights of the city played on the river like jewels, loud party boats carrying drunk and happy passengers floated past, bright lights and jazz, laughter and excitement. The night was alive and passionate, warm and over ripe, flowing. We were all moving on its currents, no longer part of our individual stories but characters in a dark and unsettling play where behind the scenes giants roamed and angels hovered overhead and magicians and witches cast spells. Grand conspiracies were being drawn out in the wings and yet here we were, happy and lost in the light, fighting back and maybe even winning for a moment.

A girl with a pink Mohawk and a sparkling faux diamond nose ring was screaming about having seen a mermaid in the river.

"She was so beautiful! So bright!" She looked around at the tourists and homeless and junkies, jazz musicians and artists, all standing there, watching her or ignoring her. "You fucking idiots! You have no idea! No fucking clue! She was right there, shining before your very eyes, and you have no fucking idea!"

I stood there, thinking, *It's like they follow me. These mermen and women. From city to city, river to river.*

"She's not the only one who's seen her," Ian said. He was standing behind me. I could feel the warmth of his body.

"What?"

"The mermaid. She's not the only one who's seen her." He took a swig from a bottle of whiskey and then handed it to me. "Kids have been seeing her for years. I heard an old fisherman tell how he'd seen her out in the bayous wrestling an alligator. She won. Guys who navigate the oil rigs through the bends in the river say they can hear her late at night singing to them. Calling to them."

I thought back to when I was a child and my mother and I were on the Brooklyn Bridge. She pointed to something in the distance. And in that moment, I swore I saw a giant fin, and the flickering light of golden hair, and then she was picking me up and telling me that all you had to do was look and the world's magic would reveal itself.

And I thought of Raphael, who had once believed the Hudson was full of magical creatures, before the world broke him, before he gave up magic for something else.

"She looks high to me," Amber said. I hadn't known she was standing near us.

"Doesn't mean she didn't see it." He paused and then took a stray cigarette from behind his ear and lit it. "I saw her once."

"Of course."

"I did. I was all alone. I had come out here to sleep." He looked at me, his eyes connecting to mine, and he smiled. "I like to sleep by the river sometimes. Instead of the squat. It's quiet. I feel like I'm part of it." He handed me the cigarette. I took it and inhaled. "I was lying, looking up at the stars and I heard her. Singing to me. You think you know something. You think you understand how the world works. And then she's there proving it all wrong." He turned to Amber, and I could feel the intensity roll off him. "There is magic in the world, beautiful things like her, and ugly, terrible monsters. Both exist. Whether you believe in them or not."

I watched him as he walked over to the girl with the pink Mohawk, pulling her into him. I turned to Amber.

"You are being a bitch."

"I know. I can't help it. It's just…come on…Satan?"

I laughed. "Lucifer."

"Whatever. It's idiotic. They are dirty." She smiled. "I'm being a bitch. It's just…who are these guys? What are we doing? And Chrystal…Jesus, she's off giving the demon dude a fucking blowjob."

I looked around. Chrystal and Lucifer were nowhere to be found.

"God knows what diseases that kid has on his dick."

There was a breeze off the river. The air smelled muddy and dank and sweet all at the same time. A large, brightly lit party boat drifted lazily by.

"I'm tired," Amber said. "I think I want to go back to the hotel soon."

"You shouldn't walk alone. I have money if you want to take a cab."

She looked at me, and I knew she was disappointed. She was hoping I would, like her, see the absurdity of what was happening. She was hoping for an ally, but the absurdity of the situation drew me toward it.

"They're squatters," she said. "Homeless kids."

I laughed. "Yeah."

"What kind of an asshole goes looking to get raped?"

"I think he's just looking to get fucked."

She laughed. It sounded nice. Real. Amber was so tall and blond and Nordic looking. She could have been anywhere, with anyone, and yet here she was. For all her posturing and elitism, she found herself continually drawn to the edge like the rest of us.

"Scheduling your own rape. It's pathetic. Can you imagine what the radical dykes back at Sarah Lawrence would have to say about that?"

"I'm sure they would disqualify the whole thing. Insisting a man can't be raped. Or some bullshit."

A darkness settled, and I looked up at the moon, clouds obscuring it for a moment.

"Maybe you'll meet some sexy Anne Rice vampire on the side of the road," I said.

"Yeah. And he'll take me away from all this."

I made a promise to myself that I would go shopping with Amber. I would buy her something nice and pretty. A scarf or a piece of jewelry expensive enough to make her happy, but not so expensive that my dad would notice it on my emergency credit card.

"I brought Heidegger," she said, standing up and laughing. "Out of all the books I could have chosen on my vacation, I brought *Being and Time*."

She looked away from the river, toward the lights of the Quarter, lit up like some enchanted forest. The city was awake and drunk. I thought about the two boys we had met, both of them sexy in lost, romantic ways, like discarded royal orphans wandering the streets until finally discovered and saved.

"Be careful," she said. "Try not to fall in love with the same one." It was cynical and true.

I watched her walk away toward the burning night of the city, gorgeous and furious and abandoned.

When I turned back to the river, Chrystal and Lucifer and Ian were all sitting on its edges, passing a cigarette and a bottle of wine between them. The girl with the pink Mohawk was sitting near them, watching moonlight play on the dark river water.

I felt in my pocket for the two bags of dope I had brought with me. I made an excuse that I had to use the bathroom for more than just a piss and walked down the hill and back into the noise of the Quarter, finding a bathroom at the Café Du Monde. I snorted the bag under a burning neon light, flickering and buzzing in its own existential angst.

When I got back to the river, they were all dancing and singing, an old man playing the saxophone nearby, a blond college kid playing small hand drums, a dark-haired girl next to him in a white flowing dress dancing in the darkness like a faerie expelled from paradise. I felt lost inside the opiate haze, floating on warm currents, buried inside poetic stanzas.

Instead of joining them, I went to the banks of the river and sat, staring at the darkly moving currents. A drawing I once saw, a nineteenth century depiction of a cabalistic image of God reflecting on himself, came to mind. It was two pyramids, each meeting at the base, each with a face drawn in the middle of the pyramid. It was meant to represent creation. The moment God stared into the mirror and allowed his reflection to become the Universe, to divide into Life. This idea has always fascinated me. That we are God's reflection, that all life is an aspect of God looking at itself.

I couldn't shake the feeling that I was part of something momentous, beyond this very moment, something that reached into the past and the future simultaneously, something so huge and endless I couldn't fathom it, but I could feel it. I could sense the existence of it all around me, in me, watching me as I watched it. Somewhere in those depths lay the eyes of God and it was watching, experiencing, *living* through me.

I felt my body go cold for a moment, something stirring inside me, and I turned toward Ian and Chrystal and Lucifer. I felt the detachment of the heroin, as if I were floating alone through space and all these people around me were stars, distant, forever removed from me. I wanted to call out to them, but I didn't. I wanted to tell them something important, but I didn't have the words for what I wanted to say.

Because, as far as I can tell, the only true thing I will ever be able to say about life is that I don't know shit about anything, and I certainly don't know shit about the over-reaching meaning of existence.

So, I lit a cigarette and smoked, watching as the night fell around me, shrouding me, darkening me.

"Hey."

I turned to look at Ian. He sat down next to me.

"Are you really going to get an exorcism?"

I stared at him. He was lit in strange and wandering colors, the city aglow behind him. "Yeah. Definitely." I coughed. My throat felt sore and dry.

"Do you think you are possessed? By a demon?"

I took the bottle of bourbon he handed me. I hit it hard and instantly regretted it, my head spinning, nauseous. "I think so. It's been with me so long, I can't be sure anymore. I don't think I know what it's like not to be possessed."

He was close enough to me I could feel the heat from his body. "I think we are all possessed," he said. "In one way or another. Like we all come into this life with some kind of parasite attached to us. And we spend most of our time here fighting it."

I took his hand in mine. His skin was burning hot. The night was freezing, though I knew that wasn't possible. A veiled fog hovered over the river.

"I think we are born with a darkness we can't escape," he said. "But then sometimes I also think maybe that's not right. Maybe we just don't understand, you know? I know for fuck certain I don't understand anything."

"I know for fuck certain I don't understand fuck anything."

He laughed. "I like you, Jeff. I'm not a fag, but if you wanted me to, I'd still fuck you. Because you're a cool guy, and I want you to be happy."

I looked at him, the glow shimmering around him creating halos and expanding outlines and definitions.

I laughed. I pulled hard from the bottle of bourbon. "You don't have to fuck me to be my friend."

"Yeah. I know. But I wanted you to know that I would. If that would make you happier."

"Why don't you think I'm happy?"

"It's just a thing. I can see it. In your eyes. In the way your hands feel. You don't feel happy."

"Maybe it's the demon."

"Maybe." He turned to me. "Can I kiss you?"

"I thought you weren't a fag?"

"I'm not. But that doesn't mean I don't want to kiss you." He smiled. It was sweet and beautiful and broken.

I leaned in to kiss him, and we held each other for a moment. We were quiet, the only sounds the beating of our hearts, the rhythm of our breath. And for a moment we felt connected. Then he pulled away.

His face looked flush, as if my lips brought the blood to his cheeks. "I like kissing you," he said.

"I like kissing you, too."

"Good." He stood up. "We are going back to the Squat. I think your girl's coming too."

I could hear her, saying too loudly, to anyone who would listen, "He's so cute, don't you think? He's so fucking cute."

"Is it safe?"

"Safe enough. I'll keep an eye on her."

Chrystal ran over and hugged me. "God, he's so fucking cute, isn't he?"

"Yeah, he's pretty fucking cute." My eyes connected with Ian's and for a moment I thought about asking him back to the hotel. But Amber was there, and I knew she would kill me. Literally. She would fucking kill me.

"I'll find you guys in the morning," she said.

"Okay." I watched her walk away, her arm entwined with Ian's.

"Hey!" She turned around. "Don't leave me or anything, okay?"

"Yeah. Okay. Of course not."

The sky was turning a pinkish bruise, and Chrystal was walking hand in hand between Lucifer and Ian, off to some unknown grove where squatters slept and made love, a fairy tale land where princesses could disappear into and never return.

I stood up and as I walked away, I thought I heard a loud splash in the dark water behind me, and someone calling my name, singing it to me over the wind.

I didn't look back. I just kept walking. But I couldn't shake the feeling that those sounds reminded me of someone I once knew, someone who was gone now, forever. Someone I had once loved.

Or maybe they were from the future, calling out to me...carrying me forward...toward them...

I knew Amber was going to be pissed at me for letting Chrystal go off with Lucifer, but it wasn't like I could have stopped her. I walked through the Quarter, garbage trucks and city workers now filling the streets cleaning up the mess from the night before, the sky now an orange pink. Passing a reflecting mirrored window, I noticed I had a thin line of blood from my nose to the top of my lip, dried, muddy colored. I was pale, my eyes red.

I can't imagine how I must have looked to the concierge, stumbling and weeping, laughing hysterically, waving my arms at him, trying to convince him I was okay. Nothing strange or worrisome going on here.

I banged on the door to our room until Amber answered, dressed in light blue panties and a long white T-shirt, and let me in. Scented candles were burning, the curtains drawn, the air on freezing. There were two empty bottles of red wine. Amber was almost as drunk as I was.

"I'm starving," she said, and we burst out laughing. "You're bleeding."

She pointed to my nose. I went into the bathroom to clean up. At one point, she asked me where Chrystal was, and I told her I had no idea. She had been stolen by magical pirates and taken to a fairy tale island in the middle of the River.

This seemed to make sense to Amber, and we agreed not to talk about it anymore. Instead we finished off the pint of Jack Daniels I found in my pockets and wandered back out into the morning in search of food.

We were so young then. The idea that something terrible could happen was too far off on the horizon, a place where other people lived, not us. We were just college kids who had stumbled into some art film, some story line, some exotic moment. We were on vacation, safe in all that entailed.

My mother wasn't dying. I wasn't HIV+. None of us knew what failure was. We believed love could save us. We believed we would be friends forever. We believed we would look back on this day and laugh. Maybe while eating onion soup in the rain at some tiny bistro on Houston, or during yearly meet-ups in Seattle or Atlanta, or Vancouver. Our future was so possible. Of course, we would be successful. Of course, we would be healthy. Of course, the world would reveal itself to us, shimmering and beautiful.

We knew nothing about life. We had no idea what was coming.

We found Chrystal walking by herself down Bourbon Street, smoking a cigarette. We knew her from a distance, even before we could make out her details, by the way she walked: sultry and forbidden, distant and yet intimate.

We ate at a small diner in the Quarter. Chrystal told us about the abandoned house Lucifer and Ian lived in with a group of other squatters.

"They all sleep on the third floor. You have to be careful walking up the stairs because they are rotting, and you might fall through. The ceiling has holes in it too, so if you lay in the right spot, you could look up at the stars and the moon as they faded into the sun. Someone had drawn huge murals all over the walls, this elaborate story line. I kept trying to figure it out, but got lost in everything else. It was sensation overload. He fucked me right in the middle of the room, with everyone else around us sleeping or getting high or also fucking. He must have fucked me five times. At one point I looked over and this big guy, huge, tatted, muscled, like a crazy giant, was watching and jerking off. It made me feel so dirty. So fucking free. And I'll tell you, if that giant had started fucking me too, I would have let him. I almost wanted him to. That's how free I was."

I ate grits and bacon and drank dark, dank coffee and watched as tourists would come in and take pictures of the chef as he prepared our meals in an open kitchen, or the wait staff who would tease and harass the tourists. The windows were open. A cool breeze blew jasmine into the greasy restaurant.

I felt dark and tired. I stepped outside to light a cigarette, letting the match go too long, burning the tips of my fingers.

My belly soured. My head was pounding. I finished my cigarette, went back inside to the bathroom, and snorted the bag of heroin I had brought with me. I swallowed the strange, sickening drip in the back of my throat, and puked almost instantly, falling back slightly. I sat on the floor. After a moment, I was kneeling over the toilet again, puking violently.

When I went back to the table, Amber and Chrystal were arguing.

"It's not your business who I fuck," Chrystal said.

"Fine. Fuck who you want. Get AIDS and die for all I care. Seriously, these kids, they are legit. They are the real thing. They aren't some art project. They are real human beings."

"Get AIDS and die? You wouldn't care if I got AIDS and died?"

I looked at Chrystal, expecting her to be smiling, but she wasn't. She was sincere.

"Chrystal—"

"You wouldn't care if I died?" She was staring at Amber.

"Don't be a baby."

"Oh, now I'm a baby. A stupid, slutty, AIDS baby."

I couldn't help it. I broke out laughing. They both looked at me.

"What? That's kinda funny. I mean, you kind of are a stupid, slutty, AIDS baby. If you really thought about it. We all sort of are."

There was silence, then they were laughing too.

"Fucking great." Chrystal said. "I've probably got syphilis, too."

"Do people even get syphilis anymore?" I asked.

"If you got AIDS and died, I would be very sad." Amber said. We were all laughing again.

Amber and Chrystal decided that instead of sleep they wanted to go to the Garden District and wander Audubon Park, maybe take a tour of Anne Rice's haunted New Orleans. I wanted to go back to the hotel, turn out all the lights, turn the air on high, jerk off, and sleep.

I woke up five hours later, covered in a cold sweat, feeling like a heavy weight was sitting on my chest, suffocating me, strangling me. As I opened my eyes, I thought I saw a shape of a man in the shadows of the room, his eyes glowing, his mouth leering. But then he was gone. I got out of bed and opened the door, letting the warmth of the day settle over the chill I had manufactured.

I had a philosophy professor who insisted that our memories were not actually memories of the event we were remembering, but memories of the last time we remembered the event. He said that in the end, who even knew what event happened? Over time our memories became so convoluted, so mixed with emotion and desire, so twisted and turned and re-created, that in the end what we were remembering was a story we told ourselves about ourselves, about our lives, about who we are based on who we decided we were, and that the truth, also a form of an illusion, was probably drastically different. His point was, why bother with the truth? If such a thing it existed outside of our perception, removed from our grasp, the Truth was just as alien to our existence as a God might have been. Too far away, lost in translation, without any real physical weight.

He held up a student's blue notebook. "You say this is blue, and we all agree. Yes, that is blue. But I don't know what you see when you say blue. I just know what the word means to me. But what that word means to me, besides the agreed upon idea of color, and what that word means to you is completely inaccessible. You might see red for all I know. And I might see yellow and there will be no way of proving different. Who the fuck even knows what blue is? Maybe the word itself created the color. Maybe before words, there were no colors. How do you know what love is? When you say I love you, what you are really doing is begging for the other person to say it back. When they do, it's not their meaning you internalize, but your need. What you need their love to be. And that isn't love. It's not real. It's just perception and greed."

"But what about computers that can register color? That know what color is?"

"They know what math is. They know what they've been told color is. They might even know in their own way the idea of color, and the idea of blue, but that's all it is. An algorithm. Truth is just a story we've made up. A group of words that we've all decided we can agree form a sentence. A group of words that tell a story that we can understand. But the experience of that story, the emotion of that story, the actuality of that story: these things have nothing to do with the Idea of Truth. We are all liars. And we are all telling the truth. Our truth."

I decided to take a backpack full of books to Kaldi's Coffee.

The thing about being possessed is, you don't really know what is possessing you. It could be something from outside or some strange part of yourself, some future you, maybe, or some multi-dimensional you that is trying to get you to wake up, or maybe just some outrageous neurosis, a poison unlocked by your brain's particular psychology. You have no idea if the thing you are going to exorcize is an enemy or a friend. That is the nature of it. And that is what I was thinking as I walked down Rue St. Anne just as Ian was walking toward me, both of us lost until suddenly we were there, in front of each other.

"Where you goin'?" he asked.

"Kaldi's. Coffee. Wanta come?"

We walked slowly through the growing humidity, not talking, both of us locked inside ourselves. His fingers brushed against mine twice, but it was impossible to say if that was just a hazard of walking side by side down a crowded city sidewalk or intentional.

We ordered two café au laits at Kaldi's. Ian stood there, embarrassed, when they told us the price. I hesitated, not sure what the problem was, and then, of course, I remembered: homeless kids.

I paid for both our coffees.

"I'm sorry," Ian said as we sat down at a window looking out at Jackson Square.

"Why?"

"For not having any money."

"Whatever. I have plenty."

I felt stupid saying it. So casually. And then I felt guilty. The rich college kid patronizing the poor street kid.

"My mom's always trying to send me money. Cause she feels guilty. But it's his money, and I don't want it. I want nothing to do with him."

The night before I heard, a vague story about Ian's stepfather beating his mother, and a fight Ian and the man had where Ian finally beat the stepdad and took off. It was lost in the memories of heroin, but it radiated for a moment like déjà vu.

"She bought me a car for my birthday, thinking I would come home. But I won't. I'm not. She told me that she was sorry. That he was getting help. They were in therapy." He took a black sketch book out of the dark green backpack he carried around with him. "That's how she always tried to fix everything. My whole life growing up. She'd try to buy us shit, me and my sister. Trips and cars and toys, sometimes just giving us cash after one of his really bad benders. As if that fixed everything. As if that changed anything."

I smiled. My father had remarried a woman who didn't like me very much. That probably wasn't her fault. I was a difficult child, but the whole living situation had been a constant struggle. My mother had left my father for a man who didn't want a second family, so we were regulated to weekends only with her, and many of those weekends she spent locked in the room with him.

"It's amazing any of us got out alive," I said.

He laughed. "Tell me about your demon."

We discussed demons and possession, and then I read while he drew in his black sketch book. I went to the bathroom to snort one of my bags of dope and when I returned scratching, my eyes heavy, he asked me if I had any more. I got him high, and we walked down to the river, laying on the banks, watching the clouds roll across the massive blue sky.

I slipped my hand under his shirt, resting on his belly. It was warm.

"I know this guy," he said, "who can get hold of this shit, salvia, like mushrooms but stronger, more intense, lasts only like twenty minutes. Maybe what you should do is talk to it. You know? Before you go gettin' all heavy handed and trying to exorcize it. Maybe, I don't know, maybe you can make peace. I mean, fuck, you don't even know what it is or where it's from or what it wants."

"Who is this guy?"

"Just some dude, named Conti. He's pretty fuckin' crazy, but once you get past that…I mean, who isn't fuckin' weird…then in his own way, he's like a genius."

X

One time I showed up at Laurent's and found him playing the piano, dressed in a long silk white robe, his blond curls hanging around him like constellations. He had made divinity candy, little pink and blue puffs of sweet meringue which he displayed on a silver platter cut deep with the image of a hunting party, tiny men and children following a fox into the woods, rifles held high. When I was a child, my grandmother, Irene, had made divinity, putting walnuts in hers. The candies were sweet, melting in my mouth. He offered me tea with whiskey in it. His mood was dark. I sat quietly while he played piano. It was a beautiful, large dark wood piece with mother of pearl flowers and hand cut glass arranged in sparkling lemniscates. He had told me the piano was a present from his dead father and was considered priceless by the museum curators who often came looking for wild pieces of lost art.

Laurent was a collector of pieces as well as of people. A vast network of beauty and oddities moved through his life, and as anyone who was anyone knew, sometimes all it took to learn the location of some exotic lost piece was to spend an hour or two smoking opium-laced joints in Laurent's presence.

For a while it had seemed that Laurent might live. He had been put on some new medications that made him vomit. All he could eat was sweet candy and whiskey-infused teas, though once or twice I remember him dunking strawberries into a bowl he had filled with champagne, giggling at me while I read to him. Sometimes I brought him chocolates and airy, cream-filled pastries from the Italian bakeries on Bleeker. He always took these gifts as if they were priceless jewels, displaying them on gorgeous, antique china, fanning himself and exclaiming how wonderful it was to receive gifts from a gentleman caller.

I always felt embarrassed by these displays of his, and yet I knew he was sincere. He was always a little surprised by the gifts I brought him.

He stopped playing, a hush filling the large room, the hum from the city outside muted. I had snorted my last bag of heroin from the night before. The world felt sad and distant and beautiful. I felt detached, as if I were floating above everything, untouchable.

"I would like to set it all on fire," Laurent breathed, his hands going to his throat, one laid flat atop the other, fingers fanned, his eyes looking up at the ceiling, frozen like a character from some silent horror film. "I would like to burn it all down."

He threw himself onto the couch, sprawled there, one arm thrown over the back, one leg touching the floor, the other spread out along the couch.

"Light me a cigarette and bring me a piece of divinity." He paused, catching his breath. "The pink ones only, please. I can't seem to stomach the blues."

He asked me to read to him from a beautiful copy of Oscar Wilde's *Dorian Gray*. "I will let the museums have it when I die, but for now, it is my only connection to a past, to something beautiful, to all that sacrifice." I sat in the armchair across from him. The world felt insubstantial. I felt weightless. Laurent was like a flickering candle at a distance in the fog.

Vincent tried to page me a few times, but I ignored the beeper's incessant buzzing. I had the sense something unknowable and yet important was happening.

"Have I ever told you about my childhood?" he asked, suddenly interrupting me.

The new medications affected his continuity. Sometimes he made brownies and cookies with kief and hash to help him stomach the nausea. I was used to the fluidity of Laurent's existence, moving from one space to the next, topic to topic. We were non-linear inside those walls. We were everywhere.

"No," I said, resting the book on my lap. I liked the way the paper felt. I liked knowing that intent had gone into making the book, not just something reproduced in a factory. It had weight. Substance. Something real amongst all this unreality.

"My mother's family was Italian. From Venice. Very wealthy. My father was a scoundrel, from New Orleans. Have you ever been?"

"Both," I said. I told him I was planning a trip to New Orleans with some college friends over break.

"It is beautiful there, but lawless." He paused. "I once knew a gangster who lived in a huge house in the Garden District. Great big columns, one of those Greek Revival things. Absolutely beautiful and gaudy. The garden felt like a jungle in some fantasy novel. You kept expecting to be served tea and cheese by miniature fauns or pastries by wispy little faerie boys. Always naked, of course. Faerie boys are always naked. He was an art thief." Laurent closed his eyes and smiled. "He was so handsome. You would blush just to see him. And so rough. You could feel the dirt on your skin when he was done with you. I never showered after. I liked the dirt. The way it felt. The way it seemed to include me in its implicitness. They killed him, of course, and stole all his art." He sighed. "He was such a horrible man. The kind of horrible you crave when it is gone. He is the first man who ever taught me the pleasures of a little bit of pain."

He swished through the room, standing for a moment in front of a painting of The Hanged Man, running his fingers along the golden halo, tracing the outline of the man's body. Sunlight filtered through plantation shutters, jeweled waves of light like those naked New Orleans faerie boys serving pastries at a gangster's mansion.

"My father's first wife was very rich, and then she died mysteriously, leaving him all her money." He smiled, looking over my shoulder at something I would never be able to see. "I always suspected he killed her. He met my mother in Paris. He was still very young, in his thirties, and dashingly handsome. I have his hair and eyes. I have my mother's constitution. When she became pregnant, he ran off with some Lithuanian hotel maid he met in Barcelona.

"I spent the first nine years of my life, just me and my mother, in a palatial apartment over the Grand Canal in Venice. The place was vast, a contained universe. Twelve bedrooms for just the two of us. We spent our days running from room to room laughing." He lit a cigarette and coughed. It sounded hollow and wracking. "I think my mother might have been a little insane. Rotting fruit filled bowls, dark horrified self-portraits done over the course of sleepless nights, small little bonfires built in the middle of a room, her laughing and dancing around it, telling me we were praying to our gods, gods of beauty and love and poetry. She refused to let the servants in for weeks at a time. She fed me cakes and wine and read books aloud to me. Grand sprawling romantic adventures. I believed the world was magical and beautiful. I believed in gentlemen and ladies. And then one day I found her in the tub, both wrists slit open, the water a muddy brown, her hands cold."

He stumbled, grabbing onto the back of a chair for support. I asked him if he was okay, but he just waved me off.

"I was told my father was dead. Shot in a gambling dispute in Marrakesh. I was sent to live with his parents, my grandparents, in Boca Raton, Florida, if you can imagine. All my mother's people were dead. These were the only family I had left."

I thought for a moment about the piano he had said had been a gift from his father, but I didn't pursue it. I knew the truth was just as fluid as the stories he told me. Not important. It was the context that mattered. He was painting a picture for me, no matter if reality differed. Maybe his father was still alive, locked away in some Miami retirement community, or maybe he had been born in Detroit, his mother a waitress, or maybe everything he said was true, and the piano was just one small part of his father's estate. I had learned early on not to question those kinds of things. They weren't important to the story.

What was important was what he chose to tell me, how he painted the picture, the shades and colors, the abstractions. A person's truth is in what they see, in the stories they create, in the meaning they assign to events, real or not. I had already learned by then that the truth was just another lie we told ourselves, a prison we enslaved ourselves in. Laurent's stories, true or not, were beautiful swirling movies that played before my eyes, filling them with devouringly stunning color and light and insatiable sorrow.

"My grandfather died a year after I moved to Boca Raton. My grandmother died when I was eighteen, old enough to collect my inheritance and move to South Beach." He giggled and belched, his hand fluttering to his mouth in mock surprise. "Oh, you should have seen the parties we had there. Miami was on fire! It was Sodom and Gomorrah. It was an Eden of orgies and drugs and fashion. No one read or watched the news or knew anything about art. And they didn't care. Everyone was beautiful, and the ones who weren't all had huge cocks!" He laughed, and I laughed with him. He stood, braced against a chair as if the floor beneath him might suddenly open up and swallow him. He held his hands out, closed his eyes and danced in small circles, careful of not falling. "I can still hear the music. The feet pounding against the wood floors. The screams. It was magical. A gay fairy tale land."

When he finally did fall, I helped pick him back up, guiding him to the couch. He took a rolled joint from a glass container on the table and lit it. We smoked for a few minutes, the air filling with that musky, pungent, weed odor.

"Have you ever been out to the Island?" he asked. I knew he meant Fire Island.

"As a kid we used to go with my parents. Then a few times as an adult." I remembered drug-fueled parties, getting lost late at night on wooden boardwalks cutting through brush covered dunes, stumbling upon strange orgies and ritual fistings, losing myself under the stars.

"Everything was so trashy and beautiful. Leather and golden showers and perfect little cocktails. The air saturated with poppers and cum. I briefly dated a stripper who OD'd right on the dance floor, all those people gasping and clapping as he lay there dying. It had seemed so appropriate, so right. Now, I can't help but wonder if maybe he would have liked it if we had called for an ambulance just a little sooner. But it was such a spectacle, him dying like that, in his clothes no less!"

Laurent picked up a small wood-framed painting of a muscled naked man hung upside down, a replication of the Hanged Man Tarot card that hung on his wall, his cock huge and swollen, his eyes dazed, his mouth agape.

"I can't tell if it's beautiful or garish. I paid a small fortune for it." He smiled. "I won't tell you who the artist is. Very famous. I just want to know—beautiful or garish?"

"Both," I said, my eyes losing focus for a moment, feeling myself falling out of time and then back. I had a strange memory of this moment, of being asked this question about another painting of a hanged man.

"Yes, of course. Both. Garish and beautiful. It makes me sad, though. It hurts me to look at it. I want to rescue him, but you get the feeling he isn't interested in being rescued. He likes it up there on his cross." Laurent laughed, high and childlike. "The little whore."

x

Vincent hated Laurent, said he took up too much of my time, and yet he never seemed to have a problem taking Laurent's money. I knew Laurent paid him a huge sum for the time I spent with him, but Vincent always claimed it was the standard hundred eighty for an hour. I never questioned him about this. I knew that Laurent paid close to a thousand dollars one day. I didn't really care about the money. None of it was for the money. I was a whore for the sport of it. Money had never really entered the equation.

Which is probably why I was such a terrible whore.

x

Ian had gotten the salvia from Conti. Amber and Chrystal and I were to meet him and Lucifer on the corner of Decatur and Esplanade where they would then lead us to the "location." The idea was that I was to take the drug in some mystical setting and then get in touch with whatever or whoever was living inside me.

Amber had found a book called *The Principia Discordia* and had decided she was now a follower of Discordianism. She represented her beliefs by dressing in contradictory looks, creating a fashion image of chaos when in reality, she had chosen the outfit for the purpose of chaos and was actually quite organized and disciplined.

"I'm the very embodiment of Discordianism!" she said, standing in front of the mirror in an overly bright yellow orange and purple clown's wig, a man's dark grey suit jacket and a white summer dress, black punk cat eyes drawn sharply on her upper face and a light pink lipstick. She looked like some fantasy demon dressed for a spring social.

Chrystal had chosen to dress for my exorcism in all white, wearing a crystal necklace her mother had given her to protect her from evil spirits and emotional vampires. "I'm not wearing any makeup. I don't want to attract the attention of any potential demon suitor."

"Demon suitor?" Amber said, her tone mocking.

"This is serious," Chrystal said, looking from Amber to me. "And you…you're dressed like some child nightmare serial killer on acid and you…" She looked at me, her eyes disarmingly direct. "…you have no idea what you are getting yourself into."

"Your beliefs will imprison you," Amber said. "As we Discordians are known to say, *convictions cause convicts*."

"What does that even fucking mean?"

Amber just smiled. "Nothing. Everything. Whatever you want it to mean."

"Don't listen to her, Chrystal." I shot Amber a *give it a rest* look. "She's being ironic. Or sadistic."

"Or stupid."

Amber sat on the edge of the bed like a satanic puppet and lit a cigarette. "Or all three."

X

People always want to believe life is linear, like if you can see the trajectory, the map, from point A to B to C to D all the way to the end, you might understand how I became a junky, as if the first time I snorted heroin was the beginning of that particular storyline and not the end. If you could follow the events, you might understand how a person ends up making the choices they make.

But I'm not sure life is linear in that exact way. I am not sure we are just an accumulation of events. There is no objective path, no trajectory, that can fully explain the man I have become.

I no longer believe I came into existence a blank slate, instead the lines of my life were already drawn solidly into patterns. The patterns existed long before I came into existence.

I believe the scared boy and the scared man exist in the same temporal location. I believe the story of my life is outside my understanding. I believe I can reach back and reshape the past. Change my destiny.

There is still time left to keep the darkness from swallowing me whole.

X

Ian and Lucifer were waiting for us just like they said.

"You can laugh at my beliefs," Amber said, "but I'd like to point out that there are five of us here. Five."

"And what the double fuck does that mean?" Chrystal said.

"The Law of Five. All events happen in multiples of fives."

Ian looked at Amber and let out a sharp, surprised laugh. "Are you into Robert Anton Wilson?"

"Discordianism," she said, disdain for our new friend dripping.

"Same shit. Get this. Where we are going? The building number is twenty-three."

Amber looked at him and something passed between them, and for a moment it seemed as if maybe she might stumble and fall. She stood still. Holding her breath. Then she regained composure and laughed, though it was clear something had upset her. "Whatever. It's all still bullshit."

"Fuck, yeah it is. Everything is bullshit. But that doesn't change that we are five people going to 23 Hyperion Lane to do an exorcism on a dude—"

"What does twenty-three have to do with five?" I asked.

"Two plus three, man. Two plus three. But also, twenty-three is a whole fucking phenomenon that Burroughs first drew attention to. The whole thing…all of it…is fucking perfect."

"Even fake religions are fucking real," Amber said, knocking her clown wig off her head and onto the street, leaving it behind, as we made our way to 23 Hyperion Lane.

"The only thing I'm not into and disagree with Wilson about is Libertarianism. It's evil and not realistic and no way to live in a civil society," Ian said.

I watched Amber as she watched him, fighting with her disgust of him and her respect for what he was saying. It was a real conflict in her. She was one of those rich kids who struggled in her attempts at liberalism and her fear of poor people.

"What's your problem with Libertarianism?" Lucifer asked. "Who the fuck wants to pay taxes?"

"That's idiotic, man. You pay taxes 'cause you live in a society that values human existence. You pay taxes because you drive on roads and you go to the library and because everyone has a right to education and to medicine and to food and to a place to sleep. You don't pay taxes and suddenly the rich own the world and the poor just kind of die out or starve or become slaves."

I ignored them and took Amber's hand.

"You ever have the feeling that everything in the world is falling apart around you, only it's probably been falling apart all along?" she asked me, her hand warm and wet in the New Orleans heat.

"Every fucking day."

"I should have kept the wig. My hair must look like shit."

"You look beautiful."

"I didn't know how to dress for my best friend's exorcism."

I laughed. I didn't believe I was her best friend, but I liked the sentiment.

"Jung wrote this book on synchronicity." She was holding my hand tight, pulling me along. Her voice sounded distant. "I had to read it for a class on Eastern Religions and Western Psychology. I remember thinking, before I even opened the book, that of course it was all bullshit. The world, the universe, *We* are not connected. There is no guiding force. No fucking pattern. Now here we are, five of us, going to number twenty-three, for an exorcism, and I think sometimes the patterns are just jokes. Like someone is laughing, having a huge great big fucking belly laugh. And the punch line is us. Even if everything is connected, even if magic is real, it's still fucking pointless."

"Or it's not," I smiled. She looked at me and punched me in the shoulder.

"Shut up."

"Well, it's true. Maybe it is all just perspective. The bias of perception. The world lining up to reveal itself based on how we are perceiving it. I still have no idea what five or twenty-three means, but somehow, it feels like a good omen. Like maybe everything will be okay. Not like some big joke."

"And maybe you are just naïve."

"And maybe you're just bitter."

"I'm locked in the construct of my perception."

"We all are."

"Do you really think you are possessed?"

"I think it's as possible as anything else."

We knew we were full of shit, but we didn't care. This felt like our time, smack in the middle of our lives, and we could be as pretentious and full of shit as we wanted. The streets were narrow, the air thick and swamp-moist, and we were on the cusp of something huge and momentous. Or at least that is how it felt to us back then.

"I keep feeling like something irrevocable is coming," she said, her eyes focused on something I couldn't see. Chrystal walked ahead of us, between Lucifer and Ian, holding each of their hands. "I can't shake the feeling that everything will be changed. I dreamt last night that one of us had died, only I didn't know which one of us it was, and I kept thinking, *What if it was me? What if I'm the one who died?*" She laughed. "I feel undone."

X

Hyperion Lane was a small alley of a street deep in the Marigny. The river hung above us, green trees blew gently in the wind, cats scurried through the street, jumping onto garbage cans, onto walls, over fences. A black cat with a white chest and four white paws, stood in the middle of the street ahead of us, a strange, almost human cast to its eyes. He watched us as if he knew us, knew where we were going, knew our intentions and knew our futures, as if at any moment he might greet us by name in some strange, meowing cat voice.

    Strange designs were drawn with chalk onto the sidewalk, spray painted onto the trunks of trees. Talismans hung from the branches, an offering of chicken bones or flowers, a slice of cake on a doorstep.

    I became aware of something stirring. Up ahead, the street ended in a row of small shot-gun houses. Number twenty-three was the center house, pink with purple trim, three steps up to a silver door. The windows were shuttered. Strange figures were drawn onto the shutters. Stick figures standing around swirling vortexes, tools in hands, as if they were carpenters building a vacuum of stars. Flower petals and branches littered the steps, a white bowl filled with the bones of small animals sat in front of the door.

    Ian stopped and turned, facing me. He held out a key.

"Whose house is this?" I asked.

"I don't know," he said.

"What do you mean you don't know?"

"This is a bad idea," Amber said, squeezing my hand.

"No one lives here. Not exactly. Conti gave me the keys. It's just… it's for this kind of shit."

"It's just a house for strangers to go and do exorcisms?" Amber let go of my hand.

"Exactly."

"I don't like this." She turned to me. Her black cat make-up made her look like a character from some surreal manifesto. "This isn't how the world works."

"The world works however you want it to work." Lucifer sniffed at Chrystal's hair. "I have a boner," he whispered loud enough for all of us to hear.

"We could be breaking into someone's house."

"We aren't breaking into someone's house," Ian said.

"I want to take you out back so you can blow me," Lucifer whispered, like he was offering Chrystal some great prize, and it made me suddenly curious about the size of his dick.

"You just said you don't know whose house this is."

"I also have the key. That isn't breaking and entering." He held the key out to me. "You have to be the one to open the door."

"Why?"

"It's your ritual."

I took the key.

Amber tried to stop me. "Jeff…"

"He's right," I said to her. "I have to do this."

For a moment, I thought I heard laughter behind me, and when I turned, I saw the strange, human-faced cat sitting in the middle of the road, eyes locked with mine, and then he turned and ran away, disappearing through an alley between two houses.

Lucifer had taken Chrystal's hand and was rubbing it on his crotch while whispering in her ear. It was distracting. I felt a sudden swell of chaos, as if understanding was moving away from me, leaving me in a howling, overly bright reality of swirling madness. This sensation passed as I took the keys from Ian and walked up the three steps to the door.

"I want to learn the I Ching," Ian said to Amber out of nowhere, as if they were best friends in the middle of a conversation. "But it's so complicated, I get mad every time I try. That's a problem I have. Getting mad for no reason." He smiled at her and she looked a little stunned, like an animal trapped in car headlights seconds before the collision.

"I want you to swallow it," Lucifer's whispers to Chrystal, who giggled, deep and throaty, reached my ears as if they stood beside me.

I wanted to throw the key into the street and tell him I wanted to swallow it. I'd do it much better than her. I'd swallow that shit down to his balls.

But instead I opened the door, a looming darkness before me.

I felt a rush of cold wind, and I heard something moving inside. Behind me Chrystal was talking, Lucifer laughing. I felt Ian's hand on my back.

"It's okay, man," he said.

"Something…I thought I heard something."

"Let's get inside."

He guided me inside, his hand never leaving my back. I could feel his fingernails through the shirt.

The house was empty except for a mattress in the middle of the living room. A card table with some chairs. A few cushions thrown about to sit on. We searched each room. They were all empty except for a small room at the back of the house. Someone had spray painted a large pentagram in red on the floor. A white candle, burnt to its base, was on each point of the pentagram. A discarded bible lay in the corner, slightly charred as if someone had tried to light it on fire but had given up.

We posted up in the living room. The mattress had clean sheets on it. Lucifer and Ian had filled their backpacks with candles and incense and bags of jelly beans that they said would taste really good when I was "all done."

Ian stood next to me. "You're going to need to do a banishing spell." He handed me a bundle of sage. "You're going to go into one of the rooms, alone, and close your eyes and try to clear your head, like meditate or something, and then after a few minutes you'll light the sage and just walk through the house removing any darkness, invoking light."

Amber sighed heavily.

"Someone should remove her," Chrystal said, and Lucifer laughed a giant guffaw, pulling her to him and grabbing onto her tits, squeezing them, one hand going to her ass.

I took the sage and left the four of them, ending up in one of the bedrooms towards the back. I avoided the room with the pentagram in it. I didn't want someone else's magic to affect me.

I sat on the floor. I closed my eyes. I tried to still my thoughts. I was suddenly concerned that the strange cat from outside had gotten in and was clawing its way to me, laughing in its hissing voice, calling my name. I had the sensation of being very hot and then very cold and then neither. I felt alone and connected, and I had an intense moment of fear where I was sure someone was in the room with me, standing in front of me, watching me. I could hear them breathing, I could feel them. When I opened my eyes, I thought I saw them disappearing into the shadows.

I have had this feeling of a presence watching me throughout my life. I am never sure of its intent. Whether it is benign or malignant. Sometimes I take great comfort in it. Sometimes I am afraid.

I lit the sage. I had no idea how to banish darkness and invoke light, so instead I just talked to ~~god~~. I have done this all my life too. An endless dialogue with some unknown deity. I have spent nights alone walking through Alphabet City waiting for the dope dealers to arrive, in cold rain and the heat of New York summers, talking endlessly, praying, sobbing, begging, hoping.

Eventually I ended up back in the living room where they were waiting, Ian and Amber sitting off by themselves, separate, Chrystal lying with her head in Lucifer's lap.

"Now what?" I asked.

Ian had brought enough salvia for all of us, plus five pipes for us to smoke it in.

"Now we get high," Lucifer said, jumping up and walking over to Ian.

I looked to Amber, expecting her to object or to walk out or to say something to me about how idiotic this all was, but she didn't. Instead she took the powdered leaves and pinched it into her pipe and waited.

"So, look, this shit, it kind of fucks everything up, makes the world look really insane."

"Makes shit real." Lucifer said.

"Sure. As real as anything. But the point is, don't freak out."

"This isn't our first trip," Amber said, and I felt a little relieved the cynic was still with us.

"Like this it is," Ian said. "Remember, we are here for Jeff. To help him and to guide him and to offer him any insight we might come across during our own journeys."

All our pipes filled, we looked to each other and smiled. We lit our pipes and inhaled the herbaceous smoke.

My head exploded.

X

Once, Vincent sent me to the house of a very rich man named Cleveland in Riverdale. It was one of those large stone mansions that littered those forested hills above the Hudson.

Cleveland was short, just reaching five feet, and hairy, with a grey beard and small eyes and glasses. He wore a grey suit with a red tie, and he shook my hand, his palms hot and dry.

He had a whole room dedicated to this strange collection of dolls, wall upon wall of eyes staring down at you. His house was a sprawling tribute to various collections: puppets and kimonos, portraits of strangers' families he'd bought at estate sales all over Westchester, a room for religious artifacts and one for magical artifacts, a room full of toys and playgrounds for his twelve cats, and a room for cat portraits. His house was a maze of tangents gone too far.

He wanted to show me the basement. He said he had created a special lay out to express his various tastes.

"I like to think of it as an amusement park themed after my various fantasies." His voice was almost a whisper, with sharp edges hinting at violence.

I could smell the violence on him, feel it in the air around him. His softness was laced in fury.

I didn't want to go into his basement. I wanted nothing to do with this man's fantasies.

The door to the basement was in the kitchen. The back door was open, a screen door letting in the night air. The kitchen was large and modern, a room he rarely used.

"I'm only in here for the basement," he said. "This is cook's room." And he chuckled, a dry sound like dead insect wings rubbing together in a desert wind. It made my skin itch.

He flicked on a light switch and a bald bulb flickered into life, illuminating aspects of the darkness below, but never revealing the whole truth. Music vibrated through the walls, muffled by some kind of sound padding.

I laughed. "You gotta be kidding me."

He turned to me, smiling, as if he deemed the gesture appropriate even if he wasn't in a smiling mood. "Is something wrong?"

"What's down there?" I asked, the question phrased as if I expected him to answer, *Monsters*, which I guess, in retrospect, I probably did.

Because that would have been the truth.

"This is my fantasy," he answered, "for which I am paying a large sum. And I will tip you very well." He put his hand on my shoulder, it made me feel sick. "You will not be physically hurt."

Physically? What about in other ways? I wanted to ask, but I didn't.

I am self-destructive at times. This was one of those times.

I walked slowly down the stairs.

The basement was divided into a strange, labyrinthine warren of mazes and caves. Colored, flickering lights created a dizzying nausea. Loud, angry, chaotic music roared over speakers spaced throughout. Along some of the walls were horrific depictions of violence and mayhem, decapitations, strange rituals, children held down and raped, demons devouring and fucking. There were cuttings from newspapers about acts of violence, a collage of horror and despair. Being down there made my heart hurt. Behind me I could hear Cleveland whispering, talking to the walls, to the air, the desecrated spaces that surrounded us.

Cleveland was casting a spell. I could feel it clawing at me. His words pestilential, drawing cancerous patterns over my flesh, soaking me in their oily cadences.

The ugliness down in those dark, cavernous spaces was born from a soul so maligned I thought it must hurt to be alone inside that head, his thoughts so depraved and desperate they drove him to create rooms filled with such banality and nightmare themed terror.

We came to the end, a room at the very back of the long tunnel, empty except for a chair. A naked man was handcuffed to the chair. He was blindfolded, and his mouth covered in thick tape. His cock and balls were elaborately tied in thick roped knots, pulled and twisted painfully. On his nipples were metal clamps with heavy black balls hanging from them.

Cleveland stood behind me. I turned. In his hand was a piece of paper.

To whom it may concern. My name is Paul. I am the man tied in the chair. I am here of my own consent. Cleveland is my lover. This is a game we play. Please do not be frightened for my safety. Everything we do here we do consensually.

I returned the paper to Cleveland. He grinned.

"This could be bullshit," I said. "Take the tape off and let him tell me for himself."

"That is not how the game is played." He handed me a portable phone. "Call Vincent. This will confirm the game. And that it is safe."

I dialed Vincent.

"What the fuck is going on?" I asked, angry.

"Paul and Cleveland. I know it's weird. Play along. They are normal guys. One night it's the basement games, and the next time they will be taking you to the opera. It's nothing." Then he hung up on me.

I handed the phone back to Cleveland. "So, what do you want me to do?"

Cleveland showed more teeth. "You are very handsome. Not in the conventional sense, of course, but that only adds to your handsomeness. I would like to put you in a cage one day and show you off at one of our parties."

"Right, but what do you want me to do now? How is the game played?"

Cleveland walked up to the bound and naked Paul and smacked him, hard, in the face. He turned to me. His eyes were like tiny little balls, hard as stone, cold, depthless.

"Your turn." His voice felt like a void, cold and foreign.

"You want me to hit him?"

"For starters."

"No."

Cleveland pointed to Paul's hard, purple bruised cock. "He likes it."

"That's amazing. But this isn't a game I like."

When Cleveland laughed I shuddered as a million insects crawled over my skin. "That is even better."

He pointed to an uncomfortable-looking chair in the corner.

"All you have to do is watch. I will do the rest."

I sat in the chair. Cleveland got naked. He was hairy and formless, like an unfinished mold. His flesh was splotchy and pink in all the wrong places, sprouts of hair growing like thick weeds. His penis was small and shriveled. It reminded me of a dandelion head, nothing real or usable. I'm not sure if it ever got hard, or if it was just a perpetual shrinking weed.

For an hour I watched as he punished his lover, urinating on him, defecating and rubbing it into his face, punching him, kicking him, pulling at the ropes on his balls, elongating them into painful looking aberrations, yanking on the balls attached to his nipples. Neither of them came. Neither of them touched their dicks. There was nothing intimate or loving or kind. It was a strange and horrible thing to witness.

Afterward, Cleveland walked me upstairs and to the front door. He thanked me and gave me a three-hundred-dollar tip. We had left Paul downstairs, still tied to the chair. Alone in that strange rendition of a nightmare.

I walked through the dark, the mansions of Riverdale looming in the decay that surrounded my thoughts. A light rain began to fall. I felt cold in the summer night. Alone.

In the dancing streetlights ahead of me, I saw the angel once again. He turned, his eyes blazing, and opened his mouth to scream, and then he was gone, the rumble of a far-off train, the night breaking in two, shattering, and the sky opened up and the rain fell, and I thought, *We will all drown, if not tonight then soon. We will all drown and the infected world will be devoured.*

x

As I inhaled on the pipe, the rich, herbaceous taste of the salvia filled my mouth, and the room and my friends fell away.

A bright and violent light replaced them, filling the room, filling me. It became the air I breathed and moved through, became the blood in my veins. This light reached out across the whole planet. It moved through and was a part of everyone and everything; it reached beyond the planet into the universe and even further, to the Meta-verse. It was everything. It was infinity itself.

And I could feel it. I knew it. I *was* it.

I felt myself shrinking and expanding at the same time, disappearing and becoming.

I was the rain drop and the storm.

And then it stopped, and I was alone, naked and cold inside the poisonous rhythms of Cleveland's labyrinth.

A tall man dressed in a clown's outfit stood at the end of the hallway. His face was a raped version of joy and merriment, leering and ugly. He held in his hand a bouquet of bleeding flowers. He motioned me to follow him and the hallway grew longer, vaster, expanding. As I walked, the floor underneath me turned to a dark, inky water. Splashes of it hovered in the air with each foot step.

I couldn't see the clown any longer but I could feel him. I could hear him. He was singing songs from my childhood and sometimes I forgot where I was and wanted to sing along with him.

The water turned to clouds which turned to grass which turned to a city street, lights and noise and people. A man stood next to a store with a rainbow flag. He wore a cardboard sign that said "Revoke the Rights of the Deviant. Return to Jesus. Kill a Fag."

The clown was standing on the rooftop of a building across the street. I watched as he wiped away his make-up, tossing his bleeding flowers into the air. They turned to butterflies and then sparkles of dying flames and then into stars floating away on rivers of moonlight. I watched as he slowly undressed, his clown suit disappearing and he was just a five-year-old boy in a sailor suit, smiling and waving. I watched as giant wings sprouted from his back and his body elongated into something strange and elfin, floating to the street. He stood before me, his long pale face and sky-blue eyes, and then he turned, walking into the crowded street, turning slowly into a woman pushing a baby carriage, then a man with a briefcase, then a police officer, then a dog, running through the legs of the world. The Mopses would be so pleased with reality.

And I stood there, confused, suddenly alive in the city. I had no idea where I was or how I had gotten there. But I felt safe. I could hear the slow breathing of the world around me. The constant in and out of breath. The city felt like a river, turbulent, chaotic, but with a rhythm to it, an undercurrent of meaning I could sense, as if something else were there experiencing life along with us. It was the thing we moved through, the thing we breathed and ate.

By the time the drug wore off, I was weeping in the middle of the pedestrian roadway that ran along the side of Jackson Square. Tarot readers and psychics and tourists all kept their distance. I bought a large bag of beignets and walked slowly back to the guest house. Amber and Chrystal were lying naked in the bed smoking a joint.

They made room for me, and I curled in between them, feeling their warmth.

When I woke up, they were gone. It was our last day, and they wanted to go shopping. I showered and changed and made it outside. It was grey and hot and wet. As I neared Bourbon Street, I found Ian passed out on a patch of grass, his pants around his ankles, dark green boxers barely holding on. I knelt down and said his name. He looked at me with a kind of stunned, what-the-fuck-is-happening expression and sat up. We lit cigarettes and sat quietly for a moment. Clouds created a dark veil in the overcast sky.

Ian looked around, terrified, pulling a black backpack to him. "Fuck," he said, holding the backpack tight.

"Are you okay?"

"I thought someone had taken it."

"Where's Lucifer?"

"I fucked up." He looked at me, panic and fear radiating off him. "You gotta do something for me. It's important."

I sat in a swirl of smells and tourists, artists and musicians, the heavy *clomp clomp* of horse-pulled carriages. Ian looked different. Less light, more dark. Heavy.

"Did you see the clown?" he asked me.

"What?"

"Last night. The clown. Did you see it?"

The idea we might have shared a vision, a hallucinatory trip suddenly taking on the mask of reality, felt too much. I wanted a different world today. An easy world of books and coffee and escape.

"I don't know what I saw last night. I can't remember."

"It was dark. Man, it was so fucking dark. Like a river of poison and shit." He held out the backpack toward me. "You gotta return this for me."

I didn't take it. "What's in it?"

"Nothing." He looked around nervously. "I stole it from that dude, Conti. The one who gave us the salvia. You gotta return it for me."

Conti lived in one of those huge, decaying mansions on Esplanade Avenue. Ian walked me to the spiked, black wrought iron gate and left me looking up at the large Greek Revival style house. I opened the gate and walked up the stone path to the front door. Black tape blocked out the doorbell. In the center of the door was a large knocker in the shape of a growling lion's head.

I banged three times.

The guy who answered the door was my age, with black curly hair, hazel eyes, and light brown skin. He smiled at me, and then he saw the backpack in my hands and he instantly became wary, looking over his shoulder nervously.

"Fuck, dude, what are you doing here with that?"

He started to close the door when a booming voice called out, "Who's at the door, little *cher*?"

The man who appeared was well over six feet, with linebacker shoulders and a steroid-born thick-muscled chest. He was shirtless, tattoos weaving up his arms and over his neck, covering his chest and belly. His arms were like canons, bulging in muscles. His head was shaved, tattoos sneaking up his back and over his scalp. He smiled when he saw me, looking right at the backpack I held like some dirty bomb in my outstretched hands, his teeth capped in gold, his eyes a dark purplish blue.

"Well, look out Jesus, we got company." He talked slow and heavy, the cadence of it almost physical. Everything about him took up space. And a lot of it.

A smart man would have left the bag on the porch and ran. I was not a smart man.

I have learned in life that violence is not always something physical. It is something that sits on the air, invisible and palpable. You can taste it. Breathe it. It moves against you and finds its way inside you, poisoning your thoughts, your perceptions. It creates an edge to the world around you. Changes things. Makes them ugly.

This is what it was like being around Conti. Violence was in the air he breathed. A fury. A kind of craziness that could end up anywhere, taking everything with it.

He was also unbelievably fucking sexy. It was hard to take my eyes off him. He moved like some giant monstrous machine built from chemicals and weight lifting and ink. His eyes bore a dark, bruised quality.

He pushed the boy aside and made room for me, never asking for the backpack. I stepped in, the house dark, curtains pulled over tall windows. Despite the gloom, I saw statues of naked men and warriors with swords, tall marbled angels and bad David knockoffs. There were giant stone lions and even an elaborate *Birth of Venus* that someone had spray painted various bright and startling colors.

The boy from the door walked past us and through arches that led into a large living room with a TV and couches, chairs, various drug paraphernalia, and bodies in sleeping bags sprawled about, naked boys in corners fucking, shooting up, whispering to each other in brutal, foreign sounds. The place smelled like speed, weed, and opium, and underneath that the unmistakable smell of boy: sweat, dirty feet, and ass.

Pizza boxes littered the floor around the stone angels and gods.

Take away the drugs, the naked boys and all the garbage and tacky furnishings, and the house was amazing. Architecturally flawless with high ceilings, arched entranceways, stained glass windows, and a grand circular staircase leading to the second floor, it hinted at lost wealth and splendor.

It was the kind of place you walked into and never came out of.

Shadows moved in the darkness. The air was hot and claustrophobic. Grunts and moans and strange sobbings sounded like musical orchestrations to the melancholic gloom.

I had the feeling of Déjà vu, of synchronicity, of a structure to my life revealed in architecture, revealed in madmen and magicians, I began to feel myself as far away, outside, watching the actions before me as if in a movie. I suddenly felt like the reader of one of those choose your own ending stories, only I wasn't choosing, I just kept picking new endings, new beginnings, and new middles.

Conti led me down a hall toward the back of the house. We passed a room filled with hundreds of brightly colored caged birds, all singing, a room piled high in books, another room filled with green vine-like plants hanging from the ceiling, cots along the floor where pale bodies slept, unaware of the threat the hanging vines posed.

We stepped through a door and into a sun filled modern kitchen, the air chilled and fresh, clean and organized, a direct contradiction to the decaying decadence of the rest of the house.

"I live amongst an army of drug addicts and whores. This room, as well as upstairs, is off limits. They all know there is a heavy price for breaking any of my rules." He smiled, gold teeth flashing in the sunlight. His hands were long and thick, tattooed symbols on each knuckle.

He closed the door and locked it. Large, floor to ceiling windows looked out on a lush, overgrown, tropical garden. Bursting reds and oranges and yellows flowered amongst an endless wave of green.

"It seems you and I have a little problem." He leaned against the counter, his body massive, feral, and sexy.

Over his shoulder and outside the window, green leaves blew in gentle breezes, reds and purples, strangely colored flowers.

"Have you looked inside the bag?" he asked.

I felt his eyes exploring me like fingers.

I have found the best course, when confronted with some kind of human threat, is to remain solid. If I remain calm, my chances of survival are higher.

"Are you lying to me?"

Of course, I was lying to him. The first thing I did when Ian gave me the bag was to look inside.

I put the backpack on the table that divided us, and pushed it toward him. I wasn't there to negotiate. Honestly, I'm still not sure why I was there.

He took the backpack and opened it, looking inside. He smirked. "Seems I got my property back."

When he stepped out from behind the table and unzipped his pants and pulled out his semi-hard cock, it had seemed inevitable. I wasn't there to return the bag. That was just fate's little trick. I was, of course, there to suck his dick.

Life has a way of always coming back to this.

When he came he held my head down, and I swallowed, loving the feel of it hot and shooting against the back of my throat.

After, as I was leaving, he offered me my choice of drugs. I took six small, individually wrapped black bags of China White with the words Haze Paralysis written on them in an ominous dark red and left.

Back on Esplanade, it was suddenly hot and muggy, the air smelling of rain. I walked down to Decatur but instead of turning right and heading back into the Quarter, I went left, crossing Esplanade onto Frenchmen Street and the Marigny. I ducked into a small café with slow moving ceiling fans and dark wood floors and used the bathroom to do one of the bags of heroin. Back outside, the air was so thick it had a weight all its own. People moved slowly, a sudden, languid gloss to the world. I walked over to the small park and sat on one of the many benches. When the rain came, I just closed my eyes and let it wash over me.

It felt warm and beautiful, and I felt connected to it. A part of it. As if I were intrinsically linked to everything everywhere.

Some moments, I get a glimpse of the true nature of reality. As if someone has pulled back the curtain on a stage and shown me the real theatre in the back, where all the players and the actors and the stagehands are, as if I was allowed a glimpse at something eternal, vast and interconnected.

Sitting on that bench in the Faubourg Marigny, the rain soaking me, I felt connected to all of life. I felt as if I could reach forward or backward through time, over vast distances of space, and reconnect with different parts of who I was and who I am. I suddenly felt the strength of my linear progression broken into fragments, re-shuffled, and experienced in small bursts of bright, startling sensation.

I remember Laurent once saying to me, "We are endless possibilities, endless moments."

I went looking for Lucifer and Ian to say good bye to them, but they were nowhere. I asked a few street kids, but was only told they had moved on, hitchhiking to Austin or Atlanta. It was strange to think they were just gone. Maybe Ian was afraid I wouldn't deliver the backpack. Maybe he thought Conti would go looking for him anyway. Or maybe the demons we went in search of had grabbed hold of him that night, and he needed to get moving, back on the road.

The last time I saw Laurent was June. We sat in his brightly lit living room, reading sections from the Anais Nin diaries I had bought in New Orleans, and I told him about Ian and Lucifer and Conti. He gasped with delight when I told him how I had given Conti a blowjob on the kitchen floor.

"We are such dirty and beautiful creatures, aren't we?" he said, clapping his hands like a little lost prince discovering a world of fantastic monsters hidden deep inside his bedroom closet.

We sat at the piano together, and he played Carly Simon songs that reminded me of my mother. They were sad and beautiful and filled with jaded hope.

"I always thought I would be famous," he said, his body warm and fading next to me. "Maybe we all do. It is so hard to imagine that one day I will be just gone. As if I had never been here. I always thought, eventually someone will come along and save me." He laughed. It made me smile. It always made me feel happy to hear him laugh. I loved Laurent.

X

A month later, having not heard from him in a while, I asked Vincent if he had called again. Vincent laughed meanly. He had been doing lines of coke all night long. "Fuck that faggot. He died of AIDS two weeks ago."

I would like to find a way back in time to those brief moments, afternoons of whiskey infused tea and strawberries and champagne and little pink puffs of divinity candy. Books and chocolates and whispered secrets.

Laurent was my friend. This isn't something you come by easily. Laurent was a true Queen. Queens were so fucking elegant back in those days. Royalty.

Nights On Fire-

When I was twenty-four, I fell in love with a man named Max.

I met him on a phone sex chat line while living in a brownstone on Schermerhorn and Hoyt Street in Brooklyn. It was a ghetto back then, too close to the Gowanis projects to be cool, edgy and filled with strange Goths and artists and heroin addicts. I was a junkie back then, snorting three bags of China White a day and trying to be a writer. Chrystal was living with me at the time, and she and I were going to write plays and movies, and we were going to be famous.

Even though it was a lie, I told Max I had never been fucked, and he told me he would love to be my first. He convinced me to take the A train in the middle of another snowstorm to the West Village where he was living in a giant apartment complex on Bleeker Street. He wanted to be the first dick I ever had, and I liked the idea that he was going to teach me how to bottom. He told me a story about his brother and how he was also a drug addict. He was fascinated I had stopped in the East Village to buy bags of heroin off the street because I was so nervous to meet him.

Max had a huge cock. Like porn star huge. After fucking me, he asked if we could get high. He said he'd never done heroin. We shared the second bag and went for a walk. It was cold out, the sky that frozen kind of beautiful, the stars lit in patterns that might have told our future if we had been looking. The streets were blanketed in snow, mythical, like some kind of lost fantasy where everyone ends up happy.

People moved slowly, carefully, trying to miss patches of ice, trying not to slip and fall.

We were so high we forgot to wear hats and walked east on Bleeker toward Thompkins Square park where we sat on wooden benches covered in patches of ice and sang songs to each other. He let me climb all over him, holding his arm out so I could swing. I called him my junky jungle gym, which made us both laugh.

He was twenty-seven and tall, over six-five, and muscular. He worked at a boxing gym in Chelsea. He was Italian from Bensonhurst. "A real fuckin' guido," he said, his accent thick. He had dark eyes and a scar that ran down the side of his face from a knife fight when he was in high school.

When he laughed, the whole world felt like it was shaking. He would reach for me every time, holding on to me, until the laughter broke, and then he would kiss me. Sometimes when Max kissed me, I thought the world had gone silent.

Max's favorite movie was "Married to the Mob." He thought Michelle Pfeiffer was a genius. He would sit there holding my hand, mouthing the words along with the movie.

I remember once, sitting on his dick, riding him, and watching his face. His eyes were closed. His mouth was moving, whispering words I couldn't hear. Suddenly, right before he came, he opened his eyes and said, "I love you."

Years later I found him on Facebook. He looked too thin and sick. We talked. He was dying, he said. Some kind of AIDS related complication. I didn't know how to ask him what that meant.

I went looking for him online recently. He had died. A page was dedicated to him. It's strange to think about. We had been so in love for those few months. We sang songs to each other and went for walks, and he used to lie next to me and whisper things in my ear, about how one day he was going to be a famous actor, that he was built for fame. "It's because I'm Italian. From Brooklyn. Shit is big inside me. Too big sometimes. It needs to be out there. It needs to be in the world."

In the end, he never did become famous. All he did was die. But he was beautiful, and we were beautiful together for a while.

He once made me promise I would never do heroin again. I promised, and then I spent the rest of our time together lying to him. I would sit in the living room waiting to hear the sound of his snores and then I would break out the tiny pink packets with the black leering skulls on them and I would roll up my dollar bills and I would get fucked up and read Genet and Lorca, getting lost in the dream worlds of Hart Crane and Frank O'Hara.

Those nights in Brooklyn were on fire. You could almost believe one day we all might amount to something. I hope he believed he was my first. It meant so much to him. Even if it was all a lie.

The idea of failure or sickness seemed so removed back in those days, the idea that I might die, that life might not go the way I planned. Like Chrystal and Max, I was going to be famous. And we would all be millionaires.

And my mother would never get cancer. And I would never hear the words, "I'm sorry, the results came back positive." Back in those days Laurent would never die, and there was still a meaning to all this loss.

Back in those days everybody I loved would be safe. Forever. And no one would ever suffer.

But that isn't how life goes, is it? And that definitely isn't how love goes.

Darkness

I was in New Orleans with my grandmother, Sadie, eating dinner at a small French-Cajun restaurant in the Marigny right on Frenchmen Street, the little park just outside the window. She had ordered a Cajun dish with shrimp and okra. It had the crispiest fried green tomatoes on top, wrapped in bacon. I had rabbit and dumplings, and shrimp and grits.

"I feel haunted," my grandmother said. She smoked Salems she kept in a silver case, and she drank whiskey straight from an antique flask she carried in her purse. "Possessed," she said, deep and rusty, like rain water on a tin roof.

There's a story about how Sadie would step naked out onto the balcony of her large house, actually the top floor of a hotel she owned, and talk to the dead soldiers who came to visit her. She held séances in the basement of the hotel and ran an illegal speak-easy. She told me my uncle was a shape-shifter and that our family were witches.

I watched her closely in that Faubourg Marigny restaurant. You never really knew how these kinds of things were going to turn out with her. Once when I was thirteen, she gave me a gun and sent me into one of the hotel rooms where a trucker was beating up some hooker he had picked up on the side of the road. She came in behind me, telling me to, "Shoot the motherfucker in the balls if he moves." I'd like to think she hadn't really meant for me to shoot him, but honestly, she probably did. I think she might have liked me better if I had shot him.

"We are all possessed," she said to me. "Darkness runs in our family."

Darkness runs in my family…

My mother, Beverly, had an uneasy relationship with Sadie. Sadie was competitive and jealous and often mean to Beverly, yet she told me incredible stories when Beverly wasn't around. She told me how she had awoken late at night once to hear Beverly outside talking to someone in whispers underneath a blooming magnolia tree, shrouded in a southern moonlight.

"The moon was so perfectly placed it felt painted, placed there for the moment, its white golden light filling the whole scene with transcendence." Sadie lit a cigarette, her eyes distant, the smell of the night sweet and warm, a haunted darkness. "And there was your mother, standing underneath that giant magnolia, talking to a tiny little man. No taller than three feet. Dressed in the most elegant, gentlemanly dark suit, with impeccable shoes, one of those bowler hats men once wore, smoking a cigar. He was the strangest little man I have ever seen." She paused, blowing out a stream of white smoke. "And I have seen a lot of strange little men."

Candlelight at the room's edges, hints of incense and swirling heady incantations and whispers. Sadie wore a lime green satin robe. She unscrewed a bottle of red fingernail polish, her cigarette at an angle in her mouth, sipping from a glass of iced Jim Beam.

"Beverly was the most beautiful girl Georgia had ever seen. Men came from all over just to spend a few minutes in her presence. She never seemed to have time for any of them, or she had too much time. Some people thought she was a snob, but I always thought she was discerning. She had the luxury of choice, and for the most part, she used that choice wisely." She looked at me, paused, and I knew what went unsaid. *Until your father.* She used that choice wisely until she married your father, another strange little man.

Sadie lived in a black and white romance novel where men were tall and dashing and well dressed and heroic, and women were always beautiful and in need of saving. She lived in a world of magic and fairytales.

"Your mother, set afire in that moon light, talking to that little demon, was so beautiful it almost made me scream out, to warn him that he needed to be careful. She was casting spells, conjuring—your mother was a witch with her beauty. I stood there, fixed to my spot, unable to even breathe, and he held out his hand, thick little fingers, each with a different colored jeweled ring: sapphire and turquoise, emeralds and garnets and rubies. All those colors captured the moonlight and reflected in your mother's eyes. She had us all bewitched.

"He tipped his hat and held out his sparkling jeweled hand and she just turned from him and laughed, fanning herself with one of those black Chinese fans with red dragons on them we had bought in New Orleans. She looked up at the moon, and I swear to you, those jewels were still trapped in her eyes, and then they faded, her pale skin lighting up momentarily, as if all those colors were burning just underneath."

Sadie looked at the new red of her fingernails, fanning her long fingers out before us. She reached for her cigarettes. "He seemed so deflated. Robbed of whatever beauty he might have had. And then he was gone, a door opening in the empty spaces around him, and him stepping into it, and your mother stood, more radiant and beautiful in that moonlight than I had ever seen her." Sadie exhaled smoke, admiring her nails. "We were all bewitched by your mother. Every last one of us."

Sadie stood. She was tall, just under six feet, with long red hair, and dark, ever burning eyes. The door to the balcony was open. She shuddered and then she smiled. "You need to be careful because there are demons in the world who will try to get inside you and take over. They have hunted us all. It's a family thing. My aunt once told me a story about your great, great grandmother, a Jewess from Russia who fell in love with one of them. It's because of her that they keep coming. They are in love with us. And we fall in love with the darkness. It's in our genes. We are predisposed to love it." She sat on the edge of the bed, candlelight flickering, shadows dancing along the darkest edges of the room, cigarette smoke swirling. Her eyes were aflame. "I miss the demon," she whispered. "Even as he was killing me, like a cancer, gnawing away at my cells, at my DNA, at my soul, I loved him."

My mother once told me a strange story about a man in the shadows who would come to visit her. He was tall and handsome, and he would sit on the edges of her bed, his hands burning, his eyes dark, and he would whisper poems and secrets to her, singing songs. One night she went looking for him and she found him, at the edges of a lake. She never told me what happened after she found him. Just that a part of her loved him. And a part of her was afraid.

"You need to be careful," she said to me. "Soon he will come looking for you."

These are the women who raised me. These are the people I come from. So, is it any wonder that, sitting in that AIDS Health Care Foundation Truck in the parking lot of Faultline at a Sunday Beer Bust, learning that the counselor was sorry because my results were positive, that I immediately wanted to find some magical cure? Some deeper meaning? Some mythological explanation for the mundane?

"History is made every second," Daniel once said to me, lying in bed, listening to the first rain of the spring. I held him tightly, afraid he might break. I was always amazed by how little there was of him. As if he were just some figment of my imagination, just another magical creation to make sense out of life.

History is made every second…the past is consuming us, ever changing, evolving while the future remains the same: the same ending to every life.

No magical cure, no spell could relieve me of this. Just like no spell could have saved my mother from losing her hair, or the pain of chemo, the coughing up of blood, the dizziness, and the loss of memories.

No magical spell would save those I loved from what was coming.

"We are burning angels, lit aflame with passion and desire. We are monsters. Ugly and tainted. We are so fucking beautiful." Laurent sat perched on the edge of the couch, high, nails painted a startling orange. He giggled. "I have been loved by so many people it's almost unfair."

✖

When I was a boy, we lived for a while in a large house in a suburban town. I would lie in bed, and downstairs a woman was screaming. Howling. Breaking plates. Smashing lamps. Years later when I told my mother this story, she told me that it was her. She told me on that night she went crazy. She gave in to whatever demons were stalking her.

Years later I stood with my mother on a crescent-shaped bridge, looking out over the canals of Amsterdam. It was cold. She was shivering. I asked her if she wanted to go in. We had rented houseboats on the next canal over. She said she wanted to stay outside. She was frightened inside.

"Of what?"

"It feels like going insane. Like slipping into another you. Like falling out of this world and into another."

We went inside a bar and ate pickled herring and drank beer. She ordered a plate of fried meats. I knew something was wrong because my mother didn't like to drink with me. I was supposed to be sober. But unlike her, I wasn't strong. I was weak, possessed by desires that were easier to give in to than to control.

A fire burned, outside the window as it began to snow. My mother wore a red scarf and sapphire colored earrings. Her nails were painted black, a diamond ring sparkled in the burning light. I knew she was wearing a fortune in jewelry. The kind of fortune that amounted in a life time of work for most people.

We didn't discuss with my mother where the money came from. I once visited her in New Hope, Pennsylvania. I was at Sarah Lawrence at the time, and some friends and I wanted to stay outside the City. Over the weekend my mother asked us to carry a suitcase to the Lambertville Station.

"There will be a limousine. Knock on the back window. Give the man inside the suitcase."

My mother was scared. She had recently married a man who had used a fake name and, had stolen a great deal of money from her. Had bought houses using her name. He was a fraud.

"What's in the suitcase?" I asked.

She smiled. "Karma."

I knew it was cash. We all did. I knew what karma meant.

When he disappeared weeks later, we all knew what had happened. "People don't just disappear," someone said.

My mother just smiled. "Everyone has to go somewhere, eventually," she said sweetly, her Southern accent like peaches and sugar.

It never really occurred to any of us to question why she was asking us, her son and his Sarah Lawrence friends, to make this delivery.

Once, my mother sent me to spy on the man she was having an affair with. He and his family were picnicking on the river. My mother was married to a wealthy, famous scientist who lived in a house designed by a student of Frank Lloyd Wright.

She wanted me to deliver her lover a message.

I really didn't want to do that.

"His wife doesn't know you. I need to see him." She was near hysterical. She was on the verge of furious. "You have to do this."

As children, after my mother left our father, she would pick my brother and I up, and we would go on "adventures." These often included excursions into the darker avenues of the East Village, searching for Dan the Van Man. That's what she called him. She even made up songs about him. Dan The Van Man had bought up whole avenues of apartment buildings, all up and down Avenues A, B, and C. This was the late 70's. He slept in his van while he renovated the buildings. Everyone thought he was insane for spending so much money on those buildings. That mother fucker is a fucking billionaire now.

We would eat falafel on 10th Street and then drive slowly into the far East Village. When we found his van among all the other vans parked out there, we'd all pile inside. He'd usually have a pizza waiting, still warm. We'd eat pizza and tell crazy ghost stories and listen to the weird junkies roaming the avenues outside.

Late at night those junkies screamed at God. They really gave it all they fucking had. Those junkies were telling me my future.

Some particularly crazy nights, we would drive looking for her rich scientist, searching bars and parking lots. She knew he was fucking someone. None of us really understood why she cared. Monogamy was not her strongest attribute. When we would finally find him, she would wait silently, her car dark, my brother and I hidden in the back seat, for him to appear from whatever clandestine place he had been. And she would gun the car, chasing him down the street. We never knew if she was serious about killing him or not. Just that she kept screaming it.

We stayed out all night, wandering the Amsterdam canals, talking. She was manic. She was brilliant. She was magical and possessed. She was haunted. On nights like that, she could sweep you up in it. You never knew exactly where you were going, but I always found myself craving more afterward.

She was a witch on those nights. A time traveler.

"It's like fire," she said, snow falling around us like tiny sparkling jewels. Her eyes were bright. Consumed. "The way it eats through me. Like catching flame." She smiled. It was a sad smile. "And then it goes out. And the world...the world becomes grey. Flat. Sometimes the only thing that keeps you going is knowing that the flames will come again. That soon you will burn as bright as the sun."

"That's what heroin feels like," I said to her. "Like suddenly the whole world becomes beautiful. Everything is lit in this poetry, in this music. Everything is suddenly real."

She laughed at that. "It's such a lie, though, isn't it? Neither you nor I have any fucking idea what reality is."

"Then why isn't that reality? Why do I have to accept the gray?"

"You don't. You can let the fires consume you if you want."

That night we watched the sun come up, obscured by low, dark clouds. We had wandered all the way out to the Van Gogh Museum. We bought espressos and chocolate pastries and wandered the museum.

"I could have done it all differently," she said. We were standing in front of the painting *Skull of a Skeleton with Burning Cigarette*. "I could have stayed with your father. I could have been a good mother. I could have been a whole other person. But I am who I am. And you are who you are. And maybe we can't change that. Maybe we can't change the path we are on. Maybe one day it will kill you. Maybe you will find a way to survive it or to beat it. Who knows?"

We wandered our way to *The Potato Eaters* and then *Sunflowers*.

"People stand here and they take pictures, and then they leave and they forget and they don't see. They don't get it. He is telling us something. Something important. There are messages here. There is a way to survive in these paintings. In the poetry. In the music. In all the books. But people, they don't slow down. They forgot. Maybe we've all forgotten."

"Forgotten what?"

"Why we are here."

We took a train to Rome and met a friend of mine. My mother wanted us to go hunting Caravaggio's. She had read that you could find them in churches, worn and exhausted, and glorious.

We ran into a group of young guys from Dublin who were also searching for Caravaggio's. Later that night, we all went to dinner. My mother, the Dublin guys, my friend, and myself. We found ourselves standing in the forum drinking a bottle of wine and smoking cigarettes. I made out with one of the boys from Dublin, a red head with skin so white it was almost translucent.

Tired of big cities, we took a train to Pisa the next day, and made our way to Cinque Terre on the Italian Riviera. We ate seafood and pesto and smoked unfiltered cigarettes. My mother would stay up all night. Often, I would wake to find her on the balcony, looking out over the rocky coast line and the sea. The water was blue. The sky was flawless. My mother was crying.

"What's wrong?" I asked her.

"I can't see it anymore."

"Can't see what?"

She looked at me, despairing. "Any of it. I can't see any of it anymore."

I knew what she meant. The fire was gone. The flames had burned out. The world of magic had been replaced by the gray world of reality.

"It's okay," I said. "It's still beautiful. If you really look at it."

I bought us a round loaf of cheesy bread and a whole fried fish at a small restaurant down the street from where we were staying. My mother spent the rest of the trip reading and pulling Tarot cards. I hiked the trails that connected the five towns to each other.

A therapist of mine once said, "It must have been hard growing up with a mother like that. You seem very forgiving of her."

I didn't know what she meant. What was there to forgive? She was my mother. She was exactly who she was. She never apologized for that. Even when she would say, "I know I was a bad mother," she never followed it with an apology. Just a smile and a look, and then, "But I guess we are who we are."

I don't think my mother was a bad mother. She introduced me to magic and to beauty, to wonder. She made the night burn bright and the days seem endless with adventure.

When we found out she had cancer, I flew from L.A. to be with her. I sat with her outside, in the small courtyard behind her house. It was warm out. July. Humid.

"If I die," she said, "I don't regret any of it. Maybe that is selfish. But I don't. I feel lucky."

She told me about the three angels that hover around her and take care of her. She told me their names, and she told me the things they whispered to her.

"I am the luckiest person I know. I have lived such an amazing life." She smiled at me. "You know, you and your brother are the best things I ever did. I mean that. You are the thing I consider myself luckiest for. I always thought I didn't want children. I lived most of my life as if I didn't have them. But I don't think I could have made it this far without you. And if I die, I want you to know. We, you and me, we are okay. And I love you."

I knew she was referring to the fact that I was using heroin again. She was telling me she loved me anyway. She was telling me that she loved me for who I was, not who she thought I should be.

"You are my baby. And I will always love you. You are my luckiest thing."

We are burning angels, lit aflame with passion and desire. We are monsters. Ugly and tainted. We are so fucking beautiful.

I find it hard to reconcile the past with the present. The story with the reality. I find it hard to reconcile my life with the man I am now... *I have been loved by so many people it's almost unfair...*

Their words are like ghosts. Their memories like anchors. If I close my eyes I can almost taste them, feel their breath, their touch hot on my skin.

I have been so in love with so many people. Consumed by that love. Devoured. I have ached and cried and dreamed. I only spent seconds with some of these ghosts in some dark room, our mouths locked and hands grasping for a connection. Now, they hold me and whisper to me at night.

The man who whispered another boy's name as I fucked him bent over the urinal in Grand Central Station. The boy who kissed me and told me had tried to kill himself the day before, right as he sat on my dick, swallowing me whole. The quiet ones who never spoke, me on my knees watching them, their eyes closed, their breath deep, their cocks in my mouth, slowly getting them off. Some of them would look down before walking away. Some would just disappear, fading away back into the trees. All those men who I have been inside, who have been inside me.

All the different ways we found to connect in a world that feels disjointed and empty.

"We are the luckiest people," my mother said to me. "Even if no one else knows it. We are the luckiest people in the world. We burn bright. We are lit by fires."

Shut Up And Fuck

Kiernan loved eating at Florent late at night. Some days he would refuse to eat, waiting for the *escargot* and fries, the steak *tartare*, the *moules frites*, all served by flamboyant and bitchy drag queens on broken sidewalks in the meat packing district. We would get high and dance all night at Limelight and Save the Robots, then pour into cabs and head west, where Kiernan spent hundreds of dollars on bottles of wine and extravagant late-night dinners.

His favorite time to arrive was after 6 a.m. when all the "people" were getting up and going to work. He loved sitting there, dressed in his make-up and outrageous club costumes, smoking, eyes twitching, watching as the "humans" made their way through life. "It's trudgery," Kiernan would say, "that fascinates me most. The trudgery of the human existence." He would stand tall, well over six feet, with his broad Nordic build, and he would smash his skull-headed cane into the sidewalk and howl until tears sprang into his eyes. He would scream our names at the humans passing us, scream that we were gods, we were the only truly living things in that dying city.

Some nights he would fall into a malaise, lying naked in his Tribeca loft, high on Valium and heroin, empty packs of Marlboros and boxes of donuts littered about him. He was beautiful in that fallen way, spoiled and destroyed and glorious.

"I am waiting to die," he would wail, and I would try to hear him, but mostly I was fascinated by the thickness of his cock. He had a huge cock, which always distracted me. No matter what drama was playing out before us, I just wanted to climb on him and ride him. "I am waiting to die, and all you can think about is getting fucked. Like some whore."

He would sit up, pushing half-eaten donuts at me across the floor. After fucking, he would show me his newest work, paintings he kept hidden in the corner of the empty space, behind a black curtain. It was always the same thing. Kiernan in various stages of decay. Happy or sad, beautiful or beaten, there he was, dying. He believed he could prepare himself. Trick that existential crisis through acceptance.

Sometimes he would let me blow him while he painted. "Do you ever think about anything?" he asked me once, after cumming in my mouth. "Do you ever think about anything that isn't my cock?"

Kiernan was rich. The kind of rich that most people would never touch. He had a huge trust fund. His family owned planes and yachts and sat on the boards of museums. When his father arrived, their air was filled with body guards and private chefs and galas.

"Nietzsche was right. Hitler was right. We aren't all equal."

I hated him most at these times, his arrogance ugly and inflated as protection.

He was most beautiful in the fall, just before Halloween, lying in bed with a bottle of wine listening to the rain and Berlioz, reading poetry and telling me he was lost. "Among all this life. I am so lost. I have no direction. No place to call home. All this freedom, it is too much."

Kiernan had grown up in Amsterdam and Paris. We had met at boarding school and then again at Disco 2000 when Limelight still mattered. He had appeared so bright and shining, so beautiful. We talked about Dostoevsky and Miller and Joyce and why he hated the cold mathematics of Mann. To this day, I think he said that to upset me.

Magic Mountain has always been one of my favorite books.

We spent summer weekends at his father's house in East Hampton, a huge castle of glass and stone on the beach. We lay around eating potato chips and caviar sandwiches on Wonder Bread and Kiernan cried about the emptiness of existence. He wailed about the sorrows of life. And during all this, all I thought about was his dick. If it wasn't for that dick, I probably wouldn't have listened to him. If it wasn't for that cock, I probably would have walked out long before I did.

I could never figure out why I had to listen to him talk. I didn't care about his stupid theories and his sad wailings. The only thing I ever thought about that whole time we were together was his thick cock and how I wish we could just shut up and fuck.

Broken

When I was fifteen, I got a job at the local movie theatre where all the goth and punk kids worked. The projectionist was named Tom, a guy in his early thirties. He was short and stocky with reddish blond hair and a slight beard. He kept to himself, locked in the projection booth, playing Bowie and Iggy and Lou. All my friends had jobs at the theatre, and those who didn't would come and hang out, getting in to the movie for free, never being bothered for smoking cloves in the front rows.

Tom would smile at me and tell me stupid jokes that never really made any sense and had no real punch line. He was awkward and silly and had no idea how sexy he was. He lived in the basement of his family's huge house, locked behind a stone wall. I never really thought about why a thirty something guy was hitting on a fifteen-year-old. All I knew was that I loved him. Because that was how it felt. Like this insane clawing inside me, this unrelenting tearing, this screeching need. I fantasized about the two of us running away together to Los Angeles, where I knew life was endless and perfect. Where there was sun and freedom—and life wasn't so claustrophobic and loud.

The first time Tom invited me into the booth, we were premiering *Rambo*. People chanted, "Nuke the gooks. Nuke the gooks." One of the ushers, TJ, a wiry, muscled punk kid with a blond Mohawk and an angry sense of humor was furious about how stupid the world was. He screamed, "Fucking assholes. Ima nuke you idiots if you don't shut the fuck up!" I sat on the floor next to Tom, watching him work, and at some point, I rested my head on his thigh, watching his dick grow hard through his jeans. My heart pounded. The world seemed to open up. I had never done this before, not in this exact way. I ached. Scared and hopeful, I remember how bad my own dick hurt, pushing against my pants.

Tom let me suck him off and when he came, it never occurred to me not to swallow. He sobbed for a moment, and then told me I should get back to work. He closed the door behind me, and I heard it lock. I felt devastated. I wanted to hold him, to lick his tears, to tell him it was okay. I wanted to tell him that I loved him too. Because I did. I loved him so fucking much, in that outrageous way that only a fifteen-year-old boy can love a man too old for him, in that way that never really happens again because it was never really real.

I sat at the train station across the street from the movie theatre, my heart breaking, smoking cigarettes with TJ and asking him what I had done wrong. Why didn't he let me stay? "Fuck the world," TJ said, "And fuck him and fuck you. Get used to it. All it fucking does is hurt." TJ's dad was an alcoholic who beat his mom and sometimes smashed TJ's head in with a bottle. None of us really talked about that a lot. It was just how life was sometimes. He had a right to be angry. He stroked my head and rubbed my shoulders and whispered in my ear, "Fuck the world, man. Fuck everybody."

A few weeks later, Tom invited me to his house. His parents were in Cape Cod for the weekend. He lived in a large Tudor house, one of those vast endless mansions of stone and wood and dark corners that seemed so prevalent in much of my early life. We fucked in his bed. How bad it hurt and how much I wanted more of the pain, of him, of that pounding. I wanted to be fucked right out of my life. We fell asleep in his bed. It rained that night. It was summer. Lightening broke the sky in huge apocalyptic flashes.

The next day he stopped talking to me. I begged him to tell me what I had done. He just looked at me and shrugged and locked himself in his booth. TJ told me, "That guy, he's an asshole. A dumb fuck in his thirties living at home with his parents working at a movie theatre. He has nothing. He's going nowhere. Fuck him. Fuck the world."

"But I love him!"

"Fuck love."

A few nights later, I would show up at his house, screaming his name, demanding he talk to me. His parents were home. They called the cops. My dad had to come get me from the police station. No one asked me what I was doing there or why I couldn't stop crying. I felt like I had been broken. Like someone had held me down and beat me with a bat, with their fists, kicking at me until nothing was left.

Much of my life love has felt like being beaten so badly I can't breathe or move.

TJ snuck into my house that night with a bottle of whiskey and a pack of Merit Ultra Lights. We got stupid drunk, and he told me how sometimes he thought that none of us had any chance. No one was ever going to be able to love us enough because there wasn't enough. Couldn't be enough. Not for us. "What does that mean?" I asked him, shaking from the whiskey, dizzy from the cigarettes, my heart a little less broken with TJ next to me, picking records from my collection.

"What does it mean? Easy. Fuck you. Fuck me. Fuck the world. Fuck everybody. Got it?"

I laughed. Yeah. I got it.

Disenchanted

I had my first threesome in seventh grade with Peter, an old family friend, and Anthony, a local kid who lived on the block. Peter was the first person to ever tell me how to jerk off—mom's Nivea cold cream, rub real slow, and wait. It hurt at first, then it didn't. Anthony was the first guy to ever suck my dick. We were in the basement of his family's house looking at his older brother's porn collection. I tried to explain to him how to jerk off, and he pointed to the picture of some washed out blonde lady blowing a skinny guy in an electrician's suit and said, "Why don't I just suck you off?" I have no idea where Anthony learned to suck dick, and, honestly, I probably didn't want to think about it too much, but he did it like a pro and swallowed every last drop.

Peter lived on a large estate with a pool and long, expansive gardens. His mother fed us cheese and crackers and elaborately prepared finger sandwiches. When she would finally disappear, we would play a game called look-in-bottom which consisted of the two of us exploring each other's butts with our fingers and mouths. I must have been twelve at the time, maybe thirteen.

We were precocious children, spoiled and bored and willing to do almost anything.

My mother moved out when I was in second grade. To say that this event was formative is to downplay the vastness and the scope it had over my entire life. For years I pretended to have severe, epileptic-like fits. I was once carried out of an Atlanta Braves baseball game by paramedics and flown to the emergency room in a helicopter and elaborate and expensive tests and brain scans. My parents took hours from their lives to cater to my extensive fake illness, as did psychologists, social workers, and specialists from all over the country, me in the school nurse's office shrieking and howling and convulsing in fake agony. All to convey the absolute misery and pain, the total loneliness that was eating away at me.

All because I wanted my mother back.

That loneliness stayed with me through much of my teen years. When my father finally remarried, he and his wife would spend summers in Italy, leaving us with various nannies. One in particular, a smart, nerdy, red headed guy in his twenties named Tim, would stay up with me all night long talking and listening to music. He introduced me to Laurie Anderson and I introduced him to the Psychedelic Furs.

One night, lying on the floor of my bedroom, he leaned over and kissed me. He is not the first man to make love to me. He is not the first adult I had sex with. The Cure was playing. Incense was burning, smoke drifting in strange currents along with the flickering candlelight. His body smelled musky and darkly occultish. Magical. His breathing was heavy as he got close to cumming. Some nights he would call my name when I was downstairs and he was asleep in my parent's bedroom, dreaming of me, pretending we weren't in love.

When the summer was over, Tim went back to his life. He sent me a letter and a Yaz CD once, around Halloween. The letter read: *Dear Jeff, I remember that night we spent laying on the grass looking up at the night sky. We couldn't see the stars because of all the city lights, and you told me you were afraid, and when I asked you what you were afraid of, you just laughed and you said, of being nothing. Of being empty. Of failing. I didn't respond. I just kissed you. I should have told you you will never be nothing. You will always be full of strength and beauty and light. I have never met anyone who laughed so easily and wanted so much. You are everything. And beside you, for those few months, I felt like I was everything too.*

I was sixteen that summer with Tim. Just three years after my first three way in the guest house overlooking a sparkling pool, Peter holding Anthony's legs for me, Anthony whispering our names over and over, smiling, that look on his face saying, *I am alive. I am here. I am finally myself.*

We all knew Anthony's life was not okay. But we were kids. We didn't understand he needed to be saved. We had no way of knowing the darkness he needed to be rescued from. So instead we fucked him, and we marveled at how he seemed to know everything about sex.

And there were moments when Anthony seemed happy. When maybe even he believed we were heroes capable of doing the impossible.

x

Years later, I ran into Anthony on 8th Ave in Chelsea. I asked him how he was. He was sunken and sick looking. He spit at me. "I loved you," he said, and then he turned and walked away. When my father remarried, we moved into a larger house in a wealthier neighborhood and I forgot about Anthony. Just like that. One day we were fucking every day, and the next he was gone.

One summer afternoon hiding in a tree fort at someone's country house, Anthony and I lay naked next to each other. He was so stunning, olive skinned, black curly hair, hazel golden eyes, and we held hands, Anthony was laughing and he said to me, "Promise me we will always remember this moment."

"I promise," I said, having no idea it was a lie.

Philosophers

When I was a junior in high school, I went to Solebury Boarding School in New Hope, Pennsylvania. I met a man who worked in town. His name was Christophe. Christophe was from Belgium. He was tall with dark hair and blue eyes. He had a full brown beard and thick workman-like fingers, and he told me he was going to sacrifice an animal in the woods, down by the river, to see if maybe it might change the course of his life.

When I asked him what kind of animal, he smiled. "The bigger the better."

"Is this some kind of Satanic ritual," I asked, trying to be funny.

"People don't understand Lucifer," he said to me. "They don't understand falling. To be abandoned by your father, to be thrown away instead of loved."

X

I met Christophe in the men's room at the inside mall on Main Street. He was wiggling his big uncut cock at me, and I found myself pulled to it inexorably, as if called to my destiny. Even at seventeen, I was a cocksucker's cocksucker. It was a few days before Halloween. Cold out, winds smelling of winter, trees barren, the streets dark and moody, the air all burnt wood and chimney smoke. I had spent the afternoon at Tony's house, a friend who rented an apartment in town.

His father was a well-known mafiosa from Queens. We drank hot chocolate and whiskey and ate liverwurst and onion sandwiches on thick multi-grained dark bread.

Tony was telling me about alien artists from other dimensions who came here and drew great murals on the walls of caves. They taught the cavemen how to communicate. Alien artists mated with humans and sped up our evolution, creating mankind out of a cesspool of fear and darkness and shit.

"That is all we were. Animals in shit. Feasting on the flesh of our children. Monsters. They elevated us. Created us."

"Where are they now?" We had the heat on and the windows open, a bitter wind blowing through the large apartment.

"They're still here, waiting."

"Waiting for what?"

"For us to grow up."

Tony was one of the ugliest people I have ever met. He was so ugly that sometimes I found it hard to look at him. It almost became erotic, the deformities of his face and body taking on a strange sexuality. It was rumored that his cock was equally ugly and huge, like a gnarled baseball bat.

He was dating a local girl, though most of us suspected it had more to do with who Tony's dad was than Tony himself. She was in love with his money and the hint of power and he was in love with her tits.

Tony was nineteen. He had run away from home. Meaning, mostly, he had taken a bunch of money, his credit cards, and left Queens. He surrounded himself with canvases to paint on and books to read.

"I love my dad. My dad loves me. I just don't want to be around him. Around that." For months I had assumed he meant the violence. The illegal behavior. I was wrong. "I don't care about that. It's the tackiness. The architecture. The ridiculous women and their ridiculous outfits. Faux Botticelli angels spouting dirty water from garish fountains. Pink stucco houses and castrated Davids. I had to get out of Queens."

His apartment was up the hill, with a view over town and to the Delaware River.

On that Sunday afternoon, hours before I met Christophe for the first time in the bathroom of the mall, a rain began to fall. The smell of wet, decaying leaves filled the smoky air. This was Halloween. This smell of burning and death. Of decay and destruction. The cold wet darkness.

"Ideas are dead," Tony said. He had a thick accent that mangled his words as they escaped his strange and misshapen mouth. "No one reads *The Brothers Karamazov* anymore. TV and modern life inundate us. Destroy us. I doubt the aliens care anymore. Maybe they've already left. Maybe we failed them. Maybe we are still nothing but animals rooting around in shit."

He got like that sometimes when he was drinking, when it was raining, in the darkness. He found despair, and he clung to it like it was a blanket filled with some dejected form of hope.

"Maybe we are nothing but food for slaughter."

I watched as he pranced around the room, picking up books, picking up objects he had found, rocks and sticks and weather-beaten metals, searching for something, anything to remind him that beautiful still existed.

"Everything has become so inelegant," he whispered, and it sounded strange, mythic and glorious coming from such an ugly, inelegant face.

"I'm gonna go get my dick sucked," I said out of nowhere, and he looked up at me, his face melting into a smile. "I heard that the bathrooms in the mall get cruisy on the weekends."

He started laughing, and I smiled. "God, you faggots. You have everything, don't you? It's not fair."

I walked slowly down the hill through the rain and the cold, the river before me full and violent and black. The bridge into Lambertville was shrouded in a fog.

A muted darkness had settled. Overhead, geese flew in communicated patterns, crying out. Trees were bent and barren.

"I don't believe in the Devil," I told Christophe, a few days after I had sucked his dick in the mall bathroom. We were sitting on the large tapestried rug in his apartment in a converted factory overlooking the river. The floors were cement. The walls brick with large pipes sticking out. Huge metal tubes lined the ceiling. It was shabby and expensive and cold. Distracted pieces of modern art hung in displaced ambivalence.

Christophe had a beautiful dick. The kind of dick that overwhelmed my ability to think straight. Though to be fair, most cocks had that effect over me.

Christophe and I were sitting on the rug at a chrome and glass table eating cheese and olives and drinking whiskey.

Christophe held a deck of Tarot. He said it was one of five ever printed. His father had given it to him on his thirteenth birthday. The cards were supposed to have been drawn by Lucifer himself while inhabiting a castle on the canals of Venice, in the fifteenth century.

"Collectors and museums would pay millions for these cards," he breathed, his English lyrical and frozen due to his accent. "But for me they are more than millions of dollars. For me they are a connection to my past. To my family. To my soul."

Christophe spoke like that. Life was monumental to him. Spending days with him was like getting lost in other dimensions, in fairy tales and magical realms. Everything was real. Everything was possible.

"My father comes from a long line of Satanists in Antwerp and Brussels and Amsterdam. Persecuted for centuries by idiots who believed everything was literal, too stupid to understand that magic and God and faith were figurative, stories built out of the fog, castles built out of air. Nothing but vague outlines for things so unknowable to even pretend understanding is childish and dangerous."

You could almost believe that Christophe came from a long line of Belgian Satanists. He had that kind of devilish good looks. Philosophic and despairing. Eyes so blue they ate into you. I imagined him at my age, sitting in dark cafés reading La Bas or Baudelaire, Maturin while listening to Ravel and drinking wine so red it burned.

"When they sentenced my father to life in prison, I sold the house, most of the art that was still left, and moved here." He smiled. "This strange river town full of ghosts and witches. Magic seems to follow me, directing the course of my life. I could have gone anywhere, lived any kind of a life. Milan or Berlin, Hong Kong, or Mexico City. The world became so vast and endless that it froze me, so I let the world take me, pull at me, until I found myself in this apartment on this river. Nowhere and everywhere at once."

"Getting blowjobs from teenage boys in the mall bathroom."

He smiled, and I could feel its currents running through me like heroin and sex, like dark forgotten dreams. "We all have our decadencies."

I watched as he closed his eyes a moment and rubbed his cock. He took it out, half hard, and wiggled it at me, inviting me. My eyes locked with his, my heart beat faster. I was hungry.

A few weeks later, just before Thanksgiving break, Christophe and I walked along the canal. The water was frozen. Life was still. As if we were all waiting for something monumental to happen. Some great explosion that would destroy the world and carry us off into a new existence.

"I have something I want to show you," he said. "But it's a secret. Something no one else can know about." He stopped walking. He watched a squirrel skid across the frozen canal. The day was sullen and gray.

The previous summer, a friend of mine, Lea, and I had planned to do a séance in the town cemetery. We met at the Dunkin Donuts just down the street from the cemetery at midnight. The story around school was that Lea had once gone into the graveyard with the football team and let them all fuck her. That story occupied a special place in my early adolescence. When I jerked off, I was always Lea, being held down and brutally fucked by the town football team.

When I had asked Lea about this, she had smiled that blonde cheerleader soon to be porn star smile and said, "Not the whole football team." She had lit a cigarette, red lipstick staining the end, matching the red tips of her fingernails. "After they left me, that night, I lay there alone, half naked in the dark, the sky lit bright with lights from the city, more beautiful than stars, more alienating than all the expansive coldness of the universe and I felt them. All of them. The dead."

She spoke slowly, methodically, her voice husky, cigarette smoke like a veil. "The watchers. Feasting off me. Off my energy. I was covered in sweat and cum and spit. Why do guys always turn sex into some semblance of rape? Like it almost made them mad that I was enjoying it just as much as they were. But those dead things, those watchers, it took me a moment to realize they weren't the ghosts of the once living. They were something else. Something darker. Something bigger. Those creatures had never been human. Never been us. They fed off moonlight and destruction, off emotion, good or bad. It all tasted the same to them. It was the intensity they were going for. The spice of feeling that satiated them. I lay in that graveyard till sunrise talking to them, inviting them into me, letting them feast on me. They devoured me. And for a moment, they freed me from who I was. They set me free."

I, of course, wanted to see them too. I wanted to be devoured and freed. That was how we ended up at the graveyard at midnight on a Tuesday night. I was a teenage boy looking for Satan and magic and gang bangs, and Lea was my tour guide into her dark underworlds. Whether everything she said was bullshit or not didn't really matter. We weren't there for the truth. We were there for the ride. For life. For fucking and drinking and losing ourselves to the bigger story. The truth was for losers and middle class heteros looking for a secure job and two kids and a Volvo. I wanted as far away from that as possible. I wanted lies and stories and beauty.

I wanted escape from the suburban hell I had ended up in.

On the night of the séance, Lea had filled a small black bag with things she thought necessary. She had made the trek to Manhattan to Enchantments to buy all the essential magical elements since we wouldn't have the benefit of a gang bang to bring the hungry into existence.

To this day, I still regret not having a gang bang. I was built to be fucked by the football team.

"It's only in the darkness, in the fear, that I know who I really am," Lea said to me.

She had giant tits and blonde hair and crystal blue eyes. We would lie in her room listening to Fleetwood Mac and get stoned. We read Tarot and played with the Ouija and talked about how bored we were. One night, I sat on her bed and watched as she cut small, almost harmless incisions into her arms. She gasped in pain, closing her eyes.

"It's like cumming," she said. "Only better. Clearer."

Other girls didn't like Lea. She was the kind of girl you couldn't trust around your boyfriend.

"Everyone is so uptight," she said. "Yeah, so I blew your man. And you're pissed at me? Why don't you ask your man why he's putting his dick in my mouth if he belongs to you? But no one likes the truth. It's easier to call me a bitch and a slut than to accept that their boyfriends are cheats and liars." She laughed. "But then, I am a bitch and a slut."

She hesitated, fingernails clawing red tracks into the pale skin of her arms. "Everyone is a liar. To think you own anyone is a farce. To think you know anyone is a fucking epic deception. To think you know yourself is just as false. My father gets awards, he gets year-end bonuses, and he talks to committees on finance reform. He is asked to give lectures at universities, he leads sermons at church on Sundays and is paid to travel the world because of the kind of man he is. The kind of human being. He also cheats on his wife with whores when he does too much coke on his boys' nights out.

"Once, drunk, late at night, he stumbled into my bed and lay down and jerked off next to me. The next morning, he kissed me on the forehead and pretended we were the happy family. A week later when I was jacking off, I started thinking about my father. After I came, I ran to the bathroom and puked. I hated myself. Every human being is a dark unknowable vortex. To believe otherwise is to be an idiot. And idiots get what they deserve."

In the graveyard, she took out five candles, each with black bases, white middles, and red wicks. She poured liquid from a vial over her hands and handed it to me. She drew a circle around us with some ash-colored substance that smelled like rotting meat. She closed her eyes. She wailed. She begged. She sobbed. She broke the circle and puked on a grave stone. She pulled up her black dress and pissed on the ground. She called God a whore and Jesus a faggot. She stuck two fingers in her pussy and wiped the juice on her lips.

When she looked at me her eyes were wild. Haunted. Less blue.

When she fell to the ground, I thought she had died, and for a moment I think I felt them. The hungry. All around me. The night seemed to breathe with them. I felt their ache in my belly. I don't know how to explain to you exactly what I felt. Maybe it was just the hysteria of two lonely kids looking for a way out, but for a moment I thought I would tear the flesh from the world, devour it, destroy it.

And then it was over. She was laughing, her face pink and flushed.

"Goddamn, every time, it's better than jerking off."

We bought a dozen donuts and walked up the steep hill to where I lived with my father and his wife, and we sat in the front yard, laughing and smoking and eating donuts until the sun came up.

Something about Christophe reminded me of Lea.

When he finally revealed to me his great secret, I understood why.

We walked deep into the woods at the edge of town, across a frozen stream and up a slight hill. A small family of deer were standing, watching us as we made our way through the cold stark trees.

"My father blamed everything on Christianity," Christophe said, walking slightly ahead of me, black curls sneaking out of the grey wool cap he wore on his head. "Every atrocity in the world could be laid at the feet of religion. At God. Maybe to some extent, he is right. Maybe God and religion are a cancer eating away at us. Devouring us. Maybe the only way to enlightenment, to real freedom, is by killing all the gods. The symbolic has become the real. The story has become the reality. We created the fairy tale, and then we stepped into it and built our homes there, forgetting it was all made up. Just an elaborate lie."

Ahead of us was a circle of rocks with symbols painted in red on them. Circles had been painted onto the trunks of trees, watching eyes carved into branches. Behind us lay the river, ahead of us the trees and an old stone house fallen in ruins.

Lonely, whimpering cries came from inside the house.

I no longer found any of it beautiful. I was tired of the countryside and the people who lived in it. I was ready to be back in the city. I had found myself in a story that wasn't mine. A construct built by someone else I wasn't meant to inhabit. This wasn't my life. I had taken a wrong turn.

This idea was strong as we walked up the incline toward that fallen structure and whatever was making those strange whimpering noises inside it.

"You have to jump into the darkness," Lea had once said. "Let it consume you. Live inside the violence and the beauty. The only places that are real are the edges, frayed and beaten, walking on those thin lines between sanity and insanity, between hope and despair." Her eyes were always so wild, filled with madness and fire. "Sometimes when I'm jerking off, I imagine watching as a man is murdered by a hulking figure in a ski mask. It is horrible and violent. Full of anger and fury. And when it is over, the hulking figure turns to me. His dick is raging and hard, just as furious as his fists, and he fucks me. Straight into oblivion. He fucks me and holds me down with those murderous hands and when it's over, when I am splayed and used, his fingers turn tender, and he kisses me. I could love a man like that. So far on the edges that he is no longer human."

I stop walking. I turn to look at the deer in the distance, the terrified and trapped whining from the buried house like a scream, and I say, "Hey, I think I'm going to go back."

Christophe turns to me. I see the same fury in his eyes that I used to see in Lea's.

"Back? Back where?"

"Town. School. Home. Just back."

"You can't go back. We are already here."

I laughed. I'm not sure why. But it seemed so funny to me then. So wrong and absurd. I wasn't supposed to be there.

"Yeah. I can."

Christophe looked at me, the fury in his eyes physical, and I knew what he was thinking. I knew what he wanted to do. But I stood there, still. I am not a little guy. I am broad and strong, and I know how to fight. And I knew in that minute if he came for me, I would do whatever I had to survive. It occurred to me that I would kill him if I had to.

Instead he just turned from me and continued walking toward whatever dark destiny awaited him.

X

Later, sitting at Tony's, he told me a story. About his father. And a whore dying on the side of the road. Tony had been a little kid. They had gone to dinner with his grandparents in Manhattan. A steak house in the theatre district. The kind of place with baked potatoes and wedge salads and minestrone. Old World. Dark wood. They were crossing through Times Square, Tony swallowed up in the back seat of the limo, barely able to see outside the window, when ahead of them a man was beating a woman. It was brutal. Savage. Tony had never seen anything like it. The man used his fists like hammers. Slamming the woman's head into the cement.

Tony's father told the driver to pull over. He had a gun in his hand. Even as a boy, Tony knew who his father was. What he did. But he had never seen. He had been sheltered from those things.

"My dad pointed the gun at the man. The street was barren. Just some homeless and junkies. The guy ran. I think my dad would have shot him if I hadn't been there, wrapping my arms around his thighs. I was crying. Scared. The woman, lay twitching and bleeding, her skull cracked open. It was horrifying. You could see the meat of her brain. Her eyes were white planes, rolled into the back of her head. My father, knelt down next to her, took her in his arms, and he held her, whispering to her as she died. When it was all over and she was gone, we got back into the car.

His hands were stained in her blood. I could hear him sobbing. I refused to look at him. I just put my tiny hand in his and tried to be still. To be quiet. Something about the world had broken that night. Something impossible to repair." He bit into a cherry Pop Tart, his eyes distant. Outside I saw shadows on the street, and I thought about monsters and gods and the lies we tell ourselves.

"My whole life all I've ever heard was what a horrible man my father was. Is. And it's all true. My father has done unspeakable things. Things that are worse than what that guy did to that whore in Times Square. He sobbed, driving home after dinner with his parents, my hands in his, his bloodied, hopeless, meaningless. We are monsters in a broken world. It's good you didn't go into that buried house. It's good that you weren't a part of that."

He stood up. He changed the record from Leonard Cohen to David Bowie, "Panic in Detroit" filling the room. He began to dance. A strange dance. He really was the ugliest guy I've ever seen. He held his hands out for me, thin fingers with dark hair. I took them, letting him pull me up, and we danced throughout his room, candle light throwing shapes into distortions, and we laughed.

We might have been stoned or we might have been sober, I can't remember, but I know it was good to dance like that for a while. It was good to be able to breathe.

When We Are Famous

In 1993, I was in the middle of a vast and expansive heroin addiction. I was living in a railroad style apartment on Sackett Street in Brooklyn. Next door to me lived a Dominatrix named Candy.

"After that Velvet Underground song, 'Candy Says.'" She smiled at me, her eyes a startling, mystical green. She had red curls and long dark lashes. She was tall, but then everyone seems tall to me. She wore black leather pants and red high heeled leather boots. Candy worked in a dungeon in Chelsea where she would tie men's cocks and balls up because she was trying to save all her money to move to Los Angeles to be a movie star.

We used to sit in her apartment, which was next door to mine and connected out our front windows by a fire escape, and we'd drink cheap wine and watch old romantic comedies and smoke cigarettes on the fire escape. We would talk about our dreams and how one day we would both be famous. She would tell me how some married man paid her to tie him up and tickle him, or to call him names and humiliate him. She would tell me about the eloquence of cock and ball torture.

Brooklyn was the most romantic place in the whole world back then. It still had that old school charm.

Our building was owned by a mafia family who demanded rent in cash. Smith Street was filled with Santaria shops that had magic candles and animal heads, or glass jars filled with clear liquid and floating intestines. There were no vegan restaurants or hipster cafes. This was before cellphones and internet. We used to take long walks to the promenade and look out at Manhattan burning like some golden city set aflame by the gods, and the future seemed open, limitless.

One night, dope sick and broke, I climbed across the fire-escape through Candy's window into her apartment. She kept the money she made working as a dominatrix in a shoe box in her bedroom. I stole the shoe box of cash, close to three thousand dollars, and took the subway to the East Village where I bought a hundred dollars' worth of heroin. I don't know what happened to the rest of the money in the shoe box. I must have left it somewhere.

I can be that kind of a person. I got what I wanted. Nothing else mattered. And when I'm high, I forget that any of you exist. I forget about love.

The next morning, I woke up to find Candy standing in my room, a gun in her hand. She gave me the number to AA and told me if I ever came near her again she would shoot me. "In the fucking face."

A week later, she moved back to North Carolina, where her mother lived in a trailer on a hillside next to a lake. She was my best friend. She also probably saved my life, even though I didn't really get sober until 2011. Candy was a truly beautiful person. And she loved me. I know it because she didn't shoot me. I think that was probably a hard choice for her.

That is not the worst thing I have done. Not even close.

Sometimes we would go dancing. She liked to go to the punk clubs. She liked to throw herself into the mosh pit, slamming herself into people. We would eat borsht at Veselka and laugh at the purple bruises up and down her arms and legs. Some nights we walked up and down First Avenue in search of egg creams and coffee and sunglasses. Candy wanted a red scarf she had seen at a store on St. Marks, but we didn't have any money on us so we stole it, running wildly through the streets until we ended up in a donut shop with a group of old

Puerto Rican men playing chess. One of them had a guitar, and he was singing ballads in Spanish. Candy made me dance with her and laughed because I am a terrible dancer. By the end of the night, she had danced with every old man in that room.

She gave the red scarf to the girl who worked behind the counter. "Because I think it will look good against your skin. You have beautiful skin." The girl smiled. I don't think she had been called beautiful a lot.

We both fell in love with men who didn't know how to love us back, but we gave ourselves to them anyway. One night after midnight, Candy showed up at my bedroom window. It was raining and cold out. She was crying, black mascara leaving streaks down her face. Her left eye was puffy and swollen.

"What happened?" I asked, even though I knew. She loved the kind of assholes who thought it was okay to punch girls in the face.

"Nothing. I fell." She smiled at her lame lie. "I hit my head on an ice cream cone."

"Mean fucking ice cream cone."

"The worst. And I still sucked his dick after."

She wasn't the kind of girl who liked heroin. She was a cheap wine and whiskey kind of girl, but she wanted oblivion that night, and I was able to provide it. She sang Sisters of Mercy songs with her eyes closed, as if they were love songs, and she traced pictures in the air around us until I saw what she saw. She kept telling me she saw rainbows and butterflies.

"Everywhere I look. All these butterflies and then a rainbow shining light in all that darkness." She lit a menthol cigarette and she giggled. "God, this shit is heaven. I can never do this fucking shit again."

She was right. That shit was fucking heaven.

It's taken me a long time to realize we can't live forever in Heaven.

x

I used to buy heroin from a stoop on 7th Street between B and C. Lookouts would whistle back and forth, letting the dealers know people or cops were coming. They had a lot of different whistles, each filled with its own meaning, each causing its own reaction. King Tuts Wah Wah Hut was on Avenue A and 7th, as well as Vasacs on 7th and B. The bar at Vasacs was a horseshoe set up with the bathrooms in the back. You could cop a few bags of dope down the street then go into the men's room and get high. King Tuts Wah Wah Hut was a little trickier because the bathroom was up a few steps past the bar, but if you bought a beer and played a song on the juke box, no one said anything to you. There was a Chinese restaurant on 2nd Ave that had pretty decent beef with broccoli for $4.99 I always ended puking up.

Before I moved next door to Candy on Sackett Street, I lived on Court Street in a large three-bedroom apartment in Brooklyn Heights, between State and Schermerhorn. My bedroom window looked down onto Court. Back in those days, that part of Court Street had a slightly abandoned industrial feel. Empty. There was a bodega where I could buy egg rolls, bagels and beer, the smells of curry and Middle Eastern spices from Atlantic Avenue, Montague Street, and the Promenade were just a few blocks away.

One reckless night, before Court Street and Sackett Street, while I was still living in the dorms at Sarah Lawrence, my best friend, Annie, and I went into the East Village to visit this guy she had met. Annie was model beautiful, Italian, thin and dark and gorgeous. She drew pictures of aliens and read philosophy, and we used to get into huge, violent fights, screaming at each other, arguing down long intellectual labyrinths over books and politics and truth and sexuality. I remember there was a fist fight over Marx and someone screaming, reciting memorized lines from Frank O'Hara's *Meditations in an Emergency*. Joyce's *Ulysses* was thrown through a window, glass shattering, and Mann's *Magic Mountain* was set on fire. We were passionate back in those days.

We were beautiful.

Annie and I took the Metro North from Bronxville into Grand Central and caught the 6 Train down to the East Village. I used to love that moment, the train speeding up just a little when the lights would flicker and then go out, all of us shadows in the darkness. And then, from the opposing tunnel, another train would speed by bright as day, and I could see the other riders on that train, like people in an alternative universe, living alternative lives. They were like angels. They were full of all the possibility that life had to offer. They were a different course, another path, and all the choices I hadn't made.

We got out at Astor place and stopped for a slice of pizza. There were rituals that had to be followed, a way to begin the night, incantations made up of actions and traditions, where to get your pizza, which side of the train you rode on going downtown and which side when you went uptown, each action was part of a spell, a way we did things.

On that night, we were going to meet a guy Annie had met a few weeks ago at a club. We were all going to get high. We were on an adventure. This was something the two of us did. We went on adventures. We picked people up and inserted ourselves into their lives. We tried them on for a while. Most of the time they didn't fit, but, every once in a while, everything fell together perfectly.

I don't remember this guy's name. He looked like a Tim. Dirty jeans and dark Joy Division T-shirt, brown hair, scruffy, dark eyes, and a narrow face. Handsome in an upper-middle-class-ex-suburban rock and roller sort of way. His apartment was on 6th Street next to Wonder Bar. It was a spacious one bedroom with hardwood floors and a white futon, posters of The Cure and the Dead Kennedys, whiskey bottles and over flowing ash trays. Incense burned. The windows were open onto the street: spring time and warm, busy, loud. New York. The city was alive, pulsating.

This is what I love about Cities. The way they radiate, flicker, the way they vibrate. I love their energy. Whether it's New York or L.A. or New Orleans, Paris or Rome or Berlin, I always feel completely at home. I'm never drawn to the country, camping or wilderness. I always want to be at the center. I want to feel it washing over me, swallowing me, drowning me. I want to feel it re-creating me.

New York smelled dirty and over grown, lush. Piss and beer and pizza. Tim showed us a drawing of a man getting fucked by another man while fucking some woman with big rosy pink tits. He said that the guy in the middle was on the road to enlightenment.

His voice was too nasal, too snobbish for the life he was living. He was obviously rich. A boarding school kid pretending to be something else.

"He's complete, you see? He's inside her while some dude is inside him. It's something only a man can feel. It's at the heart of masculinity, you know? Fucking and getting fucked. The only way to really know who you are as a man is to be that guy, that asshole." He looked at us, one eye slightly lazy, wandering off in odd directions. "Do you guys think you'd be down for that?"

Annie laughed. She had this high pitched, outrageous bark of a laugh, completely spontaneous and real. She flicked her long black hair, lit a cigarette and sat down at the table. She leaned back, one arm hanging down at her side, while she held the cigarette to her lips with the other. She had that skeptical but I'm down for anything look, cold and detached and judgmental.

x

I had once watched as her boyfriend Jacob had fucked her. They wanted me to sit there and jerk off. Jacob had a gigantic dick. Probably the biggest one I've ever seen. Fat and long. I couldn't get hard the whole time. I knew they were disappointed. It wasn't just that I had no interest in pussy, but things were too emotionally complicated—my relationship to Annie, my desire for Jacob and his big fat dick. All of it was too convoluted. Later that night, I went home and jerked off half a dozen times to Jacob's dick. In my fantasies, it was all mine. In my fantasies, there was no Annie.

There was no way I was going to fuck Tim while he fucked my best friend, and I sure as fuck wasn't going to fuck Annie while Tim fucked me.

I was terrified of the way things were going. But she looked so sure of herself, and she smiled at me, like the best friend she was, because here we were again, on an adventure, on a journey neither of us had seen coming, and that was the best journey of all. I tried to imagine what we would look like, from an opposing subway car, her sitting like that, smoking, legs crossed, sexy and defiant, Tim, his lazy eye looking off at far off vistas, me, scared and nervous, not sure who or what I was. Not sure of the meaning of anything that was being said.

"How about we go out for a few drinks, first." Annie said.

We drank Jack and Cokes and smoked clove cigarettes, and the drunker we got, the more disdainful Annie got of Tim. She could be the meanest person in the world under the right circumstances. Once she had turned that gaze on you there was no escaping it. She would tear you apart, like a tiger playing with its prey, cutting it and biting at it, batting it back and forth. No one ever told her treating people that way was wrong. Everyone let Annie do whatever she wanted. She was beautiful and rich and smart. She was a Sarah Lawrence girl, a girl who was told the world was hers, and in the end, it was true. The world was hers. At least back then.

We were at Crow Bar on Tenth Street, across from Thompkins Square Park. I kept one eye on Annie and Tim and one on the guys walking in and out of the dark room. There was a huge black guy standing by the bar, I would later learn his name was Cliff, and he wore shorts, his impossibly large dick was showing through them, just hanging fat and inviting

x

A few months later I would come back to Crow Bar without Annie or Tim, when I was living on Court Street in Brooklyn, to find Cliff outside the bar. He would take me back to his apartment and fuck me in the stairway because his mother was visiting from Trinidad. His dick was long and fat and, at first, he had to go really slow. It was the kind of dick that was going to hurt no matter what, that kind of hurt that you want more of. It reached inside you and pounded away at you, until the only thing left was the fucking. That dick got so deep inside me I sometimes think I can still feel it: in my bones. In my DNA.

He didn't wear a condom, and when he came inside me, he covered my mouth with his big hand, pushing himself so far into me I felt as if I were disappearing. After he let me eat his ass and then fuck him.

When I came in his ass he told me to go back down and lick it, licking up my own cum and kissing it to him.

I read Larry Kramer's *Faggots* when I was a boy and learning all about felching, but it was on Cliff's dirty stairway in the East Village that I found out I had a cum fetish. He was over six feet, big round dark muscles, in his forties with grey hair in his dark beard and he kept calling me little blond boy. "I'm gonna tear that pink hole up, little blond boy," or "Fuck me with that thick blond boy dick."

All these years later and I am still jerking off over that guy.

Tim called Annie a bitch. I'm not sure why exactly. I'm sure it was true. She could definitely be a bitch.

She just laughed and downed her drink.

"You should just let Jeff fuck you. He's gay. You're gay. I'm not necessary."

"I'm not gay," Tim said. He must have known how weak it sounded. It was his idea to go to the Crow Bar in the first place. "If I was gay, why would I want to fuck a chick?" He looked at her, defiant.

Cliff was leaving the bar with some short, stocky white guy who wasn't so different from me. It made me ache a little inside at the time.

For two years I would go to Cliff's apartment on East 11th Street, and we would fuck. I was young and would cum three or four times. He always teased me about it. Calling me insatiable. I was. It didn't matter how often I got his big body or his humongous dick, his plump and juicy ass, I always wanted more. He smelled rich and musky. He tasted like everything I had ever wanted.

And yet, every time Cliff asked me out to eat after, or for a drink, I would say no. Attraction is weird that way. Love is weird that way. I wanted him. I loved the feeling of him lying on top of me, two hundred and eighty pounds of muscle pinning me down, taking my breath away. I should have fallen in love with him. But I didn't.

The last time we were together, he brought home some replica of me he had met at the bank. The guy and I looked at each other, and then we all went into Cliff's place. The two of us took turns fucking Cliff, then Cliff laid us both out on his bed and fucked each of us. I made him promise to cum inside me. Then I fucked the other guy. I found out later that they had eventually fallen in love and moved in together to an apartment on the Upper West Side. Love is funny like that.

Tim said he had to piss. Twenty minutes later I went to find him and discovered he had left us. This would have been fine if it hadn't been one thirty in the morning, past the time of our last train back to Bronxville.

"That bastard," Annie screamed into the crowded bar. She had thought that we would sleep at his place. Even after she had torn him to shreds. Because for her, it was just a game. She was just toying with him.

X

Annie once told me we were all playing at life. That none of it is real. It's just a big game, an amusement park where our higher selves come for a vacation. It wasn't just a philosophy with her. It was how she lived her life. I have seen her go to the darkest corners of drugs and sex and love, I have watched her play in violent, dark sand boxes, building beautiful castles out of her pain and loss, rolling around in the stink, filling herself with the filth, only to eventually shake it off. To laugh that crazy high-pitched laugh, and move on to the next adventure.

The truth, of course, is that we weren't really in any trouble. Either one of us could have afforded a taxi back to school or a room at one of the nicer hotels. But we weren't looking for safety. We were looking for life.

X

Annie sat at Vasacs drinking beer while I walked east on 7th Street to cop dope.

I did two bags of dope straight off in the bathroom of Vasacs and then leaving the bar, high as fuck, the world suddenly magical, beautiful in that poetic, black and white heroin kind of fairy tale way. We walked around for a while, talking. People were out. It was New York City in the spring. It didn't matter what time of night it was. Nothing mattered. We were all young. We were all famous. We were all beautiful.

She grabbed my hand, and we stopped before a neighborhood garden on Avenue B and 4th Street and looked at a giant statue made out of used tires and cans and other found objects. A little blonde girl was sitting next to her mother in the garden. The mother was smoking and drinking a forty with a tatted Puerto Rican guy. They were whispering to each other and laughing. The little girl looked at us and waved. Annie smiled and waved back. I felt so alive and so full and so endless. I felt the light of the city moving through me. I felt like nothing bad could ever happen to me. I was invulnerable.

"We are all connected," Annie said as we sat in Thompkins Square Park. Someone was playing the drums, and two punk rock junkies on the bench next to us were shooting up. "Everything we see and feel and do, it's all connected to everything else." I was nodding out, my head hanging back, looking up through the leaves of the trees at the endlessly lit New York sky. Somewhere out there was a moon and stars. Somewhere behind those lights was a night filled with satellites and planets, black holes and swirling galaxies, but we were under the dome of New York City, sheltered in its light, safe.

x

I have a vague recollection of a discussion in one of my philosophy classes about the world of objects, and how we assign them meaning and shape. We assign value to everything around us, but if we could strip the world of our assignments, how would it look then? If a chair were not an object of use but just an object, if everything suddenly lost its definition, how would the world be? What would it be? Who would we be?

My eyes wandered over the park, the trees and the benches, the junkies and the dealers, the people moving along the winding paths. I tried to deconstruct what I saw, to let the meaning of it fall away, but I knew I was too much a part of everything. Too connected to really see it. I was just another object of use. I had no way of being objective because everything I saw just reflected myself back at me. My assignments. My understanding. My definition.

"Let's go dancing!" she said, standing up. We ended up at Save the Robots, sitting on couches and talking, music thumping, Siouxise and the Banshees and Africa Bambaataa, dark beats I can't remember. When Malcom McLaren's "Buffalo Girls" came on, we all danced spontaneously, everyone jumping up and moving. It was that kind of a song. That kind of a night. That kind of a life.

A drag queen in a burning red taffeta dress was doing lines off an impossibly beautiful Asian boy's muscular chest. Men in suits were making out with each other, whispering silently against the beats of the music. Club kids were dancing, so high it was possible they might never return.

All of us transcendent for those few moments.

A black girl with a shaved head and purple eye shadow turned to me and said, "When we are all famous, we will meet each other again. Just like this. Because all the famous people know each other."

We were snorting No Doz and bad coke to stay awake. I had two more bags of heroin in my pocket. Annie took my hand and led me down a long tunnel and back outside. It was morning. A brightly lit kaleidoscope. The air smelled wet and green, like rain, and there were birds and people were dressed and moving, going to work.

She grabbed me and hugged me tight, kissing me on the cheek.

"We made it!" she said, laughing.

At Grand Central, we each did our remaining bags of dope and stood under that magical domed ceiling. I felt a sudden loneliness. Less connected than I had the night before. I felt lost. Those nights and those days were like that. A wave of ever changing feelings. One minute you were connected, you could feel the pulse of God. And the next you were alone, standing in the middle of Grand Central Station with all those people rushing at you, having no idea how you got there.

Those were times when the world was limitless and then it wasn't. Times when it seemed you were invulnerable and then suddenly, maybe you could fail. Those were bright and dark times, full of wonder and despair.

Gone

In my twenties, I contacted a local Chabad in lower Manhattan. I told them I was curious. I explained the situation. We were Jewish, but the emphasis was on the "ish." I had not been raised Jewish. I had no real connection to Judaism beyond the basics. Could I meet with someone, talk a little, read something?

"I am going to be in the Village this afternoon," the rabbi on the other end of the phone said, his voice raspy, heavy. "I have a student visiting from Amsterdam. He is assisting me. Maybe the three of us could meet? If you two get along, he can teach you Talmud. Torah. You can both learn together."

"Sure. That sounds great. That'd be awesome."

I was to meet them under the arches. I asked how I would know them.

"Two rabbis in black hat and beards, we shouldn't be hard to miss, huh?"

As I walked west from my apartment on East Fourth Street, the city swarmed around me, like angry bugs gnawing at me, caging me in. My thoughts moved in all directions. I was lost and looking for some kind of a connection. I was recently sober, robbed of whatever poetry and incantations heroin had brought to my life. The world was noisy and despairing. I was searching for God, for meaning. I was looking for something to take the place of heroin, to bring the beauty back.

Maybe being Jewish would be a little like being a junky, just none of the bad parts. Only the mystical swirling. The meditative purity and none of the agony.

Because you know, Judaism is known for its lack of agony.

I have always had a fetish for books. I want to hold them, to wrap myself inside them, the words swirling into complete worlds on the page. The vision of the Hasidic Jew living in isolation from the world, locked in study and prayer was romantic to me. His life dedicated to intelligence and to God. Maybe that was the life for me. I liked the idea. It felt esoteric and clean. I always think I might have been happy if I had been born into a life that was narrow and wide at the same time. A world of God and magic and a swirling canopy of heavenly creatures.

But then I liked heroin and dick too. Poetry and art. Black magic as well as white. I liked the trappings of study, the books and the dark, dusty rooms. But after, I'd want to get lost in a sex club, fucked by twenty guys, my ass beaten into submission, my brain turned off. Pure animal. My conflict in life has been the extremes. I want both sides of the coin—dark and light, intellect and animal. I want to be fucked into enlightenment. Hard

X

I was kicked out of high school when I was a sophomore. I had dropped acid with a girl named Ellen while we both had after school detention. The two of us went running through the halls screaming what I thought at the time was some pretty articulate and well thought out anti-establishment punk rock rhetoric, but what, according to the principal was more along the lines of Satanic obscenities. This was not the only reason my parents decided to send me to Solebury Boarding School. I was not a popular kid or a jock or a brain. I was a dark and moody kid prone to drugs and goth music and rebelliousness. I was a shooting spree kid without the guns. I was angry and mal-aligned and dysmorphic.

I had the kind of problems no one understood. Lithium and therapy and punishment were useless on me. I was a horny gay boy in an upper-class suburban town without enough dick or ass to satisfy my hunger. I was Iggy Pop and David Bowie and Peter Murphy and The Cure and Siouxisie.

Looking back, I was probably just an alcoholic in the making, uncomfortable and emotional, trying to get someone's attention. I wanted someone to go hide in the woods with and fall in love with. I was looking for that connection, for meaning.

Solebury was supposed to be the perfect fit for me. It was small. It catered to intelligent, creative rich kids gone bad. The only problem was they weren't sure they wanted a kid as bad as I was. I had to do penance. I had to spend the summer at a private Catholic boarding school on the coast of New England. During the school year, it was highly prestigious, but during the summer it ran an intensive summer school for spoiled rich kids of wealthy families who had fucked up and needed a little guidance.

The campus was a beautiful, ancient-looking monastery hanging on the edge of a cliff. Next to it was a modern library built to celebrate the future and the past with elegance and function. The buildings seemed to grow out of the stone cliffs and trees and ocean. The monastery itself was beyond my wildest Lovecraftian dreams of monsters and witches and dark rites. You could almost see damsels in distress in white gowns running through a pouring rain straight out of a Mary Roberts Rinehart book. I was a kid who spent a lot of time reading obscure murder mysteries at the public library, bored and looking for adventure.

The grounds were wide open fields of green running to the edges of a cliff that looked out over the ocean, or to the dense New England forests on the other side of the campus. There was a large Puerto Rican and Columbian faction at the school, not from uptown Manhattan, but actual kids from wealthy Columbian and Puerto Rican families. I met the son of a famous drug lord who was at the Abbey before going to Harvard the following year, a boy whose dad owned coffee fields, and another whose family owned vineyards and resorts.

There was a girl as well, a blonde-haired cold beauty whose father was a professor at the school. She didn't attend classes, but she was allowed to live on the all boys' campus. She had been doing it every summer since she was born.

Her name was Austen.

During my first week at the Abbey, I read *The Fall of the House of Usher*. I had never read Poe before. I loved the dark madness of the story. The lost lines where sanity and insanity met, where reality and unreality merged. "*I looked down upon the scene before me-upon the bleak walls-upon the vacant eye-like windows-upon a few rank sedges-and upon a few white trunks of decayed trees-with an utter depression of soul which I can compare to no earthly sensation more properly than to the after-dream of the reveler upon opium-the bitter lapse into everyday life-the hideous dropping off of the veil.*"

I learned there was going to be a talent show at the end of the summer. I decided, now in love with Poe, that I would recite "Annabel Lee."

I became obsessed with Austen. I followed her around, spying on her as she read Herman Hesse's *Demian*, alone on benches overlooking the finality and expanse of the sea.

"I like *Steppenwolf* better," were the first words I ever spoke to her, and they felt banal, unworthy of that cold, sad beauty. I wasn't even sure I meant it.

"Really? I read *Siddhartha* for school and thought I would try something else."

I held up a copy of Salinger's *9 Stories*. "Can I sit with you?"

She took Salinger and fingered through it. Her eyes grew soft, almost as if she might cry. She smiled.

"My mother bought me a first edition of this for my thirteenth birthday. I read *A Perfect Day for Banana Fish* and *For Esme-With Love and Squalor* and felt my whole life was wrecked forever."

She wore a black Cure T-shirt, a grey thrift store sports coat, and an ankle length black skirt. She moved over slightly, unnecessarily making room, and kicked off her shoes. Her small, pale feet rested perfectly on the manicured triangle of green grass like two tiny porcelain birds.

We sat like that for a while, quiet, each of us reading, pausing to look out at the views of ocean and cloud.

"My father said you are reciting *Annabel Lee* at the talent contest?"

"I am. I was considering doing an interpretive dance of "Bela Lugosi's Dead," but thought that might be too much."

She laughed. It was pleasant and distant, warm and detached. "You know it's about fucking his underaged cousin?"

"Peter Murphy was fucking his underage cousin?"

She raised her middle finger into the air, waving it in front of my face.

"All I know," I said, ignoring her finger, "is that at thirteen, I would have loved some older daddy coming along and teaching me how to fuck. Hell, he wouldn't even have to teach me. He coulda just fucked the hell—"

"Of course, the only handsome boy here is gay."

"I thought that was obvious?"

"It's not." She picked up her book. "You need a director."

"What?"

"For the talent show. You can't just stand up and read Poe."

"I wasn't going to just stand there. I was going to memorize it. Wow them all with my amazing brain capabilities."

"That's stupid. We need a show. Something huge and explosive. Start with Bauhaus, you come out on the stage in a black cape, dark clothes, goth make-up, and then you *perform* the poem."

I looked at her, her ice blue eyes on mine. "Who's going to be my director?"

"Me, of course."

I wanted to tell her about the strange and confusing walks I was taking with Brother Anthony, but decided against it. It was bad enough to be Jewish and gay, but fucking a monk? That was sure to get me thrown out and kill my chances of getting into Solebury.

Brother Anthony was my math teacher. He was younger than most of the other monks, mid-twenties, tall, olive complexion, with dark stubble on his shaved head, and a full black beard. I told him I was afraid to enter the church.

I'm not sure why I said that to him. It wasn't the truth. I have always been a liar. It is encoded deep in my DNA. But this lie was so strange.

"What are you afraid of?"

"I don't know. It just feels angry at me. Like whatever is inside doesn't like me."

He smiled at me and put his hand on my head. It felt warm. I wanted to fold myself into him, get lost inside his smell.

On our first walk together, Brother Anthony asked me how school was and what I was working on. I showed him the collection of Poe and I read to him from *The Fall of the House of Usher*.

"*To an anomalous species of terror, I found him a bounden slave. 'I shall perish,' said he, 'I must perish in this deplorable folly. Thus, thus, and not otherwise, shall I be lost. I dread the events of the future, not in themselves, but in their results. I shudder at the thought of any, even the most trivial, incident, which may operate upon this intolerable agitation of the soul. I have, indeed, no abhorrence of danger, except in its absolute effect—in terror. In this unnerved, in this pitiable, condition I feel that the period will sooner or later arrive when I must abandon life and reason together, in some struggle with the grim phantasom, FEAR.'*"

Brother Anthony was silent for a moment. His large hand rested upon my lap. His fingers were thick and gnarled, tufts of black hair sprouting at odd intervals. We were sitting on a bench overlooking the sea. A heavy fog was rolling in. Behind us, trees beaten by coastal winds whispered in a chilled breeze, breaking the heat of the day. I could hear the crash of waves and beyond that the silence of the church, the awe of the world, the never-ending stillness.

"The human condition," he said, his voice a low, thunderous rumble, his cadence direct. "We find it most distinctly in filth. Poe understood this."

His hand squeezed my thigh, and I felt my dick grow painfully hard. I looked at him. His eyes were closed.

In that moment I wanted him to own me. I wanted him to hit me. To throw me down. I wanted him to make me beg. In that moment I understood needs that were only beginning to surface. I had explored these avenues in the rambles, in other men, in public bathrooms and on phone sex chat lines. I had fucked and been fucked. But this was something new. This need was compulsion and desire and violence. It was about power.

This need had nothing to do with love.

Raphael once told me, sitting on our rock, "There are two ways to fuck a man."

We had spent the afternoon watching other men fuck. At one point, he had asked me if I would ever let him watch me.

"Watch me what?" I knew the answer. I just wanted to hear him say it. I wanted to hear the words.

"You know what I want, pa. You know what I like."

"I do. But I want to hear you say it."

"I want to watch you get fucked. But I don't want to hide in the bushes while I watch. I want to be there. Next to you. I want to hold you down and kiss you while they fuck you."

"What are the two ways to fuck a man?" I asked him.

"One is with love and one is with violence."

"You can't fuck with both?"

He laughed. "When I fuck you is it violent or loving?"

"I know you love me."

When a stranger fucks you in the bushes, pushes you into the mud? I want to be a stranger to you. I want to fuck you into the mud."

X

"Tell me what scares you most about being in a church? About God?" Brother Anthony asked me.

I thought about darkness, about a coercive evil, about violent and ugly desires, about piss and cum, about gang rape and murder. I thought about all the dark fantasies that ran through my poisoned mind, and I wondered if I had, in fact, been lying. Whatever lived in that church would not see me as its friend. I was an enemy; I was drowning in my hungers; I knew that there would never be enough to satiate me.

I thought about Roderick Usher, and of the darkness that, "...*poured forth upon all objects of the moral and physical universe in one unceasing radiation of gloom.*"

We were different, Roderick and I. The darkness was destroying him, whereas I wanted it. I wanted to see everything the world had to offer. All the vile beauty, the sickness and despair. I wanted to bathe in it. I wanted to lose myself in it. I would always choose the darkness over the light. The madness over the stability. I wanted chaos and startling beauty. I would sacrifice comfort and security and my soul for that swirling vortex I perceived, that chance at absolute gorgeous decadence.

I wanted to find all the beauty in this life: even in the pus-filled abscesses and derelictions, in the soul blackening horrors. I was a monster. I had known this all along. I was born this way. I wanted to celebrate it.

When I was a child, my mother would tell me that in a past life I had committed great acts of evil: sorcery and magic, human sacrifices and conjuring demons. I had bent the light into something harmful and destructive, and that I had been sent back to this life to make up for that. She warned me to stay away from magic, to be careful. Evil followed me and would tempt me.

Sitting there with Brother Anthony, his question about god, about the church swirling through my mind I thought, *Maybe I don't need tempting. Maybe I had made my choice long before.*

"I don't know," I said, lying, playing the part. "It's just…it feels really *big* in there."

"And you feel really small?"

"Sometimes I think I am possessed." I looked into his heavy-lidded eyes.

"Possessed?"

"Sometimes. Yes."

"By who?"

I put my hand on top of his. It was warm. My hand was small against his.

"I don't know."

I moved his hand, slowly, our eyes connected, to my hard dick. I am still surprised by my directness. It just felt like the right thing to do. I put my hand on his crotch. His cock felt huge, pulsating against my fingertips. He inhaled, his eyes shut tight, his lips parted, and I dropped to my knees before him, pushing his monk's dress up, freeing his cock.

I sucked him off right there, on the benches overlooking the cliffs, the cold summer New England afternoon coated in a growing fog, the crash of waves, the taste of him as he came in my mouth revelatory.

I wanted to continue our conversation, but Brother Anthony was suddenly nervous, anxious to get away. Honestly, I didn't care. I found his sudden fearful attitude to be uninteresting. He was a grown man. I didn't like that all of a sudden, after he came, he wanted to run away and hide. It felt wrong. Conflicted in ways I wasn't interested in being.

If that kind of self-hate is what god has to offer, I want nothing to do with him.

After he walked away, I knelt down on the edges of the cliff and prayed.

Not to god. But to whatever Lovecraftian monsters lived out there, in the world, whispering to it, opening myself up to it. Because if god caused grown men to whimper and run in fear from a boy, I wanted Satan. I wanted Lucifer. I wanted the Anti-Christ and all that word meant: anti-establishment, anti-fear, anti-failure, anti-boredom. I wanted exceptionalism, brilliance, gold and fame, I wanted the world to open itself up and reveal itself to me. So, with the taste of my monk's cum still strong in my mouth, I rejected god and accepted his opposite.

And it felt good.

"You are so beautiful," Raphael whispered to me as the second man forced himself inside me.

Raphael knelt in front of me, his shoulders blocking my escape, forcing me back on the guy's dick. He watched my face, every gasp, capturing my breath with his kisses.

"I'm getting close," the man said.

"Do it. Shoot it inside him." Raphael sounded like a man, not a boy. He sounded like everything I had ever wanted.

After, we sat on our rock and made out.

"It didn't make you mad?" I asked.

"Mad? How could you ever make me mad? It was so fuckin' hot, pa. You were so fuckin' hot. All I want is that you be honest about who you are. What you want…what you need. I don't want us to ever lie about those things. Ever. Okay? Promise me."

"I promise. I won't lie about who I am."

X

Austen wanted to rehearse. We were to meet at four thirty, after study hall and sports, in the theatre. She got the keys from her dad, who was the drama teacher as well as the poetry teacher. She wore horn rimmed glasses with tiny, ruby red moon shaped jewels woven into the black frames, knee high Doc Marten combat boots, a black skirt, and a white button-down Oxford. She had moved a large armchair into the center of the room, in front of the stage, and had a tape deck with Bauhaus' *Press the Eject and Give me the Tape* already cued to "Bela Lugosi's Dead."

"So, I've been thinking, a lot. I think it might be hot if you came out and just stood there, very still, while the song plays. I found a bunch of cardboard and old boxes and paint in the prop room. I thought, maybe we could build a coffin."

"A coffin?"

"For your dead girl bride." She paused and stood up. In profile, her nose was prominent, stern. Yet, she was undeniably beautiful. Classical and frozen, like a piece of elegant violin music played in a vast, domed room, its beauty always dissipating just as its truth became known, forever lingering just out of reach. "When the song is over, you will begin your poem. And I will rise out of the coffin. Dressed in a white gown."

I laughed. It was audacious. I wish I had thought of it. "A wedding gown?"

"It'll make some people think wedding gown, others innocence. As you recite the poem, I will walk over and try to seduce you. You will ignore me." She smiled. "It will upset some people. But not everyone."

I loved it.

Later, as we painted pieces of cardboard black, I asked her, "Do you believe in god?"

She looked at me. "I don't think it matters. Nothing is coming to save us. And nothing is coming to condemn us."

We were quiet for a moment. Silence at the Abbey was like a presence, always looming over you, swallowing the world. Even in the crowded, busy boy's dorms, at night Silence would fall over us, enveloping us, devouring us.

"Yeah. But I still think there is something."

"I'm sure there's something," she looked at me and smiled. "There's no way we are the top of the food chain. You aren't Catholic?"

"I'm definitely not Catholic." I looked at her, her long blonde hair falling into the paint, leaving trails on the cardboard. "Why isn't your mom here too?"

She stopped working, her head tilting downward. "She's dead." Her voice was flat, without emotion. As if she were reciting a mathematical equation she had memorized but not fully internalized. "She killed herself. She had been sick for a while."

"Sick?"

"She was crazy." She looked up at me, her blue eyes filled with a strange light. "I worry that I am like her, that I am sick too."

We painted in silence after that, building our coffin.

A few days later, Brother Anthony asked me to stay behind after math class.

"I want to see how you are feeling," he said once everyone else was gone.

I was sitting. He was standing.

I looked up at him. "How I am feeling?"

"After what happened? The other day."

I smiled. "I feel like I want to do it again. A lot." I wanted to reach out for him, to touch him. I wanted to get him hard and to sit on him, ride him, bend over and let him fuck me till I could barely walk.

I had sold my soul to the Devil, and I planned to make the most out of it.

"You don't feel guilty?" He seemed genuinely perplexed.

"No. What would I feel guilty for? Do you?"

"I feel conflicted."

I stood up. I could feel the darkness move through me, and I welcomed it. I welcomed life and adventure. I welcomed more: more dick, more love, more of everything. I wanted whatever adventure was about to come.

And I was not conflicted.

And his question was ridiculous. I had done nothing wrong, and I knew it. I was sixteen. I had enjoyed what we did. I know that I should say he had done some terrible thing to me, but I had wanted to do that with tons of guys. I was not a virgin, but I definitely wasn't the slut I wanted to be either, so, honestly, I felt like I scored. I still feel like I scored. You should have seen him. He was fucking gorgeous. When I looked at him, I felt nothing but the desire to get on my knees and suck his dick. Let him deal with his conflicted pain. I had no interest in that.

"I don't feel conflicted." I stepped toward him. "At all. I know exactly what I want." I stood on my tippy toes, pushing against him, barely able to reach his lips, and I kissed him. "I want to suck your dick again. I want you to fuck me. And I want to do it a lot."

He fell backward. Behind us was a window looking out onto the main quad of the campus. I turned. No one was there to see us. I smiled.

Feeling stronger, more powerful.

It was late afternoon fog pushed the sun into oblivion. We walked together along the stone pathways around the campus and to the cliffs overlooking the sea. I thought of Poe and Lovecraft, and of monsters that lived in the deep darkness of the sky, and in the murky recesses of the ocean, and I wondered about this new thing opening up inside of me. I wanted to reach out and hold Brother Anthony's hand. I wanted to touch the tips of my fingers to his. I wanted to bury my face in the dark hairs of his chest, to lie naked with him. I was that monster, that strange alien being, landing on the shores and crawling from the sea, hungry and searching; I felt it build inside me, the Beast, the Destroyer of Worlds.

Brother Anthony kept looking over his shoulder, making sure we weren't being followed.

"Everyone is at study hall before dinner," I said.

"They'll wonder where you are."

"It's optional."

I thought of a story Austen told me earlier in the day about a recurring dream she had. In it, she is standing alone on a beach. The ocean is a great wave of fire. Behind her is a vast forest. It is night, though the sea of fire consumes the darkness, making it burn bright. The air is filled with screams. She turns to find a woman standing naked next to her, pointing up at the sky. The woman is not her mother, but she feels like her mother. Smells like her. When the woman speaks, Austin can't make out the words. She can't make out the meaning. Austen gets very tired and lies down on the beach. The sand is strangely cold. She falls asleep and dreams she is walking through a forest. Sunlight is filtered through layers of green. She wakes up.

"What did the woman say to you?" I ask her.

"I can never remember. In the dream, I can't hear her, but I know what she is saying. I understand her."

Austen is afraid of what people are going to think when they see our recital of *Annabel Lee*. She seems upset, but she won't tell me why. It isn't like Austen to be afraid. I want to tell her what I learned out there on those cliffs about freedom, about life, about the possibility of being yourself, even if it means being the monster and not the hero. Instead I told her, "I don't care what they think. We are doing this for us."

She looked at me and smiled. She leaned in and kissed me on the cheek.

x

Brother Anthony and I stepped off the main path and followed a smaller trail down the edge of the cliff to the beach. There was a cave on the edges of the sand, hidden from anyone who might be looking down. We sat next to each other on a large rock, the ocean dark and thunderous, the sky a sheltering grey. I took his hand in mine. He was shivering. I moved in closer.

"Did you always know you wanted to be a monk?"

He laughed. It was strange and harsh. "I never wanted to be a monk. I wanted to be a scientist."

I waited for him to continue, but he didn't. "So why—"

"Because of this!" He gestured toward me, as if I alone explained the whole problem of his life. "Because I can't help myself."

"Help yourself? From what?"

He grabbed me, lifting me up and into him, and we kissed. It was sudden and violent and consuming. I could feel his heart pounding against me, his breathing deep and heavy. He pushed me to my knees and lifted his monk's habit, revealing his large, uncut cock. When he fucked me, it was rough and hard. I was bent over the rock we had been sitting on, the air cold, waves slamming against the shore in rhythm with Brother Anthony's slams into me.

He held my hips, all the way inside me, and I could feel him. As if he were pulsing through me, the beat of his heart inside me.

After, his face burned and sweaty with shame and rage, he said, "I can't help myself from you."

He turned and left me there in the cave, his cum dripping out of me.

I jerked off alone, to the beat of the ocean, and the fading sun.

After I came, I sat there in that cave, thinking about *Seymour Glass* and *A Perfect Day for Banana Fish* and wondering where I'd I end up after all this was over. Who would I be?

Who will anyone of us be when this is all over?

Years later, I would find myself in another park, in another city. Griffith Park in Los Angeles. 1998. Cruising had become a way of life for me, an art form. A way to escape. I was two years sober. I would spend hours on those dusty desert hill trails overlooking downtown and Hollywood, the smog congested streets and freeways, the endless filth and beauty of Los Angeles. I would fuck and suck and get fucked. I would stumble upon gang bangs, sticking my dick in holes dripping with other men's cum, making out with strangers. We were so hungry, so dirty, so in love with the filth. I had found a place to worship my decadent god, and I thought of pink puffs of divinity candy and Laurent and I wondered would he think this was beautiful, or would he mourn the lack of music?

"There should always be music playing somewhere in the background," he once said. "And there should always be dessert."

"Who do you think we will be in twenty years?" Raphael asked me. It was raining. We were in the Village eating falafel with money I had stolen from my dad's wallet.

"Do you think we will still be friends?" I asked him.

He smiled that insanely beautiful smile and he kissed me. He tasted spicy, garlic and hummus. "We will always be friends. No matter where we are. I will always love you."

Some days I would cruise Elysian Park. It was rougher and the boys darker, sexier. The police academy was at the bottom of the hill, so you could hear guns being shot while getting your dick sucked. It was a strangely philosophical experience. Once I saw a guy who looked like Raphael, just a little older. I followed him into the bushes and jerked off while a group of guys pissed on him. Later I saw him sitting at a bench eating nachos and reading X-Men comics. I sat down next to him.

"I'm Jeff," I said.

"Cool." He didn't look up. His voice was heavy. Stoned.

"Wanta go make out?"

He looked at me and laughed. "Make out?"

"Yeah. Make out."

"That's all?"

I thought about it. "Yeah. That's all."

He pushed his nachos toward me. I ate some. The cheese tasted sweet. It made me feel a little sick.

We made out in the bushes. After a few minutes, he pulled his pants down. I fucked him using spit. When I came I felt sad. I left him there with his X-men comics and drove home.

"I will always love you too," I told Raphael. And it is true. I have always loved him.

A few days later, I found Austen waiting for me outside the boy's dorm. She was crying. She refused to tell me why, only that she wanted to go for a walk. I led her along the edges of the cliff, passing all the spots I had been with Brother Anthony. Our fucking had become an almost daily ritual now. I led her toward the steep trail down to the cave. Austen held my hand.

"Can you tell I was crying?" she asked me as we passed other students.

"No. Definitely not." I lied.

"I don't want these fucking spoiled assholes to know I was crying."

"Austen—"

"Just take me somewhere. Hide me."

Like a stolen treasure, I stole her away to my cave. We sat on the rock Brother Anthony had fucked me on the day before, my ass still sore in that way that always makes me want more, and we talked. She told me about her father, how he would go for months sober, but then, triggered, he would start drinking again.

"He just goes dark side," she said. "I wish he would get angry, scream, yell or cry, or anything, but he just locks himself in his bedroom and drinks. He won't talk. He won't look at me. He has these pills the doctor gave him. He stores them up for his 'episodes.' I don't know what they are, but they lock him away inside his head. I used to throw fits. Cry. Scream. Break things. All the things my mother would do. And he would look at me with the same dead eyes he used to look at her with. It was like he didn't care about me, wasn't my father anymore. Now…now I just ignore him. It'll be over in a few weeks. Until then, well he always manages to hold it together." She stood and walked to the edge of the small cave, watching sea gulls dive into the water, hunting for fish. "I wish he wouldn't, though. I wish it would all fall apart on him so he'd have to really deal with it. He isn't my dad when he's like this. It's like I've lost both my parents."

"Why do you think Roderick Usher just leaves Madeline in the coffin? He hears her moving about. He knows they buried her alive, so why doesn't he do anything?"

She looked at me. Her blue eyes cast a strange light, silvery shadows danced along the edges of the sand and the cave, the waves a constant churning.

"Everyone's a little crazy," she said. "We are all just a little out of our fucking minds."

"Brother Anthony fucked me over that rock," I said, out of nowhere. There was no real context. No point in saying it. It just felt like the right time.

She jumped up. "This rock?"

I laughed. "Ya. That rock."

"Why did you let me sit there?"

"It was days ago. High tide has washed—"

"That's beside the point. Gross." Her hand brushed a strand of errant blond hair out of her eyes. "Which one is Brother Anthony?"

"He's the math teacher. Tall, dark, good looking."

"Big black beard?"

"That's him."

"You're having an affair with a monk?"

"I hadn't meant to. It just happened."

"How long?"

"I don't know. A few weeks."

"A few weeks? And you're just telling me now?"

"I was waiting for the right time."

"Oh. And this is the right time. In the middle of my break down."

"Are you mad?"

She started to laugh. It felt a little crazy, slightly hysterical. And then she stopped. "God, we really are fucking out of our minds."

"I'm sorry. I didn't mean—"

"What the hell are you sorry for? I get it. It's not the kind of thing you can just tell someone. Not only is he a monk, but it's like rape."

"I wish it were as interesting as rape. It's kind of disappointing."

"Disappointing?"

"He's so guilty and angsty all the time."

"He's a grown adult monk fucking a sixteen-year-old. Of course, he's feeling guilty."

"It's not that. That I guess would make sense. It's more like...like he's given in, defeated. He can't even fuck me without getting all emotional and moody."

"Gross." She turned away. "I wish we had cigarettes."

"You want a cigarette?"

"Yes."

"I didn't know you smoked."

"I'd like to smoke now."

I went to the back of the cave, to a small ledge where I had stashed a carton of Marlboros. I took out two cigarettes and lit them, handing her one.

"God, I don't know you at all." She let out a long breath of white smoke. "You're a complete deviant."

"Be grateful I'm a deviant or we wouldn't have any smokes. And you know me better than anyone here."

"Not better than stupid Brother Anthony."

"Way better than stupid Brother Anthony."

"Do you ever just want to run away?"

"All the fucking time. My whole life is centered around running away."

I was hoping that would make her laugh. It didn't.

"But the thing is," she said, holding her cigarette in the air like a glamorous drag queen imitating a black and white movie star. "The thing is, there is nowhere to go."

I wanted to tell her the whole world out there was full of endless possibilities, but I knew that wasn't what she was talking about.

"Maybe my mother was right. Maybe there is only one way to really disappear."

"I don't think-"

"I get it. Suicide kills. But still, haven't you ever wondered?"

"Of course, I have. Who hasn't?"

"He feels guilty because of God," she said. "Which is stupid. If one thing is clear, if there is a God, which I strongly doubt, he definitely doesn't give a fuck about any of us."

She flicked her cigarette into the encroaching waves. "Let's go rehearse. This is getting morose."

I smiled. "Because playing a dead Annabel Lee to Bauhaus isn't morose?"

She hugged me, suddenly bursting into tears. I held her close, containing as best I could the howling of her sobs and the shaking of her body.

x

After Raphael disappeared from my life, I pretended he was watching me. Whenever I was sucking some guy off, or getting fucked, or fucking some hairy daddy bent over a rock, I always imagined Raphael was hiding in the bushes, watching me.

It made the loneliness a little less consuming.

Raphael was more than my lover, he was my friend. I imagined the two of us leaving New York City together, traveling the world, fucking anyone and everyone we wanted. Sharing love and food, sharing the darkness at night, the sunshine in the morning. I thought we were going to have the biggest life full of all the most outrageous adventures.

I thought Raphael was going to be my everything. I would like to say I was naïve because I was fifteen, but I have believed this about guys all the way up into my forties. I have spent most of my life searching for my everything.

But then one day, Raphael was gone and I was alone, cruising the trails around our secret spots, places where he had held my hand, bushes he had kissed me in, the taste of him lingering forever.

I arrived at Washington Square Park early. I found a bench with a view of the arches and waited. The park was busy, drug dealers and students, artists and drummers and skate boarders, a concoction meant to evoke a sense of burning possibility and stunning beauty

I knew him immediately. He was tall, with curly reddish-brown hair and a full, brazen beard. He was dressed in a black suit, white tzisit strings dangling from inside his shirt. He reminded me of the guys who used to do Tefilin runs on the subways on Friday afternoons, getting their good deeds in before Shabbos, as if wrapping prayer filled boxes around biceps and over foreheads might alleviate some of the damage done.

He smiled at me and told me his name was Eitan and that his father was a Chabad rabbi in Amsterdam. He was studying at a Yeshiva in Brooklyn and assisting the rabbi I had called, doing outreach and working with other Jews.

"Why didn't the rabbi come?" I asked. We sat down on a bench on the far south west corner of the park, old men playing chess around us.

"He says his wife is sick, but I think this is a lie. His wife is tired. They have nine children. I think she just needed his help, and he is too ashamed to admit that he will stay home to take care of the kids today." He had a smile that was like being punched in the gut: the kind of smile that could make a guy like me do all kinds of things to a guy like him.

"Nine kids. Jesus."

"It is a great blessing," he said, his eyes sincere, his smile making my dick hurt.

He was in his early twenties like me. He was engaged to a Jewish girl who he hadn't met yet, but he knew her father, a very famous rabbi in Johanesburg, South Africa. I asked him how he could marry a girl he never met, and he told me that love grows from God, and that he knew that as long as he trusted God, he would know love for this girl.

"Do you have a wife?" he asked.

"No. No wife." I hesitated. I had planned my sinful confession in so many different ways that when the time came I forgot which option I had decided upon. "I'm gay." I went for short and sweet.

He smiled and shrugged his shoulders. "That doesn't preclude you from getting a wife and making Jewish babies. If you decided you wanted that."

"I'm pretty sure I don't want that." His smile cut into me, making it hard for me to think. "Is that a problem?"

"For me? No. It is no problem for me. It has nothing to do with me. In the end, you will stand alone with God, and it will be between the two of you what is a problem and what is not." He put his hand on my shoulder. I hadn't thought of Brother Anthony in years, but the proximity of Eitan and his God, his hand on my shoulder, the way his smile made my dick ache, something in his eyes, brought back those chilly New England summer days.

"Good, cos I like being gay." I stood up. "What do we do? Do we sit here and talk? Do we go somewhere? What do we do?"

He smiled that smile and stood up. He was tall and broad. He looked around. "I don't know New York City so well. Maybe we can walk a bit? Do you live near here?"

"Yeah. I don't live far."

"Maybe we can walk to your house. We can get a cup of coffee. And then we can go to your home and sit. I have some books with me. We can read together. Talk. Some place less public."

It was a week away from the talent show when Brother Anthony stopped talking to me. It was sudden. The night before we had met at midnight on the cliffs at the edge of campus, sheltered in a cluster of dense trees. Brother Anthony lifted up his habit and I sat on his dick. It hurt at first, and then it didn't. He slammed himself into me, fucking me hard and without mercy. I shot all over the ground, crying out. When he came he shuddered, and I held him, pushing back on him, not wanting to let him go.

I've always loved being able to make a man cum. It's the biggest turn on I know. It's the thing I love most when I'm bottoming. It's not about how good you fuck me. It's the fact that I can make you cum. There's a power in it.

He held me out there for over two hours. We fucked three times. Each time he came inside me. Each time, I tried to hold on to him for as long as I could.

He told me he knew at a very young age that he liked boys. His father caught him with the son of the family maid. That is when they sent him to live in the Church. It was hard for me to understand what the big deal was. It seemed so foreign from everything I had ever known.

At one point, he walked out to the edge of the cliff and I sat there, on the bench, shrouded in fog, and listened as he prayed in Latin, and then Italian, chanting over the edges of the cliff, into the darkness.

I knew we had no future. I had no illusions of the two of us running off together. I wasn't in love with him. He wasn't in love with me. But I thought, there is no way he isn't going to fuck me again.

"Why won't he talk to me?" I asked Austen, indignant and petulant.

"He's a Catholic monk. What did you think would happen?"

"I assumed he would keep fucking me till the summer ended and I went home."

We were sitting in our cave, smoking cigarettes and watching high tide come raging in. Austen's dad had sobered up. He was even going to AA meetings.

"This isn't a fairy tale," she said.

"I'm not asking for a fairy tale. I just...it was fun. I thought it would keep being fun."

"You're such an idiot." She stood up. "Nobody wants fun." She flicked her cigarette into the water. Out in the distance a lone rock stood like some fallen island, seagulls hovering loudly around it.

"I don't understand." I was a spoiled prince being denied all the best toys.

And maybe it hurt a little, too. Maybe I wasn't in love, but I liked him. I liked spending time with him. I didn't have a lot of other friends. I had Austen and Brother Anthony. He had refused to even look at me. When I walked into class, he had turned around, facing away from me. An older monk, white hair, yellow eyes, came in and took over the class. Brother Anthony just sat looking silently at the floor.

"Is he being punished?" I asked. "Do they know?"

"Of course, they know. He probably told them. Confessed it."

"Why the hell would he do that?"

"This isn't for show." She turned around. "All this, it's for real to them. It's their lives. They believe in it. If not actually God, they at least believe in the structure of it."

It was the first time I had experienced faith. And it seemed idiotic to me. Repulsive. It made my stomach hurt. It made me want to break things.

"Fuck them and their god," I said.

Sex with Eitan was consuming, hungry, and passionate. He wanted to do everything. He loved to fuck as much as I loved to get fucked. And he was built for it. He had a big fat dick and heavy balls. I found it hard not to climb on top of him. I always wanted him inside me.

"I once sold my soul to the Devil," I told him, remembering that afternoon after Brother Anthony had run off, alone on the edge of the cliffs in Rhode Island.

"And what did the Devil offer in return?" Eitan rested with his arms behind his head, his chest hairy, his stomach flat, his dick half hard and wet from my ass.

"Life."

"Do you feel it was a fair trade?"

I looked at him, running my fingers through his beard. He was smiling. His eyes closed. Content. "Yeah. I do."

"Good. It is always best to come out ahead with the Devil."

I laughed, and he kissed me, pushing me back down to suck his dick again. He was insatiable. Always hard. Always ready to cum.

x

One afternoon, lying in my bed, sore from fucking, it had begun to rain. The room had been sunny and full of promise, and then a darkness fell, and it was raining, dark and ominous, pounding. Eitan sat up in the bed. He ran his hands along my body.

"Being here with you, I wonder if I will feel lonelier now that I know, than if I had never known."

"What are you talking about?" I rested my head against his chest, listening to the way his heart beat matched the rain.

"My life will not be like this forever. Soon it will change."

I didn't say anything. I didn't want to accept what he was saying. I didn't want anything to change. Ever.

"I think, what if I had not met you? Or what if I had and I had only read Talmud and Torah with you, done Tefilin, talked about Judaism and God, and not all this...would I have missed something, or will it just add more to the loneliness that is to come?"

"Are you asking me if this was worth it?"

"I am asking myself if I will be able to survive my future knowing what this was." He laughed. It came from somewhere hidden, deep inside. It came from pain. "Do you think your Devil will make deals with me?"

x

Austen was sitting on the grass reading Walt Whitman. I watched her from a distance. She had on slim, fashionable sunglasses, a blue summer skirt with white dots, and she wore thin white gloves. She was too beautiful and harsh and stunning. She arched her head back, taking in the New England sun, and I thought for a moment I could smell her, in the air around me. Clean and cold. Autumn.

Boys around me spoke in Spanish, The Psychedelic Furs were playing in a dorm room, cold stone columns and flowering trees and cut stone pathways surrounding the sprawling campus quad.

Austen looked up and saw me. She waved a white gloved hand in the air. It made me smile. The gloved hand. She was in character today.

The thing about time for me, about memory, it always holds the quality of a movie. The 70's have a muted, sepia quality to them, a strange occult darkness. The 80's a bouncing, overly colored *Pretty in Pink* quality. In my mind, everything is hopeful and bright in the 80's. Full of possibility, like that moment when, in *The Breakfast Club*, everyone realizes that they are okay, the world is okay, and maybe, just maybe, we are all going to make it out alive. It's a lie, of course, but back then we weren't torturers yet. Terrorists hadn't shattered our particular American dream. The world hadn't come to realize that maybe it was past saving, and extinction was eminent.

It was the 80's. Boarding school. Rebels and pretty girls and love. I ran across the small patches of grass, over the stone path ways, toward Austen, beautiful and cold, like some tiny mythical statue in a lost emerald garden. I collapsed next to her, hugging her and resting my head on her perfectly crossed legs.

"You're suffocating me," she said, pushing me away. Her copy of *Leaves of Grass* fell onto the ground.

"The show is tomorrow night, and you're out here reading poetry?"

"It's beautiful out. The only men I talk to anymore are either gay, drunk, or celibate. I'm in trauma. Walt is my savior."

"Another gay man."

"Fuck you."

"I thought your dad was sober now?"

"It was brief. The desert was dry. He's locked himself in the bathroom since last night."

I sniff the air. "Gross. You're filthy."

She swats my head with the back of her hand. "I snuck into the teacher's lounge. They have a shower. I'm beyond pristine. I smell like lavender and rain."

We fell back into the grass and laughed. Carefree. Like the 80's.

"I'm going to college in a year. Princeton or Yale or Harvard. I won't be there to take care of him anymore. I used to worry about what would happen when I was gone. Now, I can't fucking wait. I think about disappearing into school and never going home again. Other times, I imagine long breaks with him too drunk to stand, pissing and shitting on himself."

We were silent. I didn't know what to say. I didn't say anything.

"I had a little date," she giggled.

I sat up, towering over her. "What? When?"

"A few days ago."

"A few fucking days ago? And I'm just hearing about this?"

"Shut up Mr. I'm dating a Catholic pedophile."

"Pedophile is too strong of a word, but fine. Who?"

"Juan Carlos."

I gasped. "The hunky seventeen-year-old whose dad runs a drug cartel?"

"His father doesn't run a drug cartel. He does something in politics."

"Same thing."

"His mother is some famous Latin American movie star."

"Where'd he take you on this date? The boy's locker room?"

"I showed him our cave."

"You whore!"

She laughed. "I feel like a whore. In the best way possible. He fucked me on the same rock Brother Anthony fucked you."

I was shocked. Or at least I pretended to be. She smacked me, it was soft, and we laughed. It felt good. I was only a little jealous she had gotten fucked by the hottest guy on campus.

Next to our cave, the Theatre was the only other space on campus we felt was truly ours. It had once been the Abbey cathedral and had high ceilings, stained glass windows of pained martyrs and dysmorphic virgins, dark and chilly and built out of stone cleaved from the side of the cliffs. It was romantic and ancient and mostly ours to haunt in any way we wanted.

Austen had stolen a couple bottles of red wine from her father, and we were going to get drunk and rehearse.

x

One night, in the rain, Eitan and I walked all the way from my apartment in the East Village to the Brooklyn Bridge. He had a bottle of Russian Vodka a friend had sent him from Sweden.

I thought about my sobriety. I thought about the vodka. I thought about life and all the things I would lose and gain from taking that first drink. I was not well prepared for thoughts like that.

"He is the only one who knows about me, in my community," he said, taking a deep swig from the bottle. We sat on the walkway between Manhattan and Brooklyn, suspended over the world, floating in fog and light, the rain a soft mist in the warm summer night, and we looked out at the lights of the city, obscured by the gathering fog. "He is my best friend. He let me kiss him once, when we were boys. I gave him a blow job. Neither of us liked it very much." He smiled and wrapped his arm around me. "I always liked it better on the receiving end." He passed me the bottle. It was still cold.

And I thought, *Fuck it.* That first sip was like being able to breathe again. Like being set free. That first sip burned through me and released me.

"I always thought that being gay meant having sex with men. Now, I think maybe I was wrong. Being gay has very little to do with the sex. I will fuck my wife. I will make Jewish babies. But I will never love her. Being gay, for me, means loving men. Fucking is just a thing. Just this act we do. It defines no one. Loving is what defines us."

"Why do it? Why give up love?"

"Because I have given myself to a greater love."

"I don't accept that. If there is a god, he wants us to be happy, to be in love. If not, what is the point of god? Fuck a god who wants me to give up my life and the people I love here, now, in this place, just to prove something to him. I believe loving someone else fully, as many people as I can as fully as I can, is the way god loves us. Anything else makes god petty and irrelevant."

The sky lit bright with lightening, the night rumbling around us, and for a moment, the whole world seemed to explode and fall in on itself. He took my hand in his, and we kissed up there, suspended above the earth, floating. And in that one instant, we were in love. It wouldn't last. But for that one moment, it was perfect.

We walked back to the apartment slowly. The rain had stopped, the city shrouded in a strange, embracing mist: holding hands.

I felt like I was in a dream. Moving from one moment of my life to the next, outside of space and time, outside the limits of physics, the rules of nature. I moved slowly through each moment, down avenues, through the haze of the golden city, hands held with all of them, each of them, everyone I have ever loved. The future and the past and the present seemed to merge into one everlasting, endless, potentiality of a moment, this one love growing into everyone I will ever love in my whole life. Connecting all of us. Connecting me to each of them. In those strange, overlapping moments, time stood still. Eitan stopped, somewhere on Broadway north of Houston, and he kissed me: it was full of longing and hope and wonder. It was full of love and desire: it was full of loss.

And then we kept walking, the fog slowly dissipating.

Back at the apartment, Eitan fucked me long and hard. Each time he came, he stayed inside me, his dick pulsating, hard, relentless, until he was ready to go again. Breathless and sweaty, he said,

"I leave tomorrow. In two months I will be married."

He held me, whispering magical stories to me all night about god and love and about the dreams he had had his whole life, about who we would be in this moment if none of the things that were real mattered.

I wanted to tell him it didn't matter. Nothing mattered. Love mattered. That feeling in that moment, the two of us standing in the rain. That was what mattered, but I knew he wouldn't hear me. He was already gone. He was already locked in the cage his life would become.

x

The night of the show, Austen made me go with her to our cave. We held hands and said a prayer to the ocean and to the monsters who lived in the deep dark spaces of the Universe.

"Promise me," she said.

"Promise you what?"

"That you will never give in. To any of it. Promise me you will live as big as you can."

I smiled. "Of course. I don't think I have a choice."

She had gotten a few joints from Juan Carlos, and against our better judgment we got high and then we were naked, laughing and dancing around, kicking our feet in the sand and in the ever encroaching ocean.

We lay together and she said, "I love you."

"I love you, too."

"Even if we suck tonight, we are the coolest people I know."

"Fuck ya!"

She rolled over onto her side, her head propped on her hand. Her eyes were the color of some atavistic ice age landscape. Her lips were bruised and pouty from long make out sessions with Juan Carlos. Her breasts were plump, nipples small and hard.

"We will never have this exact moment again, no matter how hard we try." Her voice was deep and lyrical, matched in elegance by the slow rhythm of the ocean.

Austen stood up and ran to the edges of the cave, the water rushing over her toes, and she spread her arms, raising them to the rising moon, and she screamed, "I love you!" She turned to me and fell to the ground laughing and sobbing and screaming. "I love you!"

x

I thought I saw Raphael once, years later. I was with a boyfriend of mine at the Ollie's Noodle House on the Upper West Side. He was sitting at a table with a group of other guys. They were eating and drinking beer. Laughing. He looked happy. He looked over at me just as my boyfriend grabbed my hand and whispered in my ear.

I have no idea if he recognized me. I thought about going over to him but what would I say? "Hey, it's me, Jeff. I loved you once. I loved you so much I thought I would die if I didn't get to see you again. But I was wrong. I didn't die. And neither did you."

But he was happy, and I was with someone who loved me. Seeing him like that was enough. Knowing he hadn't died out there on the streets. Alone.

The talent show was uninspired. We stood stoned and giggling in the wings waiting our turn.

After it was all over, the audience sat stunned and silent. I couldn't tell if we sucked or were so brilliant they just didn't get us, but either way, we ran out of the theatre exhilarated and thrilled. The following day a few of my classmates told me "It was cool," and that Austen and I were "fucking crazy" but that was about it.

The next day we sat in the library and she said, "I feel like Seymour Glass."

We only had two more weeks left in the summer. My mom and brother would be driving up to get me. A few weeks after that, I would be starting at Solebury School. I suddenly felt sad. I had a sense that change was coming faster than I was ready for.

She took my hand under the table and held it.

I wondered if I would ever see her again. Our lives were about to spiral in different directions, into new worlds.

We would never be these people again.

X

A few years after my brief affair with Eitan, he sent me a letter. In it, he told me his heart was broken. He would never be in love with his wife. He had begun to hate her. That god had failed him, or maybe he had failed god. He would disappear into Amsterdam's gay sex clubs some nights. I imagined the endless orgies followed by days of anguish and guilt. He told me that he liked to imagine my life. He liked to imagine that he was free, like I was, but he kept insisting ~~god~~ must love him so much to give him such a struggle to overcome.

He signed the letter Love. Love Eitan.

X

I think a lot about Brother Anthony and Rabbi Eitan, and I wonder where they are. What their lives are like. I think a lot about the choices we make in life, the roads we find ourselves compelled to travel, and I think about the idea of ~~god~~, and how pointless it is to try and make this thing so far beyond our comprehension happy. I honestly believe that if there is a ~~god~~, he does not care who we love or how we love, or even why we love: just that we love.

It breaks my heart to think of Eitan and Anthony forfeiting love and happiness to a ~~god~~ who doesn't even care. That's the thing about ~~god~~. It doesn't matter if he exists or not. It doesn't change anything. If there is a ~~god~~, he would probably rather we forgot about him and got on with our lives.

And if I'm wrong, if ~~god~~ does care? Well, fuck him. I've already sold my soul to the Devil anyway.

We are all on this sinking ship full of strange and beautiful things, and we are all going down together. We might as well make the best of it.

And I think of Austen. Who meant more to me over that summer than Eitan or Anthony, or most men, have ever meant to me. I think of the way she would laugh, or cry, or bust out screaming. She slinked out of the coffin in a white gown, Peter Murphy distorted and wailing, creeping her way over to me, until all was silent and I recited Poe's *Annabel Lee*; the way she grabbed my hand before either of us could bow when it was over and dragged me out of the theatre, running and laughing through the school, forsaking everything and everyone for just a few more minutes of freedom.

I wonder where she is now. I never did hear from her again. I think I might have written her a letter a few months after that summer, but then we disappeared into life, and I think *I will never know any of these people again.* They are forever lost to me. And I will never know that Jeff again, that person so full of endless potentialities, narrowed down to just one. Me. Now.

And Darkness Will Prevail

It is late here in Los Angeles. 3 a.m. I like the late nights when everyone else has gone to sleep. It is easier to pretend I am alone. It is quiet. The noises of the city fade into the background.

Earlier in the night, a coyote had gotten trapped in my front yard. It must have come down from the hills in search of food or water. The day was hot, over a hundred degrees, the sun punishing, the sky cloudless and burningly blue.

Lately the days have ached from the heat, the lack of rain, the dirty desert brown of the hills.

L.A. is a paradise in a constant state of apocalypse.

My mother called me. I was standing looking out onto my yard, watching the coyote pace back and forth. I considered going outside and opening the gate, but I had no idea how dangerous coyotes were. I had heard stories of them sneaking into yards and tearing apart little dogs. Killing joggers in the hills. Children. But I had no idea how real any of that was. This one didn't look dangerous. His ribs were exposed. He looked sick and hungry. Maybe he was dying.

We are all dying, I hear Laurent say, *I'm just doing it a little faster. Maybe a little sooner than I had expected.*

Thinking of Laurent makes me ache.

The older I get, the larger the past seems to loom over me, the louder their voices get. You can drown in it if you aren't careful. You can get lost inside all those memories, forgetting the present, forgetting the future.

Watching the trapped coyote, I wondered if he would die tonight. I wondered if he could survive another night without food or water. How desperate was he?

"They took me to the emergency room tonight."

"What? Why?" Seven years since we were told she would be dead from Stage IV cancer, it is hard to gauge how my mother is doing. But it's seven years none of use expected to have.

"I was coughing blood again." Her voice is raspy, painful to hear. I wonder if it hurts. My mother is strong. She has spent seven years fighting a battle she knows she can't win. But she has fought longer and harder than most. And she has won more than anyone would have thought possible. "They say the tumors haven't grown. The blood is from a sinus infection. A fucking sinus infection. I thought I was dying."

I am sober again, five years now. This time feels more solid. Real. It has brought her closer to me. We talk every few days. I tell her how I recently had the flu. How even though I know that with all the new medications and my undetectable status, the flu isn't likely to kill me, I can't help but think this is it, every time anything goes wrong. This is AIDS. This is me dying.

"And yet we aren't dead," she says.

"Not yet."

I push a bowl of water out the front door and close it again quickly. I don't want the coyote's last hours to be spent in my front yard. I'm not even sure what I'm supposed to do if it died. Is there some city department you call? Or do I just dump it into the garbage can and wait for it to be taken away?

I notice it is one in the morning. Four in the morning her time. "Did you just get back?"

"From where?"

"The ER?"

"Oh, no, honey, that happened this morning."

"What are you doing awake so late?"

"I can't sleep."

My mother has never been able to sleep. It is a family affliction.

"I've been having such strange dreams," she says. "I'm sure it's the meds. But they scare me. The dreams."

"What are they about?"

"Just dreams of the past. Of people I once knew. Often it's just a cocktail party. It's always at the bar at the Algonquin Hotel. Isn't that strange? Why there? I have no connection to that place. Just one night with some man whose name I can't even remember." I've learned not to press her when she makes offhanded comments like this. The answers often lead to wild tangents far from the original story. "And all these people from my past are there. And we are all telling each other stories. And there all these people I love. Mario is there. Do you remember Mario?"

I did. He was my mother's best friend. A gorgeous gay man who I loved as a teenage boy. He died of AIDS. I used to fantasize that he and I would run away together. Somewhere far away. Safe.

My mother had cried. She had refused to go to the funeral. I never really understood why. And then one day, I asked her.

"He wouldn't have been there. Mario wouldn't be there. Mario is gone. And I didn't want to stand around with a bunch of queens crying over someone they didn't even know. I loved him." She said it fiercely, proudly. "I loved him and now he is dead. And I didn't want to go standing around in a room where he wasn't. I wanted Mario, and if I couldn't have him, I just didn't see the point."

"I remember Mario," I say.

"He is telling me some joke. It's the same joke he always told me when he was alive. Only this time it actually seemed funny. This time we couldn't stop laughing. We never laughed at the joke when he was alive. Somehow…I don't know why…but it had always seemed a little sad. But in the dream…well…it was hilarious."

I can hear her breathing on the other end of the phone. It is deep and painful. She coughs, and for a second I am afraid.

"When it is time for everyone to go, a few of us aren't ready. We decide to go for a walk. It is snowing outside. New York City is one of the most magical places in the world in the snow. People are out. Everyone was in that kind of mood that only happens on special nights. You could feel it in the air. The whole city was buzzing. Excited. Mario held my hand as we walked toward the park. A woman I had only known as a child held my other hand. She was eating a bag of nuts she had bought from a street vendor. She had a beautiful voice. She was one of those kind people." My mother laughed. "I've never been a kind person. So someone as kind as she was always amazed me. At 79th Street, right before we were going to enter the park, she said goodbye and kissed me on my cheek. She was crying. I didn't know why. And when I turned to Mario, he was already gone. Just like that. Without even saying goodbye. And then I was alone, and the city was quiet. It was just me on the streets. The world blanketed in snow and light. And I could feel the darkness coming." She pauses. Coughing. "I wake up and it hurts so bad. The loneliness." She laughs, but it turns into that hacking cough again. "You think how lucky you are to have loved so many people. You forget how much it's going to hurt when they are all gone."

"Do you regret it?"

"Loving them?"

"Maybe."

"No. Not at all. It's worth the pain to have known Mario. To have known all of them. I just wish there was a way to have said goodbye. To have known that I would never see them again. I just wish the final moments together had been a little more elegant."

"I wish a lot of things in life were a little more elegant."

"It can all be so ugly and messy. But that's part of the fun. The mess."

"I've been thinking a lot about people," I say. "People who are gone. The ones who are here. How one day they will be gone. How one day I will be gone."

"Let's make a promise to each other."

I laugh. I can always tell when my mother is about to make something happen. Change the course of things. "What is that?"

"To not forget that we loved each other. The odds are we won't be able to say goodbye. Or to say I love you one more time. Or that I forgive you or that it's all okay. So I'll say it now. I love you, Jeff. You are the perfect son. And the perfect friend. And I am sorry I wasn't a better mother to you and to Damon. But I did the best I could. And I never for one second stopped loving you. You are my greatest thing."

I feel myself tear up at the words, the words that are just mine and hers. *You are my greatest thing.*

"Now you say it," she said.

"What? What am I supposed to say?"

"Goodbye."

"I don't want to say that."

"But one day you'll wish you had."

"I love you, mom. More than any one person I have ever known, I have loved you. You are the perfect mother for me. You have been my friend and my support, and you have loved me through my whole life. You have loved me no matter who I was. You are the only person in my life who has loved me unconditionally. And I'm sorry for all the pain and fear I caused you. I'm sorry for all the years I was a drug addict. For all the lies and the hurt. I wish I had been a better son, but I did the best I could. You, mom, are my greatest thing."

She is silent a moment.

"I should go to bed," she says. "I can't escape the dreams forever." She begins to cough. It sounds like it will never stop. It makes me want to scream. It makes me want to tear the world apart. It makes me wish I were there with her. It makes me wish for the one thing that isn't possible. That I could save her. "Now let's not forget. You and me, honey, we are okay."

"I promise," I say. "That I will never forget."

After we hang up, I cry. Not just for my mother, but for everyone I have ever loved. For the ones I love right now in this moment. For the pain we cause each other. For the hurt and the loss. For all the things I wish I could give them but can't. I wish that I could save them all. But I can't. That is the one thing we can never do.

I go out the back door and through my back yard and down the drive way, and I open the gate to the front yard and then I quickly run to my car, getting in. And I wait for the coyote to leave. It takes him a few minutes. He is cautious. He walks in a zig zag. Confused. A little stunned. I want to feed him, but I know that is a bad idea.

He will just keep coming back for more. He is dying.

After he leaves my yard, walking into the middle of the busy street I live on, I stop watching and go back inside.

It is three a.m., and the ghosts will not leave me alone. Not tonight. They are hungry. They are lonely. They want to be loved. They want me to remember.

I can't even say Daniel's name out loud. Or Raphael, who may or may not be swimming with mermen. Micah or Annie. Laurent. All those people I loved so hard, all those people who were supposed to be my everything. My true loves.

My soul mates.

It's always Laurent's voice I hear late at night. He likes to laugh at me. To remind me how silly I am.

We are so lucky, he says. Beautiful and dirty and glorious. Love them all. Fuck them all. One day you will be dead. You might as well have burned as bright as possible. Leave them begging when you go. When I die, no one I have ever loved will be able to forget me. You will all remember Laurent. I will haunt every last one of you till you finally come to the party on the other side. I promise there will be music and cake and all the most beautiful boys will be there. Waiting with me. Waiting for all of you to come and dance. We are warlocks. We are magical. ~~God~~*, we are such beautiful and filthy creatures.*

And it makes me feel safe. Thinking they are all just there, dancing and eating and loving and fucking.

My mother is right. The more you love, the more it's going to hurt. But ~~god~~, it's worth all the fucking pain.

And so tonight I will dance. With Laurent and Elly and Ian and Daniel and I will love them. And tomorrow I will wake up and I will hold those closest to me and love them with everything I have. And I will fuck and eat cake, and I will fall in love, and I will burn as bright as possible.

Until it's over. Until the darkness comes.

About the Author

Jeff Leavell is a writer who lives between Los Angeles and Berlin. He has written for *Vice, Them, Hornet,* to name a few. His blog, *The Discerning Daddy*, ranks as one of the top LGBTQ blogs on Queer Sexuality, Culture, and Politics. You can find more of his writing at jeffleavell.com.

CPSIA information can be obtained
at www.ICGtesting.com
Printed in the USA
LVHW09s0431130918
590014LV00001B/285/P